You Call That *Love*

You Call That Love is a work of fiction. Names, characters, places and incident are products of the author's imagination or are used fictitiously. Any resemblance to actual events, locales or persons living or dead, is entirely coincidental.

Cover Design by Durrock Knox/ Polished Content

ISBN 978-0-9890982-0-5

10 9 8 7 6 5 4 3 2 1

Printed in the United States of America

You Call That *Love*

RAI

Right About It

Publications

Dedications

I dedicate this to my grandfather's Sam and Robert Lee may you rest in peace. You may not be here physically but your spirit and wisdom lives on. Thinking of you, missing you daily, but holding on to your wisdom.

Grand pop Sam, you would say, "If I help someone along the way then my living was not in vain." Grand Pop Robert Lee you would say. "It's nice to be important, but more important to be nice."

Your words stay with me. I was blessed to have both of you in my life. Just as you inspire me, I hope to inspire others.

Acknowledgements

I thank you, God.

This has been a long, long, long, long process, but it truly was worth it. From three publisher to none to me finally doing what I should have done all along, self-publish. I can honestly say sometimes you may not get what you want when you want it, but you do when you're ready. There were many sleepless nights, a lot of frustrations and even more tears. I know now had this book been published when I wanted, I wouldn't have been ready. I'd been lost and confused with no direction. The delay had a purpose and my vision is now clear. I'm ready. All the pieces are falling into place and I see the big picture.

Mommy, thank you for supporting over the years with everything from emotionally to financially. Your love is priceless.

Antoine, thank you for your encouragement, yes you truly do get on my nerves but I know it's because you know I can do it. It is appreciated, just stop talking so much and listen, lol.

To my kids, Ziah, Ke'Niah and Yohan, I love you and do this for you.

To the one and only Queen Nyki, you are one of a kind. You are on your way. The world will soon know the Queen. Are they ready?

Lil bro keep doing your thing. Make Grand pop Robert Lee proud and show him the man he raised you to be.

Lorenzo, act your age and stop fussing all the time. Thank you for irritating me enough to make this happen. I thank you for the rides and the ideas.

I'd like to thank Musa Ego. You are the best buddy. I thank you for having my back, encouraging me and although it took six years I finally did it.

My Reeky Reek, Rico, you are my oldest and craziest friend. We go way back and you are an inspiration. The stories I could tell on you, but don't worry I won't. Looking forward too many more crazy adventures and experiences with you on your quest......

To my grandmothers, thank you for your love and support.

Cretia and Cool Press you keep me rolling. Your support with everything means so much.
Joel from Paradise Books, you were the first to read this manuscript and started me on this journey. I wish you the best and hope I can work with you again.

Karen Quinones Miller, you are a gem. Your advice and wisdom are wow, no words just awe. I look at you as a mentor. I'm so grateful that I had the opportunity to speak with you and learn priceless publishing gems.

To the readers, thank you for reading this book. I hope you enjoyed Yasmin's journey on her quest for love. I hope you were able to relate to Yasmin, feel her pain, laugh, cry and overcome with her. I hope her story and future stories are able to encourage and give insight on life obstacles.

P.S.
Yasmin story continues…
Love Me Right coming soon……

Check out my website www.rightaboutitpulications.com for updates.
Also check out: www.ghostmoneyent.com .Get the latest entertainment news and check out artist.

1
Get It Together

After five long years, today, May 4, 2002, my life was beginning. Earlier, I received my undergraduate degree in business administration, with a concentration in finance, from the University of Maryland at College Park. In two weeks, I will be starting my position with Legg Mason as a financial advisor. Life is good, everything was going as planned, and finally, I decided I was done trying to please others. India Arie's, "Get It Together" was my anthem.

Who am I? My name is Yasmin Elaine Sinclair. I stand 5 foot 11 with a golden honey complexion, hazel-green eyes, and thick, long hair that hangs just past my shoulders. I am not petite but just right, a size twelve. I don't think of myself as pretty, but people always tell me I am. I've always hated the reflection that stared back, especially my hazel-green eyes. This impression of self stems from childhood.

Growing up, let's just say, was an experience. I am the black sheep. I've always felt my parents tolerated me because they had to. I knew they were counting the days until I got O.U.T. All of the affection in the house was solely directed at my sister, Ashley, who is four years younger. From personalities to looks, my sister and I are complete opposites. Ashley is the outgoing one, always on the go, while I am more reserved. The differences continued with our appearance. Ashley owned a rich mocha complexion, standing 5 foot 4 with a petite frame. Her short, wild hair matched her personality. To my parents, she is perfect. Ashley is the pretty one, the smart one, and the can-do-NO-wrong one.

Graduation was my wake-up call. I was going to forget that my father didn't even show up for the ceremony, or that my mother and Ashley only made a brief appearance. I was not getting depressed, so enough about the family.

This is my life, and it was time to take control. Today, I am going out to celebrate me.

I walked into the door of my Silver Spring apartment and began peeling off my graduation attire. I threw everything in the hamper and proceeded to my bathroom. I ran my bathwater adding Milk & Honey bubble bath and bath salts. Easing my way into the warm bathwater, I let the aroma take me away and reminisce about the last couple of years. My best friend, Landon, and I had had some fun over the years. I smiled as I thought about the first time I met her.

It was my junior year of high school, 1996. We had just moved out of D.C. to Takoma Park, after my father got a supervisory position at the Washington, D.C., Metro Transit Authority. I was the new girl, a loner, and preferred for it to stay that way. However, since I was the new girl and quiet, people assumed I was a bourgeois stuck-up bitch. I was never one for drama and knew how petty females could be so that title never bothered me. All I needed was a good book, some music, and I was happy.

One cool October day, the school decided it was a good day for a fire drill. As I was waiting for school administration to give the OK to go back inside, a fugly (fucking ugly) character and his entourage approached. This guy was about 5 foot 8, 140 pounds, light skin with a bad case of acne and a big KRS-ONE nose. He was wearing clothes that made him look like a crayon box, representing every damn color. I turned around and prayed he wouldn't say anything to me.

"What up, Shorty? Let me get ya number," this fugly guy said to me, looking me up and down.

I thought, *Not today.* Something told me he was going to be a pain. I replied, "I have a boyfriend."

"So, I ain't asking you if you had a man. I just want to talk to you," he persisted.

"Well, I'm not interested."

"Yo, I told you she was a dyke. She trying act like she got a man," he laughed. "I ain't never see her with no man. What she need is some of this good dick. I'd turn her straight, but this broad ain't worth my time. She a'wight, but she ain't no bomb."

By now we had a show. A few of the students had gathered around to see what was going on.

I turned around and looked at the fool. "Look, I was trying to be nice to your fugly ass. Look in the mirror. Just because someone doesn't wanna talk to your corny ass doesn't make them a dyke. But while we're on the subject, you're the one walking around here like you going to gay pride. You have on every color of the damn rainbow, and if that's not enough, your rap game is weak."

He looked around at the crowd, but remained silent.

I went into my Coach bag, pulled out my eyeliner, and took a step to Mr. Fugly. "And one more thing. Why would I want you? I could play connect the dots on your face with my pencil."

The group of students that had gathered was laughing and teasing Mr. Fugly by now.

"Damn, she straight-up clowned you," someone laughed out.

"Fuck you," Mr. Fugly said to me before walking away with his entourage.

I know I should have let him walk away, but I had to get the last word in. "I know you want to, but like I just told you, that's not going to happen."

Just as I was walking away, this girl approached me. I recognized her from my second-period class. I didn't remember her name, but I did remember her staring at me. She looked at me like she knew me, but I just brushed it off. Normally, when I saw her she was with a lot of guys. The rare times I saw her with a female, they were arguing.

As she got closer, I looked her over. We had a lot of similarities: same complexion, long hair, hair color, and even the green eyes. She, however, was petite and resembled the late R&B singer Aaliyah.

"Hi, Yasmin, right?" she laughed.

I looked at her. "Is something funny?"

"My bad," she pointed to herself. "I'm Landon. I was laughing at how you told him off. The things you said sound like something I would say. You surprised me. I didn't think you had it in you. You seem more like the quiet type. I wasn't expecting you to say anything."

I had to laugh myself. "A lot of times people assume they can talk to me any way. That's a big mistake. I am quiet, but if you try me on the right day, I will tell your ass off."

We both laughed. From that day we've been like two peas in the pod. Now don't get me wrong. We have our share of arguments. After all, we both have smart-ass mouths, but I love her like a sister.

Just as I was stepping out of the tub my phone rang. I knew it was Landon. I grabbed a towel, being careful not to slip on the marble floor of my rust and gold bathroom. Of course when I made it to my bedroom, the ringing stopped. Glancing at the caller ID, it confirmed Landon.

Instead of calling her back, I chose to dry off and get dressed. What to wear? It's early May, but the temperatures had been in the nineties earlier. However, according to the weather channel, it was supposed to drop into the low seventies tonight. I rummaged through my closet, deciding to be pretty in pink.

Splashing on Victoria Secrets, Pretty in Pink body splash and lotion, I followed with Issey Miyake perfume. I settled on a loose-flowing pink and brown print skirt that stopped just below my knees, a pink tube top with a brown beaded choker attached, and brown sandals. I pinned my hair up, letting some curls hang down. The final touch is my Mac lip gloss. Taking a glance in the mirror, I saw toned legs and my 36 DDs were in check. Yes, I was satisfied.

Just then my phone rang again. Assuming it was Landon, I picked up the phone.

"Yes, Land, I'm ready."

"Where you going?" he asked.

It's Derek, my ex. Derek and I broke up eight months ago, but he wouldn't move on. I silently cursed myself for not checking the caller ID.

"I'm going out with Landon."

"Where y'all going?" he asked.

"Out," I roll my eyes as if he could see me.

"I know out, but where? I'm saying, I'm trying to spend some time with you. You know you miss me. Why don't you just let me come over and give you some of this good dick?"

"Listen, Derek, you and I are not together. Where I go is none of your business. Like I told you before, we're going to different places. Well, I'm going places, and you're stuck. And for the record, your dick ain't all of that. So stop wasting your time and mine. Don't call me anymore," I said before hanging up on the fool.

The phone rang again. This time I checked the caller ID.

"Yes, Landon?"

"Are you ready?"

"Yeah, where are we going? I need a drink."

"I was thinking about going to Dream. I feel like dancing. Why do you sound so irritable?"

"I just hung up with Derek."

"Ill . . . Why are you still talking to him? You like those inner-city thugs. Why?"

"For your info, Landon, I picked up the phone thinking it was you."

"Oh, well, why you wasted your time in the first place with that thug is beyond me."

"All right, Miss Uppity, just come on and pick me up so I can celebrate. You're driving, right?"

"Of course," she said before she hung up on me.

Landon was against Derek and me from the beginning. She thought he was ghetto and wasn't going anywhere in life. I admit, this time, Landon was right. I met him a year and a half ago when I took my 2000 Honda Accord coupe in for an oil change. Landon acknowledged a guy if he made six figures. Derek's income was well below her salary criteria. Therefore, she never gave him a chance. He was the mechanic that worked on my car and came over to give me a summary of what he did. I knew he was trying to get my number and wasn't usually this friendly with customers. He kept looking at me, saying anything to keep me there longer.

"Miss Lady, I checked over everything. Everything is in order, no defects. The coupes are nice. The engine is . . . (blah, blah)."

He was telling me important stuff about my car, but I was only seeing him. He had my attention. He had sexiness about him. He was tall, brown with an athletic build. He reminded me of Method Man. Just looking at him was making me horny.

Playing along, I said, "Well, I'm glad to hear that. If my car broke down, I wouldn't have anywhere to take it. I could just bring it back here, but the dealer is so expensive."

"Yes, you would. You can just call me. My name is Derek," he said, handing me a business card.

"Thank you," I said never taking my eyes off him as I took the card.

"Make sure you use that card. Cars aren't my only specialty," he said, giving me this sexy smile.

"Really? Well, I may have to see about that," I replied walking away, all the while making sure he got my runway strut.

I called Derek three days later. He seemed to have his life in order. I found out he was from Baltimore and recently had graduated from TESST College. I told him I was working full time and going to school at night and weekends. He was twenty-five. I was twenty-two at the time. He made a decent salary and seemed to be cool peeps. Unlike Landon, it didn't matter to me where you were from as long as you knew how to treat me and act in public. We can't always choose where we're born, but you don't have to be a victim of the environment.

We went out a couple of times, and I had a good vibe. He was a gentleman opening the doors, pulling out chairs, taking my hand. Conversations were nice, no pressure. I decided, why not take things to the next level? Like I said earlier, his dick game was all right. It wasn't that he was lacking in size or width. His dick was a good eight inches. It was his rhythm. We would get into a good rhythm, and he would stop because he was about to cum. Then he would start some other rhythm. I'd get into that, and he'd stop again. Now his tongue game, *that* was on point. He took his time and did everything right.

Another issue I had with him was money. He was always crying broke. Every time I wanted to do something, such as take a trip or dinner, he was broke. I couldn't understand why he stayed broke. He didn't have any kids, and he stayed with his mother. According to him, she needed him financially. That should have put me on alert right there. Instead, I stayed naïve. Soon, he was inquiring about *my* money. This was the day before our breakup.

"Why you have all this expensive stuff? I thought you didn't make that much money?" Derek asked.

"What expensive stuff? Why are you worried about my salary?"

"You're the one always counting pennies, but you have Louis Vuitton, Coach, Gucci shoes, and lot of other designer shit. Last time I checked, you couldn't buy that at Walmart. You stealing or is some other nigga buying you shit?"

"Are you serious?" I asked, looking at him like he bumped his damn head.

"Did I stutter?"

I looked at him real good and counted to ten before responding. "First of all, don't say 'nigga' in my house. There are no slave masters in here, and the word should be abolished."

"There you go with those big words."

"'Abolished' is not a big word. All I'm saying is it wasn't cool then, and it certainly is not cool now. But, back to my stuff. Just because someone has nice things does not mean they're stealing or some man is buying it. A lot of my extra money comes from grants. I work full time and pay for everything I have. My pay is decent, and none of your damn business. As far as counting pennies, that is called 'managing money.' I only spend what I can afford. Everything I buy is on sale. My designer 'shit,' as you called it, came from New York. I go there once a month with Landon."

"Oh, that trick," he said.

"Excuse me? You don't talk about my friend like that. You don't know her like that."

"And I don't want to know her stuck-up ass. She's walking around like she fuckin' royalty."

"Whatever. She's still my friend. I haven't met any of yours, so I can't talk about them."

I did have to admit the one time Landon met Derek she was a little snobbish. She acted like Whitley from *A Different World* in her earlier years. She asked him, "What are you? A thug? Gangsta? I bet you listen to 50 Cent all day. What up, yo?" she said while laughing.

I know Derek wanted to go off on her, but didn't because she was my friend. I later blamed it on the liquor, but knew she would have said it regardless. I was glad she didn't say more.

"Yasmin, come here. I apologize for getting a li'l loud earlier. I like you, Ma. I'm feelin' you."

"Whatever, Derek."

"Come on, Ma. I'm sorry. Bring your sexy ass over here so I can slurp you up. You know you want this tongue and dick up in you."

When he started talking dirty, it did turn me on. Something about this thug turned me on. Dumb, yes, but he had my panties wet.

"You wanna go to a cookout wit' me tomorrow?" he asked.

"Whose?"

"My peeps. I wanna show off my girl."

We'd been dating six months. I was curious to meet his peeps, so I agreed. "OK."

*

The next day, he picked me up in his Chevy Impala and took me to this park called Druid Hill. It definitely was different. Never had I been to a park where there weren't any sliding boards or swings for kids. It looked like one big fashion show for adults. I should have run then.

His mama was straight ghetto. They said forty was the new twenty. Not over here. This forty-year-old woman was just a hot ghetto mess. Did I mention her son is twenty-five? She looked like Shenaynay. She was a decent size, an eight, but was squeezing in a size two. She had on these white, tight, bikini shorts. Yes, I called them bikini because I could see her pubic hair. She had on a ripped-white tank top that was cut at the bottom. The top had *"SEXY"* written on it to match the tattoo across her breast. You could see the stretch marks from her six kids. She needed to sit down with her bright orange lipstick-wearing self. If that wasn't enough, she had a bright orange bikini top underneath.

Her extralong acrylic nails with bright orange rhinestone designs matched the acrylic toes in her four-inch bright orange sandals. The hair—oh, where do I begin? Because she was wearing orange she felt the need to coordinate. There were bright orange streaks throughout her hair. At least she used tracks. How do I know? The tracks were showing. Her hair was styled in two spiraled ponytails on each side with Chinese bangs.

I can't forget the nose ring, the gold tooth, the gold rings on every finger, and big gold hoop earrings. She definitely looked like the female version of Dennis Rodman.

"Hey, girl," Mama Shenaynay said.

Oh no, she has a tongue ring. Trying not to laugh, I said, "Hi, how are you?"

"Girl, that's a good weave you got. Is that the Remy Velvet human hair? I saw that at the Chinese store on Pennsylvania and North Avenue. What number is that? Is that #33? What color contacts are they? I goin' have to go get me some of those too."

Either she wasn't paying attention to my face or didn't care to acknowledge my shock of how blunt she was. Before I could respond, Derek spoke.

"Nah, Ma, this my baby real hair and eyes."

"Ya mama or daddy must be white. Derek then got some jungle fever."

"Nope, my father is dark skin and my mother is a shade darker than me."

She just looked at me like, "Yeah, right."

The rest of day was even worse. I felt like I was in a Maury Povich audience. A person can get tired of hearing about baby daddy and baby mama drama. Then there were his cousins that tried to talk to me, slipping me their cell numbers. One cousin said dumb stuff like, "I would give you my house number, but my baby mama don't have nowhere to go so I'm letting her stay with me. She be getting jealous and causing a whole lot of trouble."

Another one said, "Fuck Derek. You need to be with a real man. He can't make you cum like me. Besides, by the time he finishes paying all that child support, the only thing he can buy you is a Happy Meal from McDonald's."

At that point I was pissed and ready to go. I could deal with the cousins, but this motherfucker told me he didn't have any kids. This would explain why his lying ass was always broke. I just smiled at the cousin and said, "No thanks."

I didn't see Derek so I just sat and tried to relax. I was going to eat until I saw everything came from Murray Steakhouse. Doesn't Murray's have a recall on meat like every month? Anyway, I was not taking any chances.

After getting crazy stares, I decided to go look for Derek. I overheard one of the females yapping. "She think she cute. She know that's not her real hair."

I started to respond, but I thought, why bother. I knew she was upset because her man was one of the fools who tried to talk to me.

I finally found Derek and told him I was ready to go. He didn't look pleased, but fuck him and his lying ass.

Well, this fool started cursing and acting out of character. He told me he wasn't leaving yet.

I realized he was drunk, but I was beyond mad and pissed. I didn't want him talking to me or taking me home at that point so I just called a cab.

While I was waiting for my cab, I had the unfortunate pleasure of experiencing other members of this Jerry Springer clan. I thought I had to run for cover one time. While sitting there looking at the fashion show, all of a sudden I heard this loud noise that sounded like a machine gun. I was in shock and couldn't move. I was praying to God that I didn't die, scared out of my mind. Well, come to find out it was Derek's grandfather. He got up, started to rub his stomach, and scratched his balls. Then he said, "Whew, I knew I shouldn't ate those beans. They sure was good though. I'mahavagitmore." Yeah, toward the end, it became difficult to understand him because his teeth fell out. Apparently he didn't have any more Fixodent. He did get some more of those beans, however. He tore it up, gums and all. Later on, he had a repeat explosion, but this time, something leaked out. Then he said, "Well, better out than in."

But the one who took the prize was Uncle Peanut. Uncle Peanut was a drunk that you could smell from miles away. Not only did he stink, he looked a mess. He had his shirt off, exposing his big beer belly which had him looking like he was ten months pregnant. He had on a pair of shorts that were so tight and funky, I could literally see the imprint of his testicles. His ass looked like it was begging for air. If he had taken off the shorts I'm sure they would have stood and ran. His ass got its wish that day. Uncle Peanut was dancing to "Pass the Courvoisier," getting his groove on, when he dipped down low, fell on his ass, and busted his pants. To make matter worse, when he stood up, we found out he wasn't wearing any underwear. Oh, my bad. He was. It was a big crusty dookie stain. I guess he had the beans too.

Later that night, the fool called me trying to apologize, saying he would make it up to me. I cussed him out and told him forget he ever knew me. He came by my apartment a few times, and I ignored him. I even started taking my car to a different dealership. Problem was he didn't understand no, so I threatened him with a restraining order. *That* got his attention. He said he couldn't jeopardize his parole, more newfound information. The calls, however, continued. He used to call every day; now he's down to once a month. Just thinking about Derek put me in a bad mood. So that's enough about him.

Tonight, I am going to unwind. Today is my new beginning. I am leaving all the negativity behind. I am focusing on Yasmin, my career, and financial stability. Relationships could wait. But if I did meet someone tonight, it will be someone without the drama.

While waiting for Landon, I took the opportunity to tidy up my apartment. It wasn't dirty, but I like for everything from my apartment to my life to be organized. Living alone is an independency I loved. My parents never showed much concern for anything that I've done. So I never had attention or company to miss. When I moved out it was the same nonchalant attitude I was used to. Actually, I take that back. My mother said, "Don't be a slut." In my spacious two-bedroom two-bath oasis, there was no tension. Here, I didn't feel like a guest overstaying my welcome.

Just as I was about to call Landon I heard a beep.

Looking outside, I saw Landon in her silver 2001 Mercedes CLK320. Landon is an only child, and S.P.O.I.L.E.D. describes her best. Her lawyer parents had their own law firm. The car was her graduation gift.

When I got to the car, Landon was on her cell lying to her latest victim about how she loved him and missed him. I admired her cream BCDG tube dress that stopped above the knees. Her hair was cut in a short fly do, spiked with blond highlights. She had long, dangling earrings and a necklace to match. Her stilettos were classy, yet said "fuck me." Topping it off, she wore her signature scent, Ralph Laurens, Romance.

"Where are we going, Landon?"

She put up a finger, shushing me.

"I'm sorry, sweetheart, that's my friend. I was trying to keep it as a surprise, but she's helping me out. I want to get something special for you."

I rolled my eyes. This girl needs to stop.

"OK, sweetie, I'll see you tomorrow night. Bye."

"Landon, you are so full of it. Who was that?"

"That was Eric."

I hunched my shoulders, "Who?"

"Eric Ayers. He plays for the Washington Wizards. I told you about him. We've been talking for about two months. Do you listen to me?"

"Like I can keep up with all your men. Where did you meet him?"

"Whatever. Don't hate. Unlike you, I date men with a future, not inner-city thugs. He's new to the area and was looking for a home."

Landon is a real estate agent in the area. She sells only to the elite. Meaning, for Landon, your salary must be a minimum of $100,000. Another criterion is that the clients must be looking for a home at a minimum of $500,000. I love Landon, but sometimes she can get above herself. I try to tell her to calm down or be nice, but Landon has a mind of her own. Like I said, she's an only child, used to getting what she wants, when she wants. Since she never had to share or fight for anything, at times she showed no empathy. My family was not poor, but like I said earlier, I am the black sheep. I had to share and work. College was partially paid for, which is why it took me five years, rather than four, to finish. It was also expected for me not to receive anything lower than 3.5 GPA.

"Let me guess, your parents did some legal work, and, of course, they had to refer you."

"Networking is key. Well, connections work best, but enough about me. This is your night so let's go party. Any requests?"

"You're right. Tonight is the beginning of my life. Time to let go!"

"Well, it's about time! Dream, here we come."

2
Dreamin'

D ream was a new club in the D.C. area, and the hottest spot in town. Of course, when we arrived, the line was ridiculous. However, I was with Landon, and waiting was not an option. We strolled to the entrance, she gave her name, and we were in. Dream was definitely *the* place to be. The four levels of partying and the men that I'd seen so far were HOT. My mind was racing, thinking of the things I'd like to do with them.

"What level should we go to?" Landon asked, breaking me from my trance.

"Let's go to the second floor. I need a drink." As we made it to our destination, it seemed as if the men were getting finer. I was definitely ready to have some fun tonight.

"What can I get you?" the bartender asked, winking at Landon. He wasn't bad looking either. He stood about 6 foot 1, with dark skin, a muscular build, dark ebony eyes, his hair was cut in a Caesar, and he had straight white teeth.

I caught Landon rolling her eyes. "Apple martini."

Never taking his eyes off of Landon, he asked for my order.

"I'll take a Malibu Paradise."

After the bartender left to get our drinks, I took the opportunity to tell Landon to be nice.

"Landon, please be nice. I don't want any drama. Today I'm celebrating, all right?"

She looked at me like, *What the hell are you talking about?*

"I know you see the bartender all in your face. I just want you to be nice when you reject him, okay?"

Before I could get a reply, the bartender returned.

"Here you go, ladies," he said as he placed the drinks in front of us. Then he returned his attention to Landon. "How you doing, sexy? How about you give me your number? I can make you a special drink."

"Sexy, I am," Landon smiled. "How about you give me yours, and I'll give you a call."

I almost choked on my drink. Purse $200, shoes $100, Landon being nice PRICELESS $$.

The bartender wrote his number down and handed it to her. "Sexy, what's your name? When are you going to call?"

Landon looked over at me and mouthed, *"I'm sorry."* Turning toward the bartender, she said, "Call you? For what? Obviously, you're a little slow. I was trying to be nice, but you had to push it." She then turned, backed away from the bar, and spun around. "Look at me. You said it yourself. I'm sexy. Nothing on me is cheap. What can you do for me? I like the finer things in life. Make me a drink. This apple martini is weak like your rap game. Next time, try something original. Again, let me reiterate, your rap game is weak. This drink is weak, so I know the sex is weak." Landon then twisted her face in a look of disgust and grabbed my arm.

"Come on, Yas, let's go."

"Landon, all of that was not necessary. You did not have to go there. All you had to do was say, 'Okay,' and throw the number away. I knew you being nice was too good to be true."

Landon looked at me. "Are you done yet?"

This bitch was pissing me off. I love her like a sister, but sometimes I wonder how we remain so close.

"Landon, remember, this is my night. No drama. Leave the divatude back there."

Landon laughed. "I tried. OK, now I'm on my best behavior."

"Good. Let's go get a table."

We lucked up and were able to get a good table that allowed us to see who was leaving and coming on the floor. We sat there for a while checking out the scenery.

"Damn, Landon, messing with you I left my drink at the bar. Go get me another one." Before she could protest, I said, "You owe me, and I want the same thing."

Landon pouted but went.

I sat back enjoying the music. They were playing Nelly's "Hot in Herre." It definitely was the truth. I decided to let my eyes scroll around the club. As I was scrolling I saw him, and I swear, my heart skipped beats.

He didn't have a name right now, but my mission was to find out. I've seen him a couple of times at Starbucks. Always too scared to approach him, I stayed in the background. Besides, he always looked to be in a rush, or he was on the cell phone running out the door. Either way, he took my breath away then, and he definitely is now. I don't think he ever noticed me. Tonight was going to be different.

I took this opportunity to really check him out. He stood 6 foot 4 with a smooth caramel skin complexion. He had the muscular build of an NBA player. His straight black hair was cut in a Caesar, and he had the sexiest goatee to match. His eyes were the most beautiful shade of grey. His brown slacks and button-down cream shirt complemented his complexion. I wanted him. Just looking at him gave me chills. I could feel my panties getting wet. Just when I thought it couldn't get better, he looked up and our eyes connected. I felt an instant surge of sexual energy, and it kept increasing. I had to have him; no substitute would do. My dream was becoming a reality tonight.

"Yasmin, are you okay? Yasmin," I heard Landon say. However, it didn't register until I felt her poking me.

"What?"

"Are you okay?"

"Yes, I was trying to get a love connection with Mr. Sexy before you interrupted me."

Landon followed my gaze and saw my eye candy. "Nice."

Sexy was still there stealing glances at me as well. It looked as if he was going to approach me. *"Yes Yes Yes!"* my mind screamed, but it abruptly stopped when I heard,

"Hey, pretty women, what are you two up to?"

It was Kevin, a friend of ours. He's cute, a 6 foot 3 bronze Adonis with a six-pack to match. Dark ebony eyes, pretty white teeth. He definitely has model looks, but instead, chose a career in law, working at Landon's parents' law firm. Kevin wanted to date me, but I told him I didn't want to mess up our friendship. Truthfully, I didn't feel a sexual or love connection. Kevin still tried, but I just didn't look at him that way. He is more like a big brother. Talk about bad timing.

"Hey, Kevin," Landon said while hugging him and turning toward Mr. Sexy. "Yasmin has her eye on a guy over there."

"Who, Braxton? Yasmin, you can do better than that."

I turned around, smiling at him. His words gave me hope. "Braxton I like, so you know him. Give me the facts. Introduce me."

"Well, hello to you too, Yasmin, and no," Kevin said.

"Sorry, Kevin. Hello, and why can't I meet Braxton?"

"I don't know him that well. We went to high school together. He always kept a lot of women. You're too good for him. You need someone like me."

That's when I knew to ignore Kevin and figure out a way to meet Braxton on my own.

"Congratulations, graduate. So, Yasmin, can I have a dance?" he asked.

"No, and thanks. Go dance with Landon. She needs to cool off."

"Excuse you?" Landon said.

I looked at Landon, pleading that she would go along with the flow. I needed to meet Mr. Braxton. She caught the hint and grabbed Kevin's arm.

"Come on, Kevin, show me what you got. Let's go upstairs to the loft." She turned around to me. "Now *you* owe *me*."

I laughed. "Thank you."

Once I made sure the coast was clear, I gathered my nerve and made it to the dance floor. The DJ must have been reading my mind because Destiny Child's, "Bootylicious" was playing. I danced with myself and prayed Mr. Braxton was watching. I was shaking my jelly, and I knew I was doing it right because several guys approached me. Unlike Landon, I smiled and said, no thank you. The record was over, and my hopes of dancing with Mr. Braxton were over as well. The DJ now played "Hey Ma" by Cam'ron. I was making my way back to the table when I felt a strong, firm hand grab mine.

"Can I get a dance?"

Braxton.

"Be calm, don't act a fool, keep it together," I told myself.

Smiling, I replied, "Sure."

He chuckled. "I was a little nervous to approach you. I saw how you were turning brothers away."

Damn, he's sexy. "Well, I didn't want to dance with any of those brothers."

"So, you saying you wanted to dance with me?"

"I'm dancing with you, aren't I?"

He turned me around so that my back was on his chest and pulled me close. "I like your style, straight to the point. What's your name, Beautiful?"

I arched my back a little, tilting my neck so he could get a better view of my 36 DDs. "Yasmin, and yours?"

Pulling me closer with his breath tickling my ear, he said softly, "Braxton."

Damn, he feels so good; this feels right. He even smells good wearing the men's version of Issey Miyake. My body melted into his. I was praying he never lets me go. As he gyrated his hips, I moved my body to match his. The DJ was so on point tonight. "Bonnie and Clyde" by Jay-Z and Beyoncé was now playing.

"What are you doing here tonight, Beautiful?"

I loved the way he called me beautiful, and if he kept breathing on my neck like that, I was going to have an orgasm.

"I'm out celebrating with my best friend, Landon. I graduated today from College Park, and you? What brings you to Dream?"

"Congratulation, Yasmin, and today's my birthday."

Perfect. He's a Taurus. I'm a Capricorn. We're the perfect zodiac match.

"Thank you and Happy Birthday." I knew he was about to ask for my number, and I was ready to give it.

"Yasmin!"

I turned around to see Kevin and Landon. He really was pissing me off, messing up my hookup.

"I see someone is trying to get your attention. I'll talk to you later, Beautiful," he said kissing my cheek before walking away.

"Kevin, why did you go and do that?"

"Do what?" he asked with a smirk.

"Okay, so you're playing dumb now." I walked off the dance floor, grabbing Landon.

"Did you get his number?" she asked.

"I was until asshole Kevin messed it up." Just then, Kevin came to the table with a drink like everything was cool.

"I know you're still not upset about me interrupting your dance. You want to dance? Come on and dance with me."

I gave him an evil look and went back on the dance floor. I knew if I didn't give him a dance he would bother me the rest of the night. We danced to a couple of songs. Kevin, realizing I wasn't into it, finally gave me mercy.

"Yas, I'm going to head back over there with my boys. I'll catch you later." He kissed me on the cheek before walking away.

I walked back to the table to see Landon had company. She was talking to this guy, very cute but not as cute as Braxton; still, not bad at all. He was about six feet, chocolate, had wavy hair and deep dimples.

"Hello," I said, sitting down.

"Hello," Mr. Sexy Chocolate said. Staring at me a little too hard, he began to make me feel uncomfortable.

"Will, this is my friend, Yasmin."

"Anyone ever told you that you two look like sisters?"

"Yes, Yasmin and I get that all the time, but we're just the best of friends."

"So, ladies, what can I get you tonight?" Will asked.

"I'll take an Amaretto Sour, and you can get Yasmin Grey Goose with cranberry."

Will walked away to get our drinks.

"Very cute, Landon. What's the occupation?" Knowing Landon like I do, I knew Will was paid.

"Yassy, that's William Mathis. He plays for the Pittsburgh Stealers. Did you listen to me? Did I teach you anything? I keep trying to tell you stop wasting your time with minimum-wage mechanics. The guy, Braxton, you were talking to earlier, I don't recognize him from any NFL or NBA stats I have. He was dressed decent enough in Sean John, but that could be his only outfit. What line of work is he in?"

Rolling my eyes at Landon, I said, "I keep telling you I don't date guys based on their bank accounts. I don't need a guy to buy me anything. I have my own money. I don't know anything really about Braxton. I didn't get a chance to find out because you couldn't keep Kevin occupied."

"Yasmin, I occupied Kevin for twenty minutes. Such a shame you really don't listen to me. How many times do I have to tell you, you should know the occupation within the first five minutes? This way, you know if he's worth the time. Life is too short to be spending it with someone who can't provide for you."

I just shook my head. I didn't feel like getting into this battle with her. I looked up to see Will returning with a friend. His friend was okay looking, but I was not interested. I wanted Braxton. The friend is about the same height as Will, with a medium brown complexion and bald head. He had no facial hair and a gap in between his teeth. Overall, he did nothing for me.

"I'm back, ladies. I hope I didn't keep you waiting too long. This is my friend, Charles."

Will grabbed Landon's hand. "Charles, this is Landon." He looked over at me. "That's her friend, Yasmin."

Charles said hello and took a seat next to me. I saw him winking at Will like they were scheming something.

I moved closer to Landon. "Hello."

"Baby, you don't have to move over. I don't bite," Charles winked.

"No, I'm all right where I am."

Just then I looked up and saw Braxton across the room. He looked at me, smiled, and then walked away. From what I could see, he was leaving the club. I wanted to run over there, but remembered Charles was sitting next to me. Shit! Why can't these guys get the hint I don't want them? First Kevin, now Charles. I was really about to be a bitch now.

Landon played the oblivious role. "Will, I haven't seen you before. Do you live here in D.C.?"

"No, Charles and I are just visiting. We decided to stay for the night. We have rooms at the Renaissance. It's getting crowded in here. We can go back to our rooms and talk, if you want."

I saw Charles smirk.

"No, I have to get up early. If you or Charles are ready to go, go ahead. Landon and I will be fine."

Landon quickly spoke up. "Will, can you go get me another drink?"

Catching Landon's hint, the two men got up to get more drinks.

Landon got straight to the point. "What's your problem?"

"Nothing. That's your thing. I am not going anywhere with them. You say you don't waste any time with men without money. I don't waste my time with men I don't like."

"Remember, you owe me," Landon reminded her.

"Landon, it's obvious they want sex, and you know I don't do that. I have to like the person and feel some type of connection. And especially not with someone I just met at a club."

"There you go. No one is trying to get married. We're twenty-three. I'm just trying to have a good time. Nothing serious. I just need to unwind. Sex is just what I need. You get attached too easily."

"Landon, you need to just chill. This is not the time to get into it, so if you want to go, then go, but make sure you wrap it up."

"Of course. No glove no love."

Instances such as this make me question my friendship with Landon. She and I have had this argument many times before. Although Landon irks the hell out of me, I still remain friends with her. In the end, she is my girl. We have this crazy bond. She brings out my wild side, and I try to tame her wild side. Unfortunately, I'm usually not successful. Despite her bitchiness and rudeness, Landon is a good person. She could be more tactful, but overall, she's a good person. I knew if I needed her she'd be there.

Landon is a sex addict. She loves sex and can't get enough of it. I constantly warn her about getting pregnant or catching an STD. But she just says condoms are always worn, and if she got pregnant she would be compensated. That's why she only messes with men with money. The men she chose know Landon has money and assume she only wants them. They think she genuinely cares for them and easily let their guard down—big mistake on their part.

"Well, you, Will, and Charles can go do whatever, but I need a way home," I said.

"You can take my car," she offered.

"No, you take your car in case you need a getaway."

I swear Landon is so smart in many ways but can be naïve in other ways.

"Well, I'll drop you off and meet up with Will later. We can just hang out here a little while longer."

"Cool."

When Will and Charles returned, Landon grabbed Will and headed right to the dance floor.

Charles took this as an opportunity to get close to me. "Yasmin, what do you have to do so early in the morning? Is your man at home waiting for you?"

Rolling my eyes, I said, "Let's just cut the bullshit. I don't have a man. I'm just not interested in you. So you can stop trying to make a love connection. It's not happening. There are a lot of females in here; help yourself."

I could tell he wanted to say something but decided not to. Charles got up and headed to the dance floor.

Kevin approached. "Are you okay over here? It looked like that guy was giving you a hard time."

"Now you come to my rescue after he left. I see you're backward tonight. I was doing just fine dancing with Braxton. You broke that up. Yet, you allowed me to sit with someone I didn't like."

Kevin laughed. "I told you earlier, Braxton is not good for you."

"Kevin, I told you, I love you like a brother. I don't want to date you. I don't want to mess up our friendship."

"Okay, if you want Braxton, then fine."

Hugging Kevin I asked, "So tell me all you know."

Shaking his head, he replied, "I didn't say I was going to hook you up."

"Kevin!"

"Yasmin, really, I don't know the guy like that. We went to high school together. He went away to college. I went away. That's it."

"OK," I said, defeated.

"Well, since you broke my heart again I'm going to find someone to mend my broken heart."

I sat at the table daydreaming about Braxton. I didn't notice Landon or Will approach the table.

"Are you ready, Yasmin?"

"Yes."

Will and Landon exchanged info, and I headed to the door. While waiting for Landon, I saw Charles with some girl. They walked past, and Charles took the opportunity to whisper, "You fucked up. You could have had me, but that's OK. I got a *real* woman now. You a little on the chunky side and don't look like you can fuck anyway."

I started to say something but figured, why bother. I had hurt his ego. Landon made her way to the door and we left.

*

Later that night, I lay in bed thinking about Braxton. I couldn't get him out of my mind. It felt so good the way he held me. I kept thinking of possible sexual positions. I didn't know this man, yet I was sprung. This is one time I wish I would have been more like Landon and got his number. I had to do something. I had to have him. I'm going to find him, and this time when I did, I would get his number.

3
Hey, You

It is the end of June. Two months had passed, and I still haven't seen Braxton. I frequented Starbucks hoping to run into him but still no luck. I was becoming obsessed with him. Okay, I *am* obsessed with finding Braxton. I finally decided if it was meant to be, then it will be. I am not going to obsess over him any longer. I parked my car and headed to Starbucks for my Starbucks fix of a Grande white chocolate mocha.

Today was going to be a busy day. My boss was taking me offsite to set up a 401(k) proposal for a local company. I've been working at Legg Mason for a little over a month and was looking forward to the experience. I can honestly say I love my job. Another bonus is I'll get to do some traveling, sometimes staying away as long as three months at a time.

I was crossing the street when I suddenly saw Braxton. Instantly, I lost my breath. I was so glad I decided to wear my sage Anne Klein suit. The skirt hugged my hips just right and stopped right above my knees. The jacket fit like it was tailored just for me. My accessories and Gucci pumps complemented the outfit. I took out my MAC lip gloss and retouched my lips and picked up my pace.

"Excuse me, miss," I heard as I felt someone tap my shoulder.

I turned around to see a nice-looking guy. He reminded me of Tyson, the model, but I was not interested.

"Miss Lady, you dropped your pen. How about you use it and give me your number?"

I smiled. "Sorry, I have a boyfriend. You can have the pen."

I turned around to find Braxton, only to discover he was gone. I was really upset. Now that I'm on a mission everyone wants me. Every time I get close to him, some guy stops me.

Twenty minutes later, I was walking into Legg Mason depressed. I headed to my office and prepared for the offsite meeting.

"Hello, Miss Yasmin Sinclair."

I looked up to see Greg walking into my office. Gregory Johnson, another financial advisor with the company, thought he was God's gift to women.

"Good morning, Greg."

Licking his lips, he said, "You look nice. Why don't you let me take you out to lunch today?"

"I've told you I don't date anyone I work with."

"I didn't say date. I relieve your stress, you relieve mine."

Just when I was about to tell Greg off, my boss walked in.

"Good morning, Mr. Rivers," I said.

Mr. Rivers replied, "Good morning, Yasmin, Greg. Yasmin, are you all set for today?"

Greg quickly excused himself, but not before winking.

"Yasmin, I told you to call me Bob. When we're at this meeting I want them to see we are a large company capable of handling their needs. But at the same time, let's show we are family."

Bob and I went over the presentation and made sure everything was in order. I was nervous because not only was a lot riding on this deal, but because it was with BET. BET is vital figure in the black community. Anyway, I could be a part of making it happen. I was glad to be of aid. Blacks needed to invest more in their future. One of my future goals is to give seminars to blacks on how to invest their money. Credit card companies are lined up ready to give any and everybody a card. I have seen so many college students graduate, only to have thousands of dollars worth of debt.

We arrived at BET, and Bob must have sensed my nervousness because he kept assuring me everything would be fine.

"Good morning. I'm Mr. Rivers, and this is Ms. Sinclair. We're from Legg Mason. We have an eleven o'clock with Mr. Simms."

The receptionist stood up and smiled. "Good morning, Mr. Rivers, Ms. Sinclair. Mr. Simms will be with you momentarily."

She then led us to a conference room.

I took the opportunity to settle my nerves as Bob and I began to set up.

Fifteen minutes later, I heard the door open. I looked up, only to lose my breath for the second time today. I wanted to scream, jump for joy. It's *him.* Here he is. Braxton! *Calm down!* I try to tell myself. But he looks so handsome in his grey Kenneth Cole suit with Kenneth Cole fragrance and shoes to match. *Get it together. Don't stutter. He is too sexy. I have on a light color suit and can't risk my panties getting wet. Yasmin, take control. This is your job. Be professional.* I glanced down at my jacket to see my nipples stood erect. Well, that did it. Embarrassed and flushed describes me.

Bob walked toward Braxton and made the introductions. "Mr. Simms, we've talked to you on several occasions, so you know who I am. But this is Yasmin Sinclair. She'll be assisting me with this account."

"Nice to meet you, Ms. Sinclair," Braxton said, shaking my hand. He then shook Bob's hand and told us to have a seat.

I took a seat and when I was sure he was looking, slowly crossed my legs.

Bob suggested I start the presentation.

I managed to get some nerves from somewhere and began to speak. I laid out our plan and explained why Legg Mason was the company to choose. I was articulate and poised. I had a very good feeling. Finally, I looked over at Bob, and he gave me a nod. I sat down and gave the floor to him. Bob recapped what I said and took questions. I'd be lying if I said I paid attention to anything Bob was saying. I silently sat conspiring on a way to give Braxton my number. Disappointingly, I was unable to come up with one.

The meeting was over, and as we were gathering our things, Braxton approached. "Ms. Sinclair, may I have your card? I may have some questions later. Bob, is that all right with you?"

"Not a problem," Bob consented.

He didn't have to ask me twice. I pulled out a business card, handing it to him, and said, "Please call me, Yasmin." *Good. I didn't need a plan after all.*

"And you can call me Braxton."

Bob and I headed back to Legg Mason. He talked, but I only halfway listened. I do know he did say he was impressed with my presentation and told me to keep up the good work.

Truthfully, I was more excited about making progress with Braxton, but wondered if he would date me or be hesitant now due to our work relationship. I couldn't wait to call Landon to get her input. Once I reached my office, I called her, but got her voice mail so I left a message telling her to call me.

I started working on other accounts and lost track of time. When I looked at the clock, I saw that it was two o'clock. I hadn't taken lunch, and I was hungry. Just as I started heading out the door, my phone rang. It had to be Landon.

"Hello, this is Ms. Sinclair, how may I help you?"

"Hello, Yasmin," a male voice replied.

"Yes, hello," I said again, not recognizing the voice.

"How are you?"

"May I ask to whom I'm speaking?"

"This is Braxton."

He sounded good on the phone too.

"Braxton, did you have any questions about the presentation?"

"Question, yes, about the presentation, no."

"Excuse me?"

"Let me get straight to the point. If you aren't busy Friday, I would you like to take you out."

Did I just hear him correctly? He's asking me out? Yes, finally!

"Hello, are you still there?" Braxton asked, breaking me from my trance.

"I apologize. I would love to go out with you. Where are we going?"

"I haven't figured that part out yet. I had to make sure you said yes first. How about I pick you up at your house Friday at eight?"

"Sure."

I gave Braxton my address and telephone number. Then I hung up and ran out of the office. I had no idea where we were going, but I knew whatever I wore he wouldn't forget.

4
Caramel Kisses

riday finally arrived, and I was so pumped. It was already 6:30, and I still hadn't decided on an outfit. I had just stepped out of the bathtub when my doorbell rang. I knew it was Landon. She insisted on coming over to help me get ready. I checked my peephole, however, to make sure it was her. I didn't need any pop-ups from Derek or anyone else. Once I told her Braxton is a senior business analyst at BET she was okay with the date. I let Landon in, and she walked directly into my bedroom.

"So where is he taking you?" she asked as she began pulling outfits from my closet.

I sat on the bed applying lotion to my body. "I don't know. He just told me he was picking me up at eight."

Landon continued to rummage through my closet. Finally, she pulled out three outfits for me to try on.

While I preferred to wear something that flowed and not cling, Landon had other ideas. Especially since it was the end of June and the weather had been terrible. Even though it was only eighty-two degrees outside, with the humidity it felt more like ninety-nine.

"Landon, it's too hot and humid to wear this. I want to be comfortable. I don't want my clothes to stick to me, and the clothes are too tight," I protested quickly, declining some bodysuit.

"Why did you call me over here if you were going to complain about what I picked out? You're just being your usual self-conscious self. You look good, Yasmin. Nothing is wrong with your body. How many times do I have to tell you that?"

I picked up the other outfits she had pulled out and put them back in the closet. "Landon, don't start."

"All I'm saying is you called me over here. If you don't need my services, let me know; I'll leave. There are a lot of people who do appreciate my services."

"I know there are a lot of men looking for a booty call tonight. You can go provide your service after you help me."

Landon laughed and sat on my bed. "Hater."

"Calm down. I call it like I see it. All I said was it was too hot for those outfits. You took that and ran with it. You got theatrical and went into your spoiled-brat mode," I teased.

Rolling her eyes, she asked, "Well, do you want my help or not?"

"I called you over here, didn't I? Just pick an outfit that's not tight."

Huffing and puffing, Landon got up off the bed and picked out three more outfits.

I looked over her choices. They were much better.

The first outfit pulled out was a Michael Kors black spaghetti strap dress that flared out at the end. I tried it on. It fit very well but not what I wanted to wear tonight. It wasn't sexy enough. "Landon, this fits well, but I don't want to wear black. I want to wear something more colorful."

The second outfit was an auburn-colored cowl-neck dress that flared out at the bottom. I tried it on and walked over to the mirror. "What do you think?"

Landon walked behind me and started messing with the collar. "It's cute, but I think the collar may be too much."

"I was thinking the same thing."

Looking at the third outfit I was hesitant. I didn't want to wear any pants, but I gave it a try anyway. I slipped on a pair of white-cropped pants that had a deep cuff on the bottom. On the upper left thigh was gold zig-zag embroidery. The top was a deep violet tube that flared out like a baby doll dress. The top layer was sheer with gold designs throughout. Looking at myself in the mirror, I then turned to Landon. "This is the one."

Landon smiled. "Okay, let's get the rest of your accessories together."

We decided on a pair of Via Spiga crystal and gold embroidered sandals. I added a long gold necklace that had a hoop at the end and large hoop earrings. I decided to pull my hair off my face and neck. It was pinned up in the back, but I let some pieces hang.

Finally, I sprayed on some of my cherry blossom Bath and Body Works and decided on Light Blue by D&G.

"So tell me, Landon, who is your employee, I mean, man of the month?"

"Yasmin, are you jealous? I'm just keeping my options open. I'm too sexy to limit myself to one man, and I haven't met anyone to make me want to commit. I like to be free and unattached. You know how I like them one minute, and then the next, they irritate me. I have no tolerance for foolishness."

"Foolishness? If your flavor of the month calls you to tell you he will be there at 12:00 and arrives at 12:30, you don't want to be bothered anymore."

"That's right. Nothing about me is inconsistent, and when I deal with someone, he needs to have his shit together. If he says he will be there at 12:00, he needs to be there at 12:00. Why? Because I took time out of my schedule to accommodate him. I could be spending my time with someone else who would appreciate me. When dealing with Landon, a guy should know I am número uno, top priority. I should not have to keep reiterating that. They have three chances and a list of rules."

Applying my MAC lip gloss and looking at her like she was crazy, I asked, "Three chances?" I wasn't trying to get into the rules. I already know they are outrageous.

"Yes, three chances. I'm not bad. The first time they violate my rules I give them a verbal warning. The second, I give him a written warning, and the third strike you are out the door. Life is too short to limit myself. There are plenty of other men in chocolate city to choose from."

"Whatever. Who are you dating, the guy Will?"

"Yes, along with Eric."

"Who's Eric?"

Landon walked over and sat on bed. "Remember, he's the guy that plays for the Washington Wizards."

"Oh, so you're into sports this season. Which sport do you prefer, basketball or football?"

"Right now, I'm loving both. It's hard trying to juggle both, but that will be simplified soon."

I looked at Landon. "You are choosing one?"

"What did I just tell you? I'm not settling. Well, you know Will is in the NFL, so he'll be going to training camp soon. He'll be tied up until February. And if Eric is still around, he has a verbal warning right now. In February, Eric will be doing his NBA stuff."

I shook my head. "You're scandalous."

"Scandalous? I let Will and Eric know I am not looking for anything serious. I told them let's just enjoy each other's company and we'll see where it goes."

"Alrighty then, Diva."

"Let me tell you about Will. He's fine, as you know. He likes to party and is very spontaneous. Last weekend he called me up and told to pack a bag. Well, he took me to Vegas, and we gambled and sexed all night. His dick is average, eight inches, and is OK in thickness. The sex was just average, like him. He's good to hang out with. However, if you want good sex, then you need a drink and some toys."

I laughed. "You ain't right."

"Now, Eric's a sweetheart. He's very affectionate. He prefers to spend time at home. He's a little too boring. I think he's a bit of a mama's boy. He must have been breast-fed as a baby because he sure can suck some nipples and a clitoris. The sex is off the damn hook. I never knew I was capable of having so many orgasms. I'm getting chills just thinking about it. I think I'll have to call him tonight. His flaw is trying to make me a housewife. That's not happening."

"Don't I know it." I finished getting ready and checked the clock on my dresser to see it was 8:17 ready.

Landon saw me. "Strike one and a big turnoff. This is your first date. That's why we have phones. He could have at least picked up the phone."

I was not in the mood for a Landon tirade. My mind started racing. *Did he get lost? Did he change his mind? Maybe this is a bad idea.* Landon was saying something, but I didn't hear, or want to hear, her. I wish she would shut up. I looked at the clock again. 8:23. *Where is Braxton?*

Landon finally broke me out of my trance. "Yas!"

"What?" I asked, annoyed.

"Don't get mad at me. I didn't stand you up. You look too good to sit in the house. I say fuck him. Let's go out and meet some men. It's 8:24, and it's his loss."

I know this is Landon's way of making me feel better, but she's annoying me. "I haven't been stood up. He's coming."

I think.

Landon looked back at the clock. "At the tone the time will be 8:25 and ten seconds. *Beep.*"

This chick is pushing it. A few more minutes passed before I heard the bell ring. I jumped up, racing to the door.

Landon quickly jumped in front of me. "It's about time. Let me handle this."

Before she opened the door, I said, "Be nice."

Landon opened the door, and there stood Braxton. I admit I was expecting to see another casual outfit. What I saw was contrast. He had on jeans, a white, white Air Force Ones, and a New York Yankees baseball cap. He was still sexy, and I did like the look, but again, I was expecting more. After one inhale of his cologne, Acqua Di Gio, though, I was turned on.

Landon's facial expression, however, said it all. She was not impressed. Her screwup face, an obvious giveaway. She stepped out of the way so he could come in. Once in and his back toward her, she held up her hand, put up two fingers, and mouthed, "Strike two."

I walked over to Braxton and could tell he was checking me out. From what I could see in his eyes, he liked what he saw.

"Braxton, this is Landon, my best friend."

I gave Landon a stern look and mouthed again, "Be nice."

"Braxton, nice to meet you. I was just leaving so, Yas, I'll catch up with you later." She grabbed her things and headed out the door.

Braxton turned to me. "I apologize. I lost track of time. Do you forgive me?"

I smiled. "I will this time but don't make it a habit."

"Have you waiting, Beautiful? Never."

"You *had* me waiting tonight."

Before he could respond my phone rang. The phone was right near where I was standing so I couldn't ignore it. I excused myself. "Hello."

"I'm not feeling Braxton. First, he shows up late and what the fuck does he have on? Your attire is sexy yet classy. He's thuggish. Tell him I'm your mother, something has come up, and you need to cancel. We can go meet some real men who can tell time and look good while they're at it."

I hoped Braxton didn't hear her. "Landon, I don't see your earring. Well, I have to go. Talk to you later." I hung up before she could protest.

Braxton laughed.

"What's so funny?" I asked.

"Is everything OK? Nothing has come up with your mother—I mean, Landon."

Damn, he heard. I guess my face showed my embarrassment because he stopped laughing.

"I see Landon's not feeling me, but I'm not concerned with her. I want to know if you're feeling me."

I didn't know how to answer that. Was I feeling him? I've been dreaming and fantasying about him since the first time I saw him. Words are just words sometimes. I chose rather to show him. I looked him straight in the eye, walked up to him, moved my index finger to indicate I want him face-to-face. Then I wrapped my arms around his neck and kissed him.

Kissing Braxton was even better than I envisioned. His lips were so soft yet firm, lips moist not slobbering wet; perfect. I began sucking on his bottom lip, and he put his tongue in my mouth. I took mine, and we started a dance. This was so sweet. I felt his hands on my ass. It was no surprise when I felt his dick growing by the second, arousing me even more. Moving his hands from my ass, he made his way to the button on my pants.

I was not giving it up that easy. I pulled away; using my thumb to wipe my lip gloss of his lips. Then I grabbed my purse, walked toward the door, and began reapplying my lip gloss.

"Braxton, you never told me, where are we going? Oh, and I am feeling you."

He smiled. "I am definitely feeling you too, Beautiful."

*

We pulled up to Dave & Buster's in Braxton's Black 745 LI BMW. There's nothing like driving in the ultimate driving machine with the ultimate man. The car handled curves so well, and the way it accelerated definitely put it in a class of its own. I wondered how Braxton's sexual performance compared. We didn't really talk during the ride; the radio was the only conversation. I guess we were both thinking about the kiss.

"I hope you don't mind Dave & Buster's. It's been so hectic at work I wanted to have some fun," he said.

"No, not at all. I'm for it," I lied. I really didn't feel like games. I agreed with Landon. I looked too good to be in a game room.

Braxton got out of the car and walked to the passenger side to open the door for me. We walked through a crowd. He grabbed my hand, escorting me to the front. He said something to the guy at the door, and we were in. Connections. Like Landon. Go figure.

"Yasmin, what do you want to do?"

"It doesn't matter."

"Can you play pool?"

"A little. I played sometimes in college for fun. But it's been awhile. So don't beat me too bad."

"I wouldn't do that. I'll make it easy on you."

We made our way to the pool room and were able to get a table. Braxton handed me a stick. "Do you need me to show you how to hold the stick?"

Looking him in the eye, I replied, "I know how to handle a stick, but if you want, you can show me some tricks."

He walked up to me and took the stick. He showed me how to move it through my two fingers. "You think you can handle that?" he asked.

I gave him a seductive look and licked my lips. "I can handle it. When holding the stick, should I move it nice and slow or hard and fast?"

"Well, it depends," he responded.

"Depends?" I asked.

"Yup, depends on what you're trying to do."

"Well, I'll just follow your lead."

He gave me the stick. "Let me see what type of skills you have. You break the balls."

"I have plenty of skills," I said, giving him a wink.

"I'm sure you do. I can't wait to see all of them."

I then walked over to the pool table. Making sure he got a full view of my ass, I bent over to break the balls. I did well, managing to knock in three balls.

"Not bad at all," Braxton smiled.

I tried to knock another ball in but didn't have any luck.

Braxton walked up to the table to take his shot. His back was turned so he didn't see the guy that kept trying to slip me his number.

I tried ignoring him, but he became more persistent. He got up and walked toward me. I moved before he could reach me.

Braxton noticed my uneasiness. "Everything okay?"

I played it off. "Yeah, I'm fine. Just trying to check out your skills."

I messed up his concentration because on the next shot he missed.

I took my turn and knocked in a ball. My outfit must have been HOT because I now had a little crowd watching me. I knew it wasn't because of my pool game. I bent over to make a shot.

"Damn, baby girl, you look real good. Your aim is on point," some guy said, chuckling.

If looks could kill, Braxton would have done the guy in. The guy got the hint and immediately stopped the chuckle.

Braxton walked up on me like he was trying to cover my body.

I tried to continue playing like the outburst didn't happen. On my next shot, I had to stretch to hit the ball. With my upper body stretched over the table, I showed more than a mouthful of breast.

That was enough for Braxton. He walked up to me, grabbing me by the waist, kissed me on the back of the neck, and said, "Let's go play some basketball."

He shouldn't have kissed me there. Doesn't he know that's my spot? Immediately I thought of Erykah Badu's song.

I want somebody to walk up behind me and kiss me
on my neck and
Breathe on my neck. Been such a long time I
forgot that I was fine

I followed Braxton and watched while he made baskets. It looked like he was shooting off some steam. Actually, he was pretty good. Yes, his build was definitely athletic, but I never thought he could play. "Oh, so you got game. Not bad."

"I played in high school, and I still play now from time to time."

I walked closer to him. "I just realized I'm out with you and don't know much about you other than your name and where you work. Tell me about yourself."

He stopped and looked at me. "I could say the same about you. What do you want to know?"

"How old are you? How long have you been with BET? Any kids?"

"I'm twenty-six, been with BET for three years. I have a bachelor's and a master's from Columbia, and I don't have any kids. What about you?"

"That's right, you just had a birthday. I'm twenty-three. I have a bachelor's from College Park, as you know, and I don't have any kids."

"Can you play basketball?" he asked.

"No."

"Come here and let me show you how to shoot."

I walked over, and he got behind me. Enjoying the feel of his body against mine I only halfway listened, making three out of ten baskets. Finally, I gave up and told Braxton to finish.

Braxton played another round while I went to the bathroom. After I used the restroom I noticed a motorcycle ride. It looked fun so I purchased some tokens. One ride turned into three.

"I like how you handle that bike," said a Shemar Moore look-alike.

"Thank you," I said getting off the bike.

"I saw you earlier. I know that wasn't your man. If he is, he's a fool for letting you out of his sight. Call me." He attempted to hand me his number.

I shook my head no. Of course, when I looked up I saw Braxton heading my way. This was not looking good. Every time I try to get close some guy jumps in my face. I hope he realizes I'm not the one initiating.

"What took you so long?" Braxton asked a little too authoritatively, but I let it slide.

Shemar look-alike walked away mouthing, "I'll holla at you later."

"After I left the bathroom I saw the motorcycle and took a ride. I lost track of time. I was just on my way to find you."

He looked at me like he didn't believe me.

I tried to lighten the mood. "So, what do you want to do now? I just bought some tokens. Show me some more of your skills. Help me play some games."

"Hmm, doesn't seem like you're having a hard time getting help," he said, irritated.

"I said I want you to show me."

"I can't tell." He walked away. "Are you coming?"

I felt like Apollonia in *Purple Rain,* the scene where Prince gets jealous of Morris Day. At first the jealousy was cute, but now it was getting old.

I followed Braxton. We played some games and got on some virtual reality ride. After a couple of games, Braxton's sweetness returned.

"Are you ready, Beautiful?"

I'm beautiful again, I thought. "Yes."

"Are you hungry?"

"Yes."

Braxton looked at his watch. "I didn't realize it was so late. It's 1:00 A.M. I don't think anything is open."

"We'll find something."

Braxton grabbed my hand, leading me out the door.

Once outside I felt the humidity. "The weather has been terrible. It's too hot and humid."

"You don't like the heat?" Braxton asked.

"No, do you?"

"I don't like wearing a lot of clothes, so I prefer the warm weather. You like it cold?"

"Warm is one thing. Hot is another. But I do prefer the cold weather. It's easier to deal with, and I like the feeling of being wrapped in my blankets."

"You like the feel of blankets?" he asked.

"Well, maybe this year I'll have someone to wrap up with," I countered, surprising myself with my boldness. Braxton made me feel comfortable, plus, I wanted to make sure this is not our last encounter.

We got in the car and rode around looking for somewhere to eat. The only thing open was a 24-hour diner.

"I wanted to take you somewhere nicer, but I apologize, I lost track of time."

"I see telling time is not one of your better qualities," I said.

"I'm not looking good tonight." He laughed.

"I wouldn't say all that."

"So are you enjoying yourself tonight, Yasmin?"

"I am."

"I'm glad you are. Let's go in and get something to eat."

We went into the diner and ate. We conversed, nothing too heavy, and he told me how he enjoyed working at BET and how one of the perks is getting concert and game tickets. I told him how I was enjoying my position at Legg Mason. Everything was going fine . . . until he went to the bathroom.

"Baby girl, you look real good. I've been watching you since you came in here. And those eyes! Let me get your number so I can take you out," the guy said.

"I have someone," I responded. The guy wasn't bad looking. He was about 6 foot 2, light skin, medium build, and curly hair. But I wasn't interested.

"What your man got to do with me?" he said.

"Look, I'm not interested."

"Baby girl, I bet he can't make you cum like I can," he challenged.

"Well, I guess I'll never find out. And really, I have no desire either."

"Is there a problem?"

I looked up and saw Braxton standing there.

"Nah, man, there's no problem." Mr. Talk Shit lost his nerve and walked away.

"Yasmin, let's go," Braxton said with attitude. He placed some money on the table and walked to the door.

Here we go again, I thought. I got into the car and remained silent, hoping he would calm down by time we got to my place. When we arrived Braxton was still upset. I took off my seat belt and faced him. "Thank you for taking me out. I enjoyed your company."

"Really, I can't tell. Every time I turned around, you had some man in your face."

"I know we don't know each other well, but I never initiated any of those incidents. When they did occur, I never encouraged it to go further. That's not my style."

"Yeah, whatever."

I really liked Braxton and felt the chemistry, but I didn't have the time to put up with his jealousy.

"Braxton, have a good night." I got out of the car and walked to my apartment. When I opened the door I noticed Braxton behind me.

"Yasmin, can I come in?"

"No."

"Yasmin, I apologize. I was out of line. Tonight hasn't been one of my better moments."

"I agree." I walked in leaving the door open for him to follow.

Braxton closed the door and took a seat on the couch. "I see you are in high demand."

"What is that supposed to mean?" I asked, offended.

"Calm down. I just see you attract a lot of guys. When I saw you at Dream, men were lusting after you, and even tonight. I don't like to share. You'll have someone fighting every night."

I took a seat opposite Braxton. "That's not a typical night with me. You know how it is. When you're by yourself no one approaches, but when you show interest in someone, everyone wants you. And who said anything about sharing?"

"How long have you been single?" he asked.

"Almost a year."

"Why so long? Why did you break the man's heart?" he questioned.

"I don't know why I've been single so long. I was focusing on school and career. I didn't break his heart. He had no ambition, and we were going in different directions."

"What's your story? Why are you single?"

He thought about my question. "I never really have been in a relationship. I just date a lot."

The male version of Landon I thought. Go figure.

"Never really have been in a relationship? What does that mean?" I asked.

"Truthfully, I haven't met anyone I wanted to get serious with. I dated the same person at the longest, three months. But it wasn't exclusive."

"Braxton, when you say it wasn't exclusive, was it a mutual decision or a decision only Braxton made?"

He laughed.

Kevin wasn't lying when he said he was a lady's man.

"I plead the Fifth," he stated.

"You know you are wrong, but by taking the Fifth, you've answered my question," I said.

He got serious. "I admit it was a decision only I knew about."

"Braxton, I appreciate your honesty." I looked at the clock. It was 3:02. "It's late. I don't want to keep you out too long."

Braxton laughed again. "Is this your way of politely putting me out?"

I looked at him seriously. "Yes, you like to share the love. I'm not into having casual sex. I need more. You said you don't like to share, and neither do I."

"Who said I want casual sex from you? I admit I've never been in a serious relationship. However, I definitely feel something with you. Are you still ready to put me out?"

I laughed. "Yes. No, you can stay. So what do you want from me?"

"Yasmin, I just want to get to know you. Let's just see where that leads us."

"Okay. Would you like something to drink?" I asked, getting up and turning on the radio to 104.3.

"No, come here and sit next to me," he said.

I sat down, crossing my legs. When Braxton put his arm around me, I snuggled closer. We sat there for a couple of minutes just listening to the music. The sexual tension was building, but I was dealing with it. That is . . . until Floetry.

Once "Say Yes" was on, it was over.

> *There is only one for me*
> *You have made that a possibility*
> *We could take that step to see*

I don't know who started kissing whom, but it was on. I kept telling myself to stop, but it wasn't working.

Braxton lay me down on the couch, getting on top, still kissing me. This time he sucked on my bottom lip. I started rubbing my hands up and down his back. The kiss intensified more. He inserted his tongue in my mouth and began tickling my tongue. I put my tongue in his mouth, and he started sucking mine. *Damn,* I thought. With labored breathing I wondered what else he can suck so well.

Braxton stopped kissing my lips, making his way down to my neck. When he started sucking on my neck I almost screamed. That's my spot. I was thinking *STOP! NO, DON'T STOP!* This felt good. He placed light kisses down to my chest, on my chest. He had one arm around my neck and the other caressing my ass. My nipples were hard and begging him to suck. I couldn't hold it any longer. The moaning started.

He got up off the sofa, pulling me with him. I could see the bulge of his dick pressing against his clothes, and I was ready to jump on it. Braxton took off his T-shirt, exposing his six-pack. Just when I thought he couldn't get any sexier, he proved me wrong. *Yasmin, stop! You can't give it up the first night. He told you he's a freak.*

Braxton pulled down my tube top and took a step back to admire my 36 DDs. He licked his lips and came in. First, sucking my left nipple, next, my right, then he mashed them together, rotating his tongue to lustily lick them both.

I started to rake my nails lightly up and down his back. *"Yasmin, stop! You're not into casual sex. You need more!"* my conscience screamed.

Braxton moved his hand to the back of my neck.

"*Ouoooooooooo,*" I moaned.

Fuck it. This feels too good. I'm not the first person to sleep with someone on the first date, and I won't be the last. If he doesn't call me afterward, I'll get over it. I am, however, going to make it worth my while.

"Hmm, Braxton, that feels so good."

I stopped raking my nails on his back, moving my hands to his stomach. I pushed him back a little, directing him to the chair. Once he was seated, I straddled him. I tilted his head back and began to lick the back of his ear, licking him all the way to his chest. When I reached his nipple, I began to tease it with my tongue. I could feel his dick jumping as I played.

"Yasmin, damn, you got skills."

He shouldn't have said that. I started sucking on his nipple, starting with just a little nibble, but then I took my teeth, adding a little pressure.

Braxton must really like that because next thing I know, he was standing up with my legs wrapped around his waist.

Lowering my legs to the floor, Braxton went straight for the button on my pants. He pulled them down, exposing my purple and gold thong.

Braxton gave me a seductive look. He put his hands on my hips and began pulling my thong down. Once my thong was midway, he got on his knees and began nibbling on my navel, using his hands to remove the rest of my thong.

Once it was off, he got up to retrieve his wallet, pulling out a condom. Braxton walked back over to me and began to kiss me once more.

Continuing the kiss, I unbuckled his pants and allowed them to drop. His dick felt like it was aching to come out. So I took my hands and slid down his boxers. Once they were down, I took the opportunity peek at his dick.

Mesmerized described me at this moment. He had the prettiest dick I've ever seen. It was long, thick, and caramel, just like him. His dick reminded me of the candy, Sugar Daddy. I remembered how you would put it in your mouth, immediately tasting the sweetness. How it would stick to the top of your mouth and you could suck it all day long and that's just what I wanted to do to his dick. But first, I needed to feel him inside of me. I wanted him bad. All I needed was three pumps. I *needed* to feel him.

Braxton was thinking the same thing. He quickly ripped the condom wrapper and slid it on. Then he pulled me close and began caressing my back. He moved back and sat in the chair. He wanted me to ride him. Hmm, was I up for the challenge!

I was ready. His dick was calling my name. I looked and saw the condom stopped three-fourths of the way up. He was a big boy. At least nine and a half inches, and, boy, did he have width! Woo. Nervousness swept my body for about five seconds. I took one look at Braxton and knew I had to ride the pony. Wasting no more time, I straddled him.

Pain is the first thing I felt. It was really tight, and at first, it was really difficult penetrating me. After a little rocking, though, he was in. I began to slowly rotate my hips.

Braxton pumped.

"Mmmmm, Braxton," I moaned. I moved my hips up so that only one-fourth of his dick was in.

Braxton pumped harder.

"Yasmin, baaaaby."

I moved my pussy up again, this time contracting my vaginal muscles and pulling my pussy completely off his dick.

Braxton still pumped. "Shit," he said. He began to shake.

What the fuck? Did I say three pumps? I meant three hundred. I know he did not cum. It's been eight months for me. I don't believe he's a just a ten-second man. I knew he was too sexy and had to be flawed. I assumed the temper and punctuality, not the sex.

Damn, Braxton, you sexy as hell, but I can't mess with you. No wonder you've just been dating. No one can get serious with you with a dick game like this. Shit, did I say it's been eight months and I'm horny as hell? Where are my toys? Got me all worked up. Play it cool, Yasmin. Don't hurt his feelings. What I'm going to do is tell him that I feel sweaty and need to freshen up. I can take a shower, put the showerhead on hard pulse, and let it hit my clit, finish what he started and couldn't finish. Yeah, that'll work. I hope my facial expression doesn't give me away.

I stood up being extra careful not to pull the condom off. On my way to the bathroom, I turned off the radio. Turning around, I gave him my sincerest look. "Braxton, I'm a little sweaty. I'm going to take a shower and freshen up."

Braxton, in turn, stood up retrieving another condom. "I'm not done with you yet."

I looked at him, and then his dick to see it had risen for the occasion.

He slipped on the condom and came behind me. Then he slowly entered me from behind. He started out real slow, bending me over my bathroom sink so I could see my face.

"Don't close your eyes. I want those pretty eyes of yours to see how good I fuck you."

Braxton then proceeded to fuck the shit out of me, speeding up his pace. I was looking at myself make some crazy faces, but I didn't care. His dick belonged in my pussy. He was working it, and I was enjoying every minute. My hair, previously pinned up, was flying in all directions. Hairpins were falling out, and my hair now looked a disheveled mess.

Braxton took one of his hands and pulled my hair back so he could see my face. He tilted my head back to get a better view. Once he was satisfied he began to tap my ass.

"Oh shit!" I yelled.

"You like that, Beautiful?" he asked.

"Uh-huh," I moaned.

"I can't hear you, Beautiful."

"Hell, yeah, I like that," I moaned.

He slapped my ass this time, causing me to arch my back. My kitty kat told me to purr. "Meow."

"You thought I couldn't fuck, didn't you? Thought I was out for the count. Nah, I wasn't letting this pretty ass off that easy. I going to fuck you like you never have been fucked. How you like the feel of my dick now?"

"It feels . . . damn, I love your dick!" I screamed.

"Show me."

I started backing it up, squeezing my vaginal muscles around his dick. Next, I rotated my hips. He started pumping me like he was in a boxing match with my pussy.

"Oh shit, Braxton, I . . . I . . . ." My legs gave as I came.

Braxton turned me around and lifted me up, putting my butt on the sink. My legs were positioned with one on each side of him. He entered me slowly, taking nice long strokes.

Damn, did he have some Viagra and Red Bull stashed?

Braxton started kissing my neck, making me immediately aroused again. We continued pleasing each other. I wrapped my legs tightly around his waist. Once I did that, he was done. He began to shake. And I was too tired to move.

Braxton looked at me and smiled. He picked me up, then carried me to my bedroom, gently laying me on the bed. After that, he climbed in bed with me, wrapping his arms tightly around me, making me instantly feel safe and secure. Five minutes later, I heard him snoring lightly in my ear. I said a quick prayer before drifting to sleep. I prayed he would be there when I awoke.

5
Ready for Love

When I woke up the next morning from the wild sexcapade, Braxton was there. In fact, his arms were still wrapped tightly around me, and it felt so good. We've been sexing and going out consistently for the last couple of weeks, but nothing was official, even now, the end of August. I admit I wondered if he was dating me exclusively or if he has someone on the side. But I doubted that because I see him at least four times a week and talk to him on the phone every day. But you never know. I wanted to ask him, but I learned a long time ago, don't ask questions you can't handle the answer to. So I left it alone.

My cell phone rang as I was driving into work. It was Landon.

"Hello," I said.

"Hey, Yasmin."

"What's up, Diva?"

"Nothing. I'm calling to see what you're doing tonight. You're not going to be with him, are you?"

Landon was very jealous of Braxton. Often she throws slurs about him monopolizing my time and his "two strikes." She has slacked up on him, though. I guess she realized I wasn't paying her any mind. She's only met him that one time. I keep telling her to give him a chance, but it falls on deaf ears.

"No, Landon, I'm free. Do you want to go out?"

"Yes, Kevin and I haven't seen you in a while."

"Kevin too? When did you start hanging with him?" I asked.

"I didn't. I just ran into him this morning at my parents' office. He asked about you. I told him I would call to see if you wanted to hook up," Landon replied.

"That's fine. Where do you want to go on a Thursday night?" I asked.

"I'll decide something later. I'll be picking you up at 6:30."

"That's fine, see you later."

After hanging up with Landon I walked into work and headed straight to my office. We got the BET account so today, Bob and I had a meeting there. Staying in professional mode with Braxton would be a challenge.

I checked my appearance. This morning I carefully chose my outfit, deciding to keep it classic, settling on a Jones New York cream wraparound dress that stopped midcalf, cream slingback heels. Pearl earrings and necklace completed the outfit. The weather was a surprising sixty-eight degrees so I decided to let my hair down. Satisfied with my appearance, I began to gather my paperwork.

"Good morning,"

I looked up to see it was Greg. "Good morning, Greg."

He took my greeting as an invitation to come in. I was not in the mood. After countless rejections, Greg was still trying to hook up, but I was not having it. Braxton is sexing me quite lovely, thank you.

"You look nice today, Yasmin. What are doing for lunch?"

"Thank you, Greg. Bob and I have a meeting at BET."

"What about dinner?" he asked.

"Busy," I replied.

Defeated, he responded, "So you're still not going to give me a chance."

"Nope," I said, giving him a serious look.

"All right, you win. I'll leave you alone . . . for now," he said cockily.

I rolled my eyes. "Good-bye, Greg."

Another typical morning. Greg still isn't giving up. Thankfully, he only asks every couple of weeks now. Just when I was getting situated, Bob walked in.

"Yasmin, are you just about ready to go to BET?"

"Yes, I'm just going over everything to make sure it's in order," I said, gathering my things.

On the way over to BET Bob and I made small talk. He complimented me about my work. He was impressed on how well I was adjusting to the position. He also talked about his family, the wife, kids, and the dog, telling me he wanted to spend more time with them. It wasn't long before we were at BET, and I put on my best business face.

No sooner than I did, Bob threw me a curveball. "Yasmin, I want you to conduct the meeting. I'll observe. I know you can handle everything."

I kept the business face on, but inside, I was starting to have a panic attack. I calmed down a little once I reached the receptionist. "Good morning. I'm Yasmin Sinclair. This is Bob Rivers, and we're here from Legg Mason."

"Yes, Ms. Sinclair, Mr. Rivers, they're waiting for you inside the conference room," the receptionist replied and led us to the room.

They? I thought.

I walked in to see Braxton sitting at the table along with another gentleman and a female. They all stood up.

The gentleman was very handsome, about 6 foot 1, had dark chocolate skin, a bald head, with a muscular build. He looked to be about thirty. The woman was about 5 foot 7 with brown skin. She was all right looking. I automatically felt intimidated. Some type of woman's intuition told me there is an attraction. Question is, whether it's one-sided or two-. More importantly, did anyone act on it?

I pushed my insecurities aside to walk up to the woman, made eye contact, and shook her hand. Next, I proceeded to the other gentleman. "Good morning. I'm Yasmin Sinclair, and this is Bob Rivers." Last was Braxton.

Braxton then took over and made the formal introductions, introducing the gentleman as Mr. Sean Daniels, and the woman as Lisa Stevens.

Everyone took a seat, but I remained standing, handing out the packages I prepared. "On behalf of Legg

Mason, I would like to thank you, BET, for entrusting us to handle your financial needs. I will make it my personal mission to ensure you receive nothing but quality service. Additionally, I have created a financial analysis of where I project BET to be in the next six to nine months. Finally, I have the list of companies I recommend we invest in."

"Excuse me, Ms. Sinclair," Ms. Stevens interrupted.

"Yes? Call me Yasmin, please."

"Yasmin, I'm concerned about a couple of the companies you have listed, particularly company XX."

I looked at Ms. Stevens. I had a feeling she was going to be difficult. "Ms. Stevens, XX is a new company. Right now, their stock is very reasonable. Their sales have been steady and have received nothing but rave reviews in the business journals. Actually, there's an article about them in *Forbes* listed in your package." I wanted to say, "Leave this to the professionals."

Ms. Stevens countered. "I did see the article, but this company has only been in business for five years. I would prefer a compare with more longevity."

Ping-Pong. The ball was now in my court. "That is true; however, the company sales have doubled each year since its existence. If we invest now while the stock is still reasonable, I'm confident we will have an ample profit."

I looked at the others. "Gentlemen, do you have any concerns about this or any other company?"

Braxton and Mr. Daniels looked over the package.

Mr. Daniels spoke up. "No, Yasmin. I'm sorry, may I call you Yasmin? Everything looks good."

He was looking at me like he wanted me. He tried to be inconspicuous, but Lisa, I mean, Ms. Stevens, caught him looking. So did Braxton, and he quickly straightened up.

I don't know if she was pissed about him not agreeing with her or him looking at me like he did, but the bitch was definitely pissed.

"Yasmin is fine, Mr. Daniels."

"Call me, Sean," he replied, smiling.

"Well, Ms. Stevens, Sean, Braxton, if you don't have any other questions regarding the investments I have chosen . . ." I paused to allow questions. There were none, ". . . then I would like to discuss the beginning date of the contract."

Ms. Stevens quickly spoke up. "I would like the investment contract with your company to begin October 1st."

I looked over at Bob. He gave me a look that said, "No way."

"Ms. Stevens, at Legg Mason, we strive for accuracy and, most importantly, customer satisfaction. However, the October 1st date is not feasible. We still need your employee database as well as payroll information. Our IT department is currently in the process of implementing a program compatible with yours. Additionally, we still need to set up a test run with your IT department to ensure everything runs smoothly. This will also give you time to update your database."

I looked over at Bob. He gave me a nod. I could see Ms. Stevens wasn't pleased, but . . . oh well. She tried to challenge me, but she was defeated. I tried not to look at Braxton, but I could see a little smirk on his lips.

"I concur with Yasmin, and you, Braxton?" Sean asked.

"Yes, I agree," Braxton stated.

"Well, Ms. Stevens, gentlemen, I look forward to doing business with you. The sooner you can provide me with that information the better."

Ms. Stevens quickly excused herself and left the conference room without another word. Bob was making small talk with Braxton while I gathered my things.

"Yasmin, I was very impressed today," Sean commented.

"Thank you," I replied.

Before he could initiate a conversation, Braxton was standing next to him. "Yasmin, it's nice seeing you again," he stated.

I quickly excused myself. "Same to you. Gentlemen, I'll be in touch."

Bob and I headed back to the office. I was not even back five minutes before my phone rang.

"Hello, this is Yasmin Sinclair."

"I'm going to have to ask you to stop coming to my office looking so good. I had a hard-on the entire meeting," Braxton confessed.

"Boy, please, I couldn't tell," I responded.

"I'm not a boy."

"No, you definitely are not."

"I like your hair like that. You should wear it that way more often. How about you wear it like that tonight? I can pick you up at seven. You can spend the night with me."

Braxton was actually inviting me to his house. I knew where he lives but never have actually been inside. He would always go grab something while I waited in the car. I didn't want to put any pressure on him, so I never asked why I'd never seen the inside. Usually, when we went out, we ended up back at my house.

Could he be ready to take this relationship further? Yes, seven would work for me. Shit! I forgot I have to hook up with Landon. She will never let me hear the end of it if I cancel.

"You're inviting me to your place? You must really like my hair," I said.

"What's that suppose to mean?" he asked.

"Nothing. Just I've known you all this time, and I've never been inside."

"So does that mean you're going to wear your hair down and stay with me tonight?" he asked.

"I will wear my hair down tonight, but I can't go out with you. I promised Landon that I would go with her tonight." I left out Kevin because I knew how jealous he could get.

He sighed sounding a little annoyed. "Landon, my number-one fan."

"Yeah, I haven't hung out with her in a while. But I'll take a rain check."

"We'll see. Well, I have to get back to work. I'll talk to you later, Beautiful." Before I could respond he hung up.

*

I sat with Landon and Kevin in the Cheesecake Factory. After I got off work, I changed into a Michael Kors jean skirt that stopped midthigh, a white Michael Kors tank, and a pair of four-inch BCBG sandals. Landon wore a blue BCBGMAXAZRIA jersey dress, while Kevin had on a pair of khaki shorts with a green Polo shirt.

"Yasmin, I see you're getting a little bold," Kevin stated.

"What are you talking about, Kevin?" I asked.

"Don't get me wrong. You look real nice, but I'm not used to you dressing like that. You're showing your navel. You're generally more conservative."

Landon jumped in, "That's because she's getting dick on the regular."

I gave Landon a stern look. Kevin said he would stay out of my personal life, but I could tell he's hurt.

"So you are in a relationship?" he asked.

"I don't know about the relationship part, but she is giving up the bootie. Shocked me. I still can't believe she gave it up on the first date," Landon blabbed.

"Landon, would you just shut up."

Setting her drink down, Landon replied, "Don't get mad with me. We're all adults. She's hoping Braxton decides he wants to be in a relationship. They're just 'dating.' I told her move on. She knows that's not her style. Personally, I think she can do better, but I'll keep that to myself. I will admit, though, I do like the change in your attire. It's about time you showed off your body."

Kevin swallowed. "Braxton . . . huh?"

Putting some of the attention on Landon I asked, "And how are the men in your life?"

"My men are fine, thank you. Will is gone to training camp so that leaves me Eric. Eric is too clingy. If he didn't know how to give me multiple orgasms, he would be gone. So to put some distance there, I have a new friend. Tony. Tony is the COO of some company. He's boring, but he loves to buy me gifts. The sex is boring, just like him. I'm currently looking for a replacement."

"If I knew taking you two out would be so entertaining, I would have done this a long time ago," Kevin laughed.

I took a drink. "You haven't seen anything yet. She's just warming up," I laughed. Although irritating, Landon is fun to hang with.

Landon's cell phone rang. "It's Tony. I'll be back. I'm going to let him go tonight."

I held my drink up. "Do your thing, Landon."

Landon walked off, cell phone in hand.

"Yasmin, I know I told you I would stay out of your business, but I care about you. Are you sure about Braxton?"

"Kevin, I appreciate your concern, but I'm a big girl. So what's going on with your love life?"

"I'm dating one woman. I met her that night at Dream actually. Her name is Nicole. She works at Johns Hopkins in Baltimore," Kevin said, smiling.

"That's good, Kevin. I'm happy for you. Good luck."

Our food arrived, and Landon was still MIA so we began to eat without her. When I looked up, I immediately lost my appetite.

Braxton was being seated at a table nearby, and he had company. The woman was none other than the bitch, Lisa Stevens.

Kevin noticed my mood change and followed my gaze. "You can do better."

I lied. "Kevin, I'm OK. We're just dating, right?"

I attempted to eat my meal, hoping he wouldn't see me. However, I looked up and saw Braxton staring at me like he has an attitude, so I looked away. Who does he think he is? He gets mad because I couldn't go out, so he takes her. Is she who's supposed to replace me? I would have been upset to see him with any female, but Lisa Stevens! I was ready to go. *Where are my keys? Damn, I didn't drive.*

"I'm back. Did you miss me?" Landon sang.

She sat down. Looking at me, she immediately picked up on my uneasiness. "Yasmin, what's your problem, why are you looking all crazy? I told you I'd be back."

Trying to get my face together I replied, "I'm fine now that you're back. How did things go with Tony?"

Landon took a drink. "Well, Tony—Oh no, no, no. I *know* that is *not* Braxton sitting over there with that old homely looking bitch. Ugh. What the fuck does she have on? Does she think she's cute? She needs to know she's not. I know that bitch did not just look over here and roll her eyes at me. She's mad that I'm hotter than she, not to mention fly. That lipstick doesn't even go with her complexion, neither does the foundation. And she needs to shave her legs. Let's not even go there with the hair. Yas, I told you to leave him alone when you first went out. First, he had the nerve to be late. Then he was dressed like a thug; took you to some Dave and Busters on a first date. What kind of shit is that? That should have told you he was nothing but games. But did you listen? No! You tried to play his game acting like dating was OK with you, knowing damn well it isn't. Now you're sitting here looking crazy. You need to start listening to me and stop falling in love."

"Landon, calm down," Kevin said between his clenched teeth.

"I'm talking to Yasmin, Kevin."

"Not now, Landon," I pleaded.

"You're going to listen now. You know I love you, and I'm telling you some good shit. Leave his ass alone. He has that old homely looking Raggedy Ann with highlights. Look at her. Her outfit looks like it came from Dollar

General. Shit, he could have at least picked someone that looked decent. I'll hook you up with someone that looks better and has deeper pockets. I don't like him anyway."

"Are you done?" Kevin asked.

"Almost. I think I'll go over there. The bitch rolled her eyes at me earlier," Landon stated, as she stood up.

"Landon, sit your ass down," Kevin ordered.

Rolling her eyes at Kevin, she sat down. "Diva does not take orders. She gives them. I'll sit this time because I see Yas is upset. Besides, he's not worth my time. Yas, if you want to go we can go."

"I appreciate your concern, but I'm fine."

I looked over at Braxton and saw him and his date laughing. I hate to admit it, but Landon is right. I wanted more from Braxton. The sex is off the chain, but I wanted more. I wanted a deeper connection. I had his body, but I wanted to be a part of his mind. I want to be his only. I didn't even know anything about his family. Hell, I barely knew anything about him, other than when I came I saw the sun and the stars. Hurt I am. But at the end of the day, I put myself in this situation so I have to deal with it.

I got up. "Excuse me, guys. I'll be back. I have to go the bathroom."

"You need me to go with you?" Landon asked.

"I'll be fine. Kevin, watch Landon. Make sure she stays in her seat."

"I'm twenty-three years old. I don't need a babysitter. But while you're up, Yas, give him a runway walk. You look good. Show that dummy what he lost."

I laughed and walked to the bathroom. Once there, I splashed cold water on my face to calm down. After a few minutes, I was able to get my face together.

When I walked out I felt eyes on me. I looked up to see Braxton staring at me. I continued walking my runway strut, ignoring him.

"That's right, Yas, you're listening now. You worked it. He watched you as you were leaving and coming back," Landon said matter-of-factly.

I ordered another drink and tried to finish my meal. Landon and Kevin were talking about work, but my mind was elsewhere. Just as I calmed down, I saw Braxton and Ms. Stevens approach the table. What's he trying to do, rub it in?

Landon was the first to speak. "Yes?"

Braxton chuckled. "Hi, Landon, right? How are you?" He looked at Kevin and held his hand out. "You went to Central, right?"

Kevin put his hand out to shake Braxton's. "Yeah, hey, man, how you doing?"

Landon gave Kevin the evil eye. "Braxton, who do you have with you?"

"I apologize. This is my coworker, Lisa Stevens."

"Hello, Ms. Stevens, nice to meet you," Kevin replied.

"Call me Lisa, please."

Call me Lisa. Bitch! I see your ass is friendly to anything with a dick.

"Nice to meet you also, Landon. I met you earlier, Yasmin," she smirked.

"It wasn't nice to meet you either, Ms. Stevens," I said to myself.

Landon, never being one never to bite her tongue and always having my back, spoke. She pretended like she was whispering, but really wasn't. "Lisa, your track is showing. You should try a short do. Some people just aren't blessed with long natural hair like Yasmin."

Ms. Stevens gave Landon the *fuck you* look. It took everything in me not to laugh.

"Well, I just came over to say hi. I'll let you get back to your dinner. Yasmin, I'll talk to you soon," Braxton said giving me a wink.

"What kind of shit is that, a wink? Did he think that was cute? Who does he think he is, Billy Dee Williams? I still don't like him, and that Lisa—did you see that dead eye? She was scaring me," Landon proclaimed.

Twenty minutes passed when our waiter approached the table with a white rose and a note.

"Ms. Sinclair, Mr. Simms requested I deliver this to you."

"Thank you," I said, surprised. Once I read the note, to Landon's dismay, I couldn't hold back my smile.

Hey, Beautiful,
I missed being with you tonight.
Allow me to pleasure you tomorrow.
I'll pick you up at six.
I look forward to seeing you.
Braxton

P.S. I promise to be on time.

"Oh shit, she's gone. She's fallen for the Joker." Landon had to get another one in.

6
Exclusively

It was 5:45 when I did a final check in the mirror. The dress I'd chosen definitely accentuated my figure. Bronze in color, the silk cool and smooth on my skin. My back was completely out, meaning a bra is not an option. Since the front dipped low and I have more than a mouthful, I had to make sure to tape them down, and tie the front behind my neck securely. The bottom of the dress had slits on each side, but it clung tightly to my hips stopping just above my knees. I wore my hair down like he liked and put on a pair of long, dangling crystal earrings. The jeweled four-and-a-half inch Guess stilettos completed my outfit.

I knew Braxton would love the outfit, but I was nervous about how he'd react when other people saw me. I decided to wait for him downstairs.

By the time I made it outside I saw Braxton parking. I waited on the side so he wouldn't see me. He stepped out wearing a pair of brown slacks and button-down shirt and jacket. Good, we matched.

"Hey, you," I said walking toward him, then stopping to twirl around.

Braxton paused. He stood there for a minute without saying anything, his facial expression unreadable. Immediately I become self-conscious. Maybe this was too much. Maybe this outfit doesn't look right. I'm too fat for the outfit. I should go change.

Ignoring my insecurities, I walked toward his car, "Braxton, are you ready?"

I turned around. Braxton was still staring. Finally he spoke, "Umm . . . Beautiful, yes, I'm ready."

He walked over and opened the door for me.

Once he got in I saw him looking, so I crossed my legs. "Where are you taking me tonight?"

"I checked out your CD collection and saw Jill Scott. She's performing tonight at Constitution Hall—"

Before he could finish I spoke. "Oh my God, are you serious? I love Jill. I can't believe it." My voice began to get louder. I was so excited. "Ahh . . . I love Jill. I tried to get tickets weeks ago. They went on sale at 10:00 and when I finally got through at 10:15 they were sold out. How did you get tickets?"

Braxton laughed. "That's just another perk for working at BET."

I know I looked crazy and was out of character for my usually reserved self, but I didn't care. I love Jill Scott.

"I can't wait to hear her sing, 'He loves me.' Let's go, I'm ready. I can't believe I'm going to see Jill. Yes! Oh my God," I said smiling from ear to ear.

"Well, I thought we could get something to eat first," Braxton said.

"What time does the show start?" I asked.

"Eight o'clock."

"Do you think we'll have time? I don't want to miss anything."

"I didn't realize you were a Jill fanatic. But we'll have time. The shows never start on time."

Still smiling, I said, "I don't care where we go as long as it's close to Constitution Hall and the service is fast."

"McDonald's here we come," he joked.

"So I look like I'm dressed for McDonald's?" I joked back.

"You do look . . . umm, damn real good, but you're dressed like you're single and trying to meet someone," he said.

I turned to him and gave him a serious look. "I *am* single."

His body stiffened. His relaxed composure now filled with tension. I know he didn't like my comment, but he put it out there. He said he wanted to date and we'd see where that leads. Well, we've been dating for a couple of months, and he hasn't made any commitment. I hope he takes it to the next level, but I can't just continue to date with no strings attached. Landon is right. I can't handle the "just dating." As much as I hate to admit it, I may have to explore my options. One thing for sure, I wasn't going to let him ruin this night with his jealousy. I am going to see Jill.

Trying to lighten up the mood I asked, "What do you have a taste for?"

"Whatever. It doesn't matter," he said in a monotone.

We ended up at a small Italian restaurant. The food was good, but the conversation was minimal. Braxton obviously was still upset about earlier. The air in the restaurant was a little too chilly, causing me to shiver.

Braxton asked, "Are you cold?"

"Yes."

He stood, took off his jacket, and placed it around me. "Next time you may want to wear more clothes."

I let his comment slide because, like I said, I was going to see Jill. I looked at my watch. It was 7:30. "Braxton, the show is about to start. Are you ready? I don't want to miss anything."

"I know. We'll get there."

I stood up, handed him his jacket, and walked to the door.

Since he had to pay the bill I knew he would be awhile. I welcomed the minutes, enjoying the feel of the sun warming my skin.

Of course, while I was waiting I received some male attention.

"Excuse me, you are looking quite lovely. Why are you standing out here all alone? I know no one was stupid enough to stand you up. Look at you. You are stunning. And those eyes . . . you can have anything you want."

I smiled. *Why is it always about my eyes?*

That's the reaction I wanted from Braxton; instead, I get smart-ass comments.

Looking over the gentleman I could see he was fine, resembling Morris Chestnut. Braxton isn't my man technically. I just said I shouldn't limit myself to a man who can't commit. This guy right here, he is too damn fine. But it would be disrespectful to get his number, right? Did I mention he was fine?

"Thank you. My friend is paying the bill. He should be out any minute," I said giving him a hint.

"A pretty woman like you shouldn't be out here by yourself. Call me. I'll show how a pretty lady should be treated," he said, handing me a business card.

I accepted.

Looking at the card piqued my interest. It read PARKER FRANKLIN OF FRANKLIN HOMES. "You're an architect. Very impressive."

"Thank you. Call me if you ever get lonely. I promise I will *really* impress you." Parker turned to leave, and, of course, Braxton came out of the restaurant.

Braxton looked at Parker leaving, then me.

I stood there like nothing happened. He didn't see me taking his card. Parker could have just been asking me for the time. I'm not confessing to anything.

"Braxton, it's 7:45."

He looked at me, then shook his head. "I know what time it is."

I was not missing this concert. I grabbed his arm and walked toward the car. The ride, thank God, is short; about five minutes. As soon as the car stopped, I jumped out and waited. And waited. Braxton basically was taking his time, getting on my nerves. He finally made it to my side, and I began walking toward Constitution Hall. I was so excited. I picked up my pace and didn't notice Braxton wasn't with me. I *know* he did not leave my ass. Where is he? *Aargh,* I should have asked for my ticket.

I turned around to look for him . . . and received more male attention. OK, maybe this outfit *is* a little too much.

"Are you OK, sweetheart? Do you need some help?" too many guys asked.

"No, thanks," I said continuing my search for Braxton.

I finally spotted him talking to someone. It looked like one of the guys he was with at Dream. The guy had a female companion. She was very attractive with model looks, smooth, mocha-brown skin, long hair that stopped at her lower back, high cheekbones, full lips, and pretty brown eyes. Her outfit was cute. She was wearing a black spaghetti strap A-line dress that stopped at her calf.

I strutted over to Braxton. "Hello?"

Braxton turned around looking less irritated. "Yasmin. Yasmin, this is my friend Mike and his fiancée Tiffany. Tiffany, Mike, this is Yasmin."

"Hello, nice to meet you," Tiffany said.

"Nice to meet you, Tiffany. Congratulations on your upcoming nuptials."

"Thank you."

"When is the wedding?" I asked.

"The wedding is next year. I'll make sure you get an invite, and, girl, I *love* your dress."

Before I could respond, Braxton interjected, "All right, see you guys later. Enjoy the show."

"Thanks, man, again for the tickets," Mike said, laughing.

Before the concert started, we had a couple of drinks. Well, he had two. I had several, so I had a nice buzz. There was a line going in, and we were at a standstill for a while. During this time I got a lot of male stares.

Braxton was becoming more agitated. I want him to calm down, so I put my arm around his waist. "Thank you for the concert."

He didn't respond.

When we were finally able to get in, he led me to second-row center seats, another BET perk.

Jill came on stage, and I completely lost it. I started screaming, acting a fool, jumping. "I love you, Jill!"

I looked over at Braxton to see him laughing at me, but I didn't care.

She started out with "A long Walk." I danced a little. After a while, I decided to sit back down next to Braxton to enjoy the show.

He looked to be in a better mood now.

Jill's second song was "Love Rain." Jill was feeling the music, and I was feeling her. Part of me, though, wondered if the song would be a replica of Braxton and me.

Toward the end of the show I was really feeling the effects of the alcohol. Jill was singing "Is It the Way," and I was standing, singing, sashaying my hips, and moving with the music, oblivious to my surroundings.

I felt Braxton behind me so I turned around to dance with him.

"I'll take care of you later," he whispered as he sat me down and sat beside me.

Jill concluded the show with "He Loves Me." Closing my eyes, I allowed the words to let my mind go free. The entire show was amazing.

"Come on, Beautiful. I have a surprise for you," Braxton said, snapping me out of my trance.

"I'm beautiful again?" I said.

"You're always beautiful," he replied.

"You haven't been treating me like I'm beautiful."

He smiled at me and placed a light kiss on my lips. "You're my beautiful Yasmin. Let me take you somewhere."

Braxton grabbed my waist and led me to a room.

I walked in on a meet and greet with Jill. Now, it was my turn to be speechless.

Meeting Jill was indescribable, unforgettable. Jill was so articulate, vivid in every gesture, capturing everyone in the room like she did in the audience. She was so beautiful inside and out. I really appreciated Braxton doing this for me.

*

Since Braxton was tired, he wanted me to stay at his house. I, of course, had no objections, especially since Jill had me ready for some loving.

The inside of his place was the typical bachelor pad: white walls, leather furniture, big screen, and big stereo system. I walked over to his stereo to check out his CD collection. He had a nice collection. Some jazz from Kim Waters to Charlie Parker, Hip-Hop Slick Rick to Jay Z and a little R&B, and, of course, neo-soul.

"I didn't know you could sing," Braxton said, handing me some wine.

"What are you trying to do, get me drunk? I sing a little," I teased.

"You have a nice voice. What do I need to get you drunk for? It's not like I haven't, you know, been with you. And you've already had more than a couple of drinks."

"Excuse me?" I said, setting the drink down and facing him.

"Calm down. I just want to talk and get to know Yasmin."

"Now you want to know Yasmin? Tired of fucking me already?" I countered.

"There you go. I'm just trying to get to know you better."

"We've been doing this 'dating' thing for two months. Why ask questions now? You've been content with sex and casual conversation," I said, looking directly into his eyes.

Braxton grabbed my hands and looked me in the eyes. "Because I want more. I don't want to share you. I want to be with you exclusively. I see how other men look at you, and I don't like it. Today, when I commented on your dress, you told me you were single. Well, I don't want you to be single anymore. I want you to be mine. Is that all right?"

I smiled at him. "What took you so long?"

"So are you mine now?"

"Of course, I wouldn't want it any other way," I said.

"Well, show me how you feel."

I walked over to his stereo and put on Jill Scott's "The Way." Then I gave Braxton a repeat of my performance earlier. This time instead of stopping me he danced with me. Soon after, I was sexing my man.

7
Naughty Girl

L ooking through my closet for a Halloween
  outfit to wear tonight had proven to be a
  chore. Landon would be here at 8:00. It was
7:00 now, and I was still scrambling to put an outfit together.
Eric, one of Landon's current sponsors, is having costume
party. Normally, I would have declined since I'm really not
into crowds, but she begged me to go and gave me the guilt
lecture, complaining I forgot about her.

As if I could use more distractions, my phone rang
interrupting my search.

"Hello."

"Hey, Beautiful, what are you doing besides
thinking about me?"

"Hey, you. Aren't we a little cocky? I'm not doing
anything, just getting ready for this party."

"What you wearing?"

"Right now, a smile," I said in a sexy voice.

"Is that so?" Braxton asked.

"Yup, I'm sitting all alone anticipating . . ." I said,
letting my words drift off.

"Anticipating?"

"You."

"I can be there in twenty minutes. You don't have to
be alone," Braxton hinted.

"No, you enjoy yourself tonight. Just come by after
you hang with your boys.
I'll be waiting."

"Nah, Beautiful, you have me all worked up. You
know you want me to come over and make you scream my
name. You know you want some of this dick."

Laughing yet getting wet thinking about his proposition I responded, "I see we are really cocky today. So you think you can make me scream, huh?"

"Woman, please, I *always* do. 'Braxton, your dick feels so good. It belongs in my pussy. Put it in.'"

I stopped him. "You win."

"I know I win. I got you, don't I? Now I want some of that pussy."

"Well, Braxton, as tempting as you are, I have a party to attend. I promised Landon I would go. How about you come over tonight around 1:00? I'll have a surprise waiting for you. See you then." I hung up before he could respond.

The phone rang again, but I didn't answer. I knew it was Braxton. Smiling, I thought tonight he would definitely be in for some pleasure.

A couple of months ago Landon and I signed up for a pole class. At first I was hesitant, but when I thought about it, I figured, what the hell. It would be a good way to spice up the sex. I haven't really practiced because Braxton and I are wild enough already, but it was time to put all that practicing to use. Tonight he would be the one screaming.

I went into my closet again looking for a costume. Finally, I decided to be the queen of the Nile, Nefertiti. My costume consisted of a gold metallic-looking bikini top that had red and gold spangles, a red wraparound skirt with a gold belt, hoop earrings, and a pair of stilettos. I pulled the front of my hair in a ponytail and let the back hang. Then I added a little black eyeliner and red MAC lipstick.

Just as I was about to sit down, the doorbell rang. I peeped out to see Landon. I opened to Cleopatra Landon. She wore a gold white halter and short skirt, embellished in gold trim and costume jewels, gold jewelry, and a crown.

I bowed. "Hail to the Queen. Looking good, Queen Landon."

"Thank you, girl. You know there no other outfit suitable for a queen. I see we both are going to make the other girls look like the country bamas they are."

"I'm about ready. Let me grab my purse. So I finally get to meet Mr. Eric. Is the party at his house?"

"Yeah, I sold him this house a couple of months ago."

"Well, maybe I need to drive because I have a treat coming later tonight, and I refuse to get stranded over at Eric's."

"All that isn't necessary. If I stay, you can just drive my car back. Braxton can wait. Besides, there will be a lot of eye candy with money at the party. Landon only messes with the best. I keep saying you need to have a backup."

Landon has seen Braxton a few times since we've been together. Although she's remained cordial, she stills thinks Braxton is too domineering and possessive, insisting he reminds her of a pimp. In other words, he was the male version of her. Every chance she gets, she throws out a slur or snide remark. For the most part, I ignore her. I know she's still jealous. She's used to me always being around.

"They're you go. Braxton can't wait. Shit, I can't wait. Yasmin needs her fix of Braxton, so let's go, and I will not hesitate to take your keys."

When we pulled up to Eric's mansion it was reminiscent of Dream's VIP room. The atmosphere reeked of money. There were so many sexy men, so much temptation, albeit, money isn't the deciding factor on whether I pursue a man. However, I have to admit I could understand why Landon chose the "elite." Not saying it was right, but the men I'd seen thus far held a confidence. I could clearly see there also was a lot of egotism as well, but ultimately, they were go-getters. If I were single it would be on, umm, so many possibilities. I love my baby, but there's nothing wrong with a little flirting. I checked my makeup and checked Landon. We definitely were going to cause an uproar.

"I need to call Eric and have him stop the music so I can make my grand entrance."

"Come on, Ms. Queen. Calm down."

When we stepped out, it felt as if all eyes were on us. Of course, Landon loved it. I felt uncomfortable at first, but with Landon, my ego is boosted. We continued to do our strut until Landon stopped at this tall, dark black, wavy haired sexy man with a goatee. He stood about 6 foot 7. His smooth, dark chocolate skin was similar to a dark Hershey candy bar. His dark eyes were hypnotizing and shone like black diamonds.

"Hello, ladies," he said, giving an approving nod.

"Eric, sweetie, this is my best friend, Yasmin. Yasmin, this is my sweetheart, Eric."

"Nice to finally meet you, Eric. Landon is always talking about you."

"Landon talking about me? I don't believe it," he said laughing.

"I tell Yasmin all the time that you're my sweetheart."

"Tell me anything. You know you two look like sisters," Eric said matter-of-factly.

"We get that a lot because of the eyes, but we're just the best of friends."

"Well, you two definitely are the sexiest women in here tonight. What can I get for you two ladies to drink?"

"Thanks, sweetheart, we're fine. I'm going to show Yasmin around but don't go too far. I want to dance with my sweetheart."

"Definitely not. I'll go on the tour with you. I don't want to leave you alone."

OK, these two are getting on my nerves. This lovey-dovey back and forth can stop . . . just go fuck him . . . OK, I'm hating and missing my Braxton. I spoke up. "You two can go do your thing if you want. I'll be OK. Just lead me to the bar. I can mingle."

"Sweetheart, let me get one drink in with Yasmin. Then I'll find you and show you my costume," Landon said, giving Eric a wink.

"OK, don't be long," he said, giving Landon a light kiss on her cheek before he walked away.

"I know you did not give him a wink. Wasn't it you calling my man a Billy Dee Williams wannabe?"

"Shut up, Yas."

"All right, I'll let you slide this time. For the record, Braxton did it better. Anyways, Landon, very nice. Those lips looks like they can suck the shit out of a clit."

"Yes, they can. Don't remind me. My clit is throbbing just thinking about it. Sexy he is, but he's already trying to cling to me. I want to stay single. We're not exclusive I keep reminding him."

"Why don't you try being exclusive?"

"Yas, I told you, I'm too young for that love commitment thing you do. I want to have fun now. I'm not trying to be tied down and think years later what I shoulda woulda coulda. I'm not saying I will never commit, but it's just not for me right know. Damn, look over there. Is that Bill Kemps that plays for the Ravens? Oh, he is too sexy . . . That's one number I will be getting tonight."

"How do you plan on doing that, Diva, with Eric all up in your face?"

Landon pulled out her business card. "Landon Taylor, what you want, I've got. I'll be right back, Yas."

I shook my head as I watched her approach Bill. I must admit, when she wants something or someone she goes right for it and 99 percent of the time she gets it.

Looking from afar, I saw Bill giving her his card. *Go, Landon,* I thought. She talked to him for another two or three minutes before returning.

"I see you got the number."

"What did you expect? Let's go get a drink."

We walked over to the bar and ordered our drinks. Landon ordered a buttery nipple, and I, an amaretto sour. We sat at the bar for about half an hour drinking and laughing at the bamas.

"Let's show these bamas what *we're* working with," Landon said standing up dancing.

I joined her, following her lead to the dance floor. Landon was feeling her drink, having a good time. The DJ must have been waiting for us because he played, "Doin' It" by LL Cool J so Landon and I could do a little provocative dance.

"I see a lot of fellas in here lusting over those two sexy ladies over there. Somebody come take over. They're looking lonely, fellas," the DJ said. "You don't have to touch yourself, ladies. I'm here."

Eric walked over and grabbed Landon, kissing her on the neck. I moved over and give them a little room. Some guy came over and danced with me. He was OK, but nothing to make the panties wet. He thought he could touch, but I quickly put a stop to that, removing his hand and moving to another section.

"Homeboy struck out. She's not feeling you," the DJ announced.

Another approached. This one is sexy. He was cool to dance with . . . until he pulled me close and I could feel his dick getting hard. *Ugh.* It felt like a little pencil poking me.

He ruined my vibe, and the song was over so I went and got another drink. I sat on the couch, closed my eyes, and tried to vibe with the music. The DJ was now playing "More Than a Woman," by Aaliyah.

"You are definitely more than a woman."

I looked up to see some NBA player from TV whose name I didn't remember. He was cute, but not as fine as Braxton.

"Thank you," I said as I closed my eyes and continued to vibe.

"How can I find out just how much of a woman you are?"

"*Excuse* me?"

"Ohh, so you wanna play hard to get. I can play that game. I can show you what it's like to be with a man. You must don't have a man if your touching yourself."

I stood up and walked to the other side of the bar. I should have worn another costume. Landon can have the attention. I prefer to be left alone. This time I ordered a cranberry and Grey Goose.

Just as I was about to walk away I felt wet lips on the back of my neck. What the fuck! I admit the lips did feel good, but whomever they belong to was about to get slapped—no, fuck that—punched—in the mouth.

I turned around swinging. "What the hell is your problem?" My fist was balled, and I threw a punch. Luckily, he was fast, catching my punch.

"I see you have a good jab."

I laughed. "Well, that's because no one should be kissing on my neck."

"You've got that right, but I'm not no one," he countered.

"True that is." Feeling the alcohol and usually not that bold in public, I pulled him close and kissed him.

"Don't try to butter me up. I should be mad at you for dressing like that. You do have a man now. I didn't like your dance either. Had these fools drooling," Braxton said, pulling me closer.

I looked at him like what dance?

"Don't give me that look. 'Doin' It' and doin' it well."

"But I was thinking about you, and they can look, but they can't touch. That privilege belongs to only you."

He smiled. "I told you all that wasn't necessary. You wouldn't let me get some earlier," he said, grabbing my ass.

"Don't start anything you can't finish. You have me all wet now. What are you doing here anyway?"

"I can finish. I'm here with one of my buddies I went to school with. He plays for the Wizards."

"D.C. is small. I'm Landon's guest. She's a friend of Eric Ayers. I like your costume, Bishop Don Magic Juan."

"That's Daddy to you," he said, slapping my ass.

I turned around to show off my outfit. "You like it, Daddy?" I joked.

"That's right. You bedda have my money."

"Hey, you, you didn't forget about me tonight?"

"Me forget you, Beautiful? Never. Let me introduce you to my boy Javon."

Braxton grabbed my hand and led me to his friend.

Oh shit, not this guy, I thought. His friend is the guy who tried to talk to me earlier. Talking about he can show me what it's like to be with a man or some dumb shit like that.

Braxton stood behind me and wrapped his arms around me. "Hey, man, this is my baby, Yasmin. Yasmin, this is my friend Javon Edwards."

"Hello."

"Very nice. Hello, Yasmin," he said, eyeing me like I was on an auction block up for purchase.

I know this is Braxton's friend, but I was not getting a good vibe from him. I really didn't want to be in his presence so I made an excuse to get away. "Baby, I'm going to go find Landon. I'll catch you later."

I attempted to walk away, but Braxton grabbed my hand. "You don't have any time for your man now?"

"You know I always have time for you. But Landon is my ride. I want to make sure she remembers," I said, not noticing Landon approaching with Eric.

Javon quickly lost focus on me and eyed Landon.

"Yasmin, I was wondering where you disappeared to. I see you're occupied."

"Hey, Landon, Eric," Braxton said.

"I didn't realize you two knew each other. Hi, Braxton," Landon said.

I know she was thinking I better watch my mouth about her extracurricular activities around Braxton.

"Hey, man," Eric said, giving Braxton the handshake that men do.

"Landon, I was just about to go looking for you. Braxton snuck up on me. Last person I expected to see."

"She's not lying. She tried to punch me, but I was too fast for her."

"I heard she's a mean one. She's not giving anybody the time of day, shooting them down left and right. Good luck," Eric laughed.

"That's right. She knows who her man is," Braxton joked, grabbing me.

"Oh, my bad, man. That's you."

I intervened. "He didn't tell you the whole story. I was getting a drink, and I felt someone come behind me and kiss my neck. So I was ready. I could have knocked him out. He just got lucky."

Everyone laughed.

While Eric and Braxton continued to talk, Landon and Javon flirted. I tried to subtly to tell Landon to calm the fuck down, but Braxton was holding me. Landon definitely is too risqué for me.

After the flirting and conversing were done, Braxton decided he wanted to dance. Which I didn't mind. I love dancing with him. I love the way our bodies were in sync and how it always feels so right.

"Are you going to have enough energy for me tonight?" I teased.

"I know you're not serious. The question is, do *you* have enough energy for *me*? You know I be wearing that ass out. You be screaming, '*Braxton don't stop. You make me feel so good,*' collapsing on me. I'll have to tuck you in."

"Ha ha ha, are you complaining about having sex with me? I know you're not talking you can't get enough of this pussy. You dick starts jumping for joy when it gets a feel; it be trying to do somersaults. Your toes curl. Why? Because you're in Yasmin. Hold up, wait. I haven't even touched you, and I can feel your dick jumping now. It's knocking on my kitty kat's door. Should I answer? No, I think I won't," I teased and attempted to walk away.

Braxton pulled me close. "Uh-uh. You're not going anywhere. You can't let me walk around with a hard-on. Beautiful, you're going to have to take care of your man. Let's go. You owe me a surprise anyway."

"Did you drive?" I asked.

"No."

"Well, guess what? You are SOL because neither did I. You're going to have to wait."

"No, I don't. I'll borrow one of Eric's cars. Or we can just go somewhere. This is a big house."

"Nope. I told you I have something planned. I'll just get Landon's keys. I already discussed it with her. You sure you don't want to stay here for a while?"

"I'm sure I want you."

"You have me. While I go get the keys, go tell your ride don't wait for you. Meet me at the door."

I found Landon flirting with yet another guy, but managed to pull her away and get the keys. "No fucking in my car, comprende?"

"Like you haven't."

"Yas, don't play."

"You car is too small for all of that."

Giving me a devious smile she said, "If you say so."

I shook my head and left.

Braxton was waiting by the door anticipating the feel of my kitty kat wrapped around his dick.

"You ready?" I asked.

He grabbed me. "Where did you park? Let's go to my house because you're going to do some screaming tonight."

Once we got to his house, he pinned me to the wall and kissed my hard. Assertiveness I like.

I broke away. "Nope . . . I'm in control right now. Let's go to the basement. Actually, you go downstairs, and I'll be down. Where are your condoms?"

"Upstairs."

"Get moving."

Braxton ran upstairs, coming back with a condom. He knew we're going to need more than that. Round two will have to be moved upstairs then.

"So I can I have some of my pussy now?"

"Nope."

"Why?"

"You'll get some. I need you to just relax and wait one minute."

I left before he could protest and changed my clothes, which consisted of black lace stockings, a garter belt, one of his suit jackets, a shirt and a tie, and a hat. Lastly were my stilettos.

When I came back downstairs he didn't notice me. His back was turned, and he was drinking Courvoisier. *Good,* I thought. The moonlight was radiating through the open blinds, and with the dim lights the perfect glow was created.

I put in my CD and turned the volume up. Phil Collins's "In the Air Tonight" filled the room.

"I can feel it coming in the air tonight."

Braxton turned around looking puzzled. Upon seeing me, immediately he smiled. He then licked his lips. "You—"

Before he could finish I placed my index finger over my lips to shush him. He obeyed and my strip tease began. I allowed my body to move with the music for a while. Seductively, I walked up to him, moving my lips close to his as if I was going to kiss him. I didn't. I took my hands and rubbed them on his half-exposed chest, eventually pulling his shirt off. Wasting no time, I took my tongue and licked his nipples. I wanted to see his dick work out before I took off my clothes. So, I twirled my hips and worked it down to the floor. My knees were on the floor, my legs spread apart. Quickly, I unbuckled his pants, pulling them, along with his boxers, off. I grabbed the condom, put it on his tip, and with my mouth, rolled it down. Braxton went berserk, making subtle gestures for me to give him a blow job. I didn't. Removing my tongue from his dick, next, I moved my hands up his thighs and made my way back up rotating my hips. This time when I got close to his face I did kiss him. I ripped open his shirt, then pushed him back so he would fall in the chair. He tried to grab my clothes, but I stopped him and backed away.

I danced slowly, just moving for a couple of minutes, feeling the music. Then I took the hat off, moving it halfway down to my chest and threw it to him. Next, I took off his suit jacket, dropping it to the floor. I then started to loosen the tie. I unbuttoned my shirt, gyrating back to the floor, making my way back up, then down again. I took the shirt off, exposing a black lace La Perla thong and matching lace bra.

I stood there continuing to dance in his tie, my bra, thong, stockings, and stilettos. I turned around to give him ass, bending over and spreading my legs. I moved my hips and worked my body back up. I unhooked my bra and turned around, holding my breasts. I let them go and moved my hands to my thong, pulling it to the side so he can see my fatty. With a little wiggle and gyrating, it fell to the floor. I stepped out of the thong and with the heel of my stiletto, picked it up and threw it at Braxton.

He caught it, of course.

I stepped to the chair he was glued to, extended my leg over his shoulder, and gave him a pussy shot.

He stuck his finger in my pussy and started finger fucking me. I pulled away because this was my show. Hungrily, he took his fingers, placed them in his mouth, then sucked them like a creamed piece of candy.

I took the tie off, holding it on each end. I wrapped it around my shoulder moving it back and forth. As the breakdown of the song came, I started to quicken my pace and moved my hips more. I walked up to Braxton, straddled him, took the tie by both ends, threw it around him, and pulled him closer. Braxton tried to put his dick inside of me, but I wouldn't let him. Instead, I backed away, continuing to dance. The rhythm of the song climaxed, the drums accelerated, beat harder, playing louder, increasing my sexual desire. I jumped on his dick and rode it hard. "*Ahh!*" I yelled. I should know better to jump on Braxton's big dick, but the pain was replaced with much pleasure.

I took long strides and my pussy accepted all of his nine and a half inches.

"Umm, oh shit." Braxton stood up, and I wrapped my legs tightly around his waist. I continued to pump as he backed me to the wall and fucked me so hard, yet ohhh sooo well. Just as I started to feel my body tremble, he pulled out.

Laying me on his table, he spread my legs and dived into my pussy with his tongue lapping me up.

"Ohh, ummm oh damn, aaahhhh ooo . . . uuooo ahhh stop . . . Give me the dick. Fuck me. Fuck me hard . . . fuck me, Braxton. Fuck. Your. Pussy!"

"You want some dick? You can't handle this dick. I don't think you can handle *this*," he said, cockily.

"Let's see who can handle what. You can't handle this pussy. That's why you pull out." I grabbed him, kissing him hard and pulling his body on top of me. I felt his dick on the lips of my pussy. I spread my legs wider inviting him in.

He accepted, pumping slow and then hard, moving me closer to the edge of the table.

I wasn't going to bust my ass so I wrapped my legs tightly around his waist and pumped back as hard. Braxton sucked my nipples and neck so hard, turning me on even more. I felt something vibrating my cervix, that how deep he was, and then I felt thick, hot, sticky juices rolling down my ass. "I can handle your dick. I don't know about you handling my pussy. I'm just beginning."

"You think you handled me? Who said I was finished?" Braxton lifted me up and told me to turn around. He bent me over and proceeded to fuck me doggy-style.

I felt his dick in my stomach. He sucked on the back of my neck and back, intensifying my pleasure. It felt so good, and I backed it up, giving him more. I was taking it, but it felt like he grew and was poking a hole somewhere. I didn't know if I could handle this. I tried to turn and relieve my pussy.

"You can't handle it, can you?"

"Yes," I lied.

He continued to fuck me. He knew I was lying because he slowed it down some. Then he started to slap my ass. I know he likes to see it jiggle. So I positioned myself and started to pump a little so my ass would jingle. It felt so good. Before I knew it, I coming and screaming out his name. "Braxton . . . Brax, this is your pussy!"

"I know it is, and my pussy feels so good. Damn, you feel real good." He began pumping me hard again. This time I took it. Soon after he was coming and collapsed on my back. We stayed like this for minutes, catching our breaths. More of his thick, sticky cum rolled down my legs.

Trying to lift up I said, "Come on, baby, let me get up and get in the shower. I have cum all over my legs and butt. The damn condom broke."

"Only if I can get in with you." He got up.

"Braxton, the condom broke," I said, walking toward the bathroom.

"I know."

"Why didn't you stop and get another one?"

He gave me an *are you serious* look. "You were feeling real good. You always feel good, but raw is definitely better; besides, I don't have any more."

Automatically I got an attitude. "Why are you out?"

Approaching me and putting his hands on my shoulders, he said, "Calm down, Beautiful. I'm only fucking you. That's why I'm out. You know we go through a box of twelve in a week, if that long. I forgot to grab some."

"Oh well, no more pussy for you tonight."

He kissed me, but I stopped him.

"You're serious?"

"Yes, Braxton, no glove no love. I'm not trying to have any babies or anything else."

"Anything else? So you think I'm still fucking around? You don't trust me yet? We're supposed to be in this committed relationship."

He was right, but I've seen too many girls catch stuff. "We should have had this discussion a long time ago. I wasn't planning on sleeping with you on the first date, and ever since then, I just didn't stop."

He pulled me over to the sofa, and we sat down.

"Let's talk," he said.

"Well, other than me, when was the last time you slept with someone?" I asked.

"July."

"July?" I asked, scrunching up my face.

"You want me to be honest, right? Technically, we weren't exclusive then."

He had me there, but I was still pissed. "I assume you wore protection."

"Come on now. You know I did."

"Someone you just met?"

"No, it was just someone from the past."

"What happened?"

"We had sex. I wasn't feeling her. The end."

Coolly I replied, "So you were fucking both of us at the same time." My kitty kat lost its purr with this newfound info. The wetness was gone. I may have looked calm on the outside, but inside, I was fuming.

"Yasmin, I'm being honest. I wasn't feeling her. I am feeling you. That's why I'm with you. I have deep feelings for you. I care about you a lot."

"I do an HIV test every six months. Actually, I just got results back last week that I'm negative, and I plan to stay that way. What's your status?"

"I told you I wasn't an angel so I get tested regularly. My last test was this month, and I'm negative."

"Can you prove it?"

"What?"

"You heard me."

He got up to get something. "Can *you* prove it?"

"I sure can. I was just pulling your bluff. I believe you."

"Oh, a little trust now."

"Were there any other incidents?"

He sat back down looking me dead in the eye. "No."

"Are you going to get some condoms?"

"Why? We're exclusive. We're only fucking each other. I love you, and you're on the pill."

Did he just say he loved me? I got all wet again. "You love me?"

"Yes."

"Are you just saying that to get some pussy or do you mean it? Why tell me now?"

"Yasmin, I mean it. I'm definitely feeling you. I admit the timing could have been better, but we're talking, so I was like, what the hell."

"Feeling me and loving me are two different things. You don't have to say it because it feels right."

"Yasmin, I love you. I enjoy having you in my life. As I told you before, I've never been in a relationship. When you came, you changed all of that. You're in my face every day and haven't annoyed me. In fact, I miss you when you're not. Especially your corny jokes, and I let you leave your female stuff all in my house."

I laughed. "I am not corny. One more question. How do you know I take the pill?"

"We've practically been living between your house and mine for the last couple of months. I've seen the pills."

"Very observant, aren't we?"

He let me up, and we both showered together. Of course, we had another quickie in the shower afterward, then both exhausted, we headed to bed.

In bed I felt at peace. Braxton always wrapped his arms around me and pulled me close. Making me feel so secure and complete, I loved the feel of his body on mine, but mostly, I loved him.

*

With Braxton's arms still securely wrapped tightly around me, the next morning I woke up aching. Although I didn't want to leave this comfort, sore and all, I decided to cook breakfast. Getting up, being careful not to wake him, I threw on one of Braxton's T-shirts. In his bathroom, I showered, brushed my teeth, and pulled my hair back. I managed to go downstairs. It, of course, was a mess. As I was tidying up, I noticed my cell phone blinking. When I retrieved it, I saw I have nine missed calls from Landon, so I called her back.

"Hey, Diva, what's the emergency?" I asked.

"Finally! Can I have my car back? I *do* have some things planned for today."

"I'm sorry. I forgot. I'm at Braxton's. Can you pick it up?"

"So now you're going to inconvenience me. Why can't you get the pimp to drive you to Eric's?"

"He's still asleep, and I'm cooking."

"Now he has you cooking. Uh . . . Whatever. Where does he live?"

I gave Landon the address and directions.

"I'll be there in twenty minutes. Don't take forever opening the door," she said before hanging up.

I checked out Braxton's refrigerator and saw he didn't have much. I was able to make French toast, eggs, and home fries. I fixed a lot since Landon was coming. He doesn't have any orange juice so I made half and half (half lemonade half tea).

The doorbell rang just as I finished. I checked to see Diva looking mighty pissed.

"Good morning, Landon," I said, opening the door.

She looked at me. "You look a mess, and what the fuck is that on your neck? Turn around. I know he didn't put his hands on you. He was dressed like a pimp looking like Ike Turner. I know he didn't let that go to his head and reenact, because I will have him dealt with," she declared.

I rushed to the mirror and noticed my neck. Braxton really did a job on my neck. I have so many passion marks on my neck and chest. It looked like I was in a battle and lost.

I laughed. "Calm down, Diva. It was none of that. Just him sexing me lovely."

She rolled her eyes, then went into the kitchen to see what I cooked. "Whatever. It's juvenile, if you ask me. Passion marks? We did that when . . . middle school, and that was to let everyone know you had a boyfriend. It only shows his insecurities. If he was confident about this relationship, he would know he doesn't have to put claim and do young juvenile things like that. But you like it, so, oh well. I'm gone. I have a new client. Javon Edwards."

"Damn, Diva, you just met him. There's something about him I don't like. He seems conniving. Just watch your back."

"Excuse me, didn't he come with Braxton? You know they say birds of a feather flock together."

"Braxton is not like Javon."

"That's what your mouth says. Beside, you're looking at him through rose-colored glasses. You've been in love with him since Dream. He can do no wrong." Landon went over to the stove and took some home fries.

"That's not true. I admit, I have liked Braxton for a long time, but I've been around him long enough. I trust him. He's been honest with me from day one," I said, thinking back to our conversation from last night. I didn't want to mention to her about the pass Javon made at me so I remained mute on that.

"Look, Landon, I know you're going to do you, but all I'm saying is, be careful. I didn't get a good vibe from him. I don't know what it is, but something isn't right with him."

Before she could respond I heard Braxton coming downstairs. "Good morning, Beautiful."

Landon screwed her face but straightened it right away. "Hello, Braxton."

He just had on a pair of shorts exposing his six-pack, looking too damn sexy.

"Hey, Landon." He looked at me. "I didn't know you had company."

"Yeah, Landon needs her car. She has some appointments."

"Yup, sure do. As matter of fact, I need to get going." Landon got up and put her plate in the sink.

"Here are your keys. Call me later."

"Should I call you at home or your cell?" she asked being sarcastic.

"Call my house."

"Call her cell," Braxton said, winking at me and walking in the kitchen.

"All right, see you later." Landon rolled her eyes and left.

"I see you hooked your man up. I hope you can cook. It looks good and smells good. Let's see how it tastes."

"That wasn't even nice."

"I'm just being honest."

"You and your honesty."

"You want me to lie? Either you can cook, or you can't. If you can, that's another bonus. If you can't, my mother can. She'll teach you."

"*Excuse* you. Another bonus? What am I?"

"I'm just saying you're beautiful and so sexy. You definitely know how to please your man; you're smart, independent, the whole package. You're a keeper. If you can cook, then it's a bonus. But then again, now you have me wondering about your skeletons."

I laughed and threw my napkin at him.

"Don't try to start a food fight. If you can't cook I'll still love you."

"Fuck you."

"You already did, and I gave you props," he laughed.

He fixed his plate and sat down. "Let's see what we have here." He took a bite of my eggs and frowned. "Water!" He started coughing.

"They're not that bad." I handed him a glass of half and half.

"That's only your opinion."

"Actually, it isn't. Landon already ate. If it was that bad, she would have definitely let me know."

He laughed. "True. How long have you two been friends? You two are like day and night."

I told him the story of how Landon and I first met.

"I knew you weren't a saint," he teased.

"I never said I was. You did. And what did I do that was so bad? He asked for it."

"Nothing, I almost forgot you can be a smart-ass."

"When am I a smart-ass?" I asked innocently.

He looked at me like, *are you serious?* "What about the business meeting with Lisa awhile back."

"Who?"

"Yasmin, you know who. Don't be smart. Lisa Stevens."

"Actually, I wasn't being smart. If you remember, I'm not allowed to call her Lisa. You and Sean gave me the OK to use your first name. Lisa, pardon me, Ms. Stevens, was just a bitch, and you know she was. But while we're on the subject, that night when I saw you at Cheesecake Factory she was trying to make it look intimate. She wants you."

"No, she doesn't. She actually just got married. She just doesn't like you," he laughed.

"Ha-ha. How professional. I don't know why. I didn't do anything to her."

"She's just like that. Moody, you know how you women do."

"Anyway, that's does not classify me as a smart-ass."

"Our first date, you told me good-bye and just dismissed me."

"You were being an ass. You acted like I told those guys to approach me."

"Yeah, yeah, whatever. Another example, when we went to see Jill, I said you were dressed like you didn't have a man. Yeah, don't think I didn't see you getting that clown's business card."

My mouth dropped open.

"Yeah. You busted. You were right, I wasn't your man, but you didn't have to take his card in my face. But I know that card better be in somebody's trash."

"Well, technically, I didn't. Remember your words, 'let's go with the flow.' I didn't take his card in front of your face. We didn't become exclusive until later that night. Now I know why. You were jealous and became territorial. Now who's busted?"

"I'll admit that gave me a little push. So, where's the card?"

"I don't know."

He gave me a look that said *don't play and don't lie.*

I walked over and kissed him. "You know I love you, and I wouldn't lie."

"How do I know you love me? You treat me so bad."

"I love being with you, talking to you, and fucking you," I giggled. "I don't know where the card is. Don't really care. He can't do a thing for me. These lips," I said kissing him, "these breasts . . ." I said taking his hand and placing it on my breasts. I glided his hands to my pussy. "This pussy, all of this and then some, are yours."

He pulled me in his lap and kissed me. Quickly, he took his hand and attempted to spread my legs, but I stopped him.

I stood up. "Nope, not here, and I'm already a little upset with you."

"Why?"

"I'm sore. You have me all bruised like I was in a fight. I'm going to have to wear a scarf or turtleneck all week. And I'm scared to look at my back." I exposed my neck.

Braxton chucked. "Did I do that?"

"Ha, ha, ha, eat your food."

I fixed a plate and sat down.

He stared at me.

"What? Why are you staring?"

"I can't look at you?"

"You can, but you don't have to stare. Eat."

"I'm scared to eat. The eggs are nasty," he said shrugging up his face.

"Well, eat something else."

"I hope I don't get sick." He ate some more eggs, and then some French toast, still making funny faces.

I started to feel self-conscious. I know my food isn't that bad. Is it?

I looked over at Braxton and saw him stuffing my home fries in his mouth. He looked up. "All right, you got me. The home fries are good, real good. So are the eggs and the French toast. You make any more?"

"No, you play too much . . . Yeah, it is."

He got up and fixed another plate.

"You'll be asleep in thirty minutes."

"No, I won't. My dick will be inside my pussy."

"How do you figure? I need to go home and get ready for work. I already told you I'm sore and bruised. I have to figure out how to hide all of these marks."

"I'll be gentle. It's eleven now. We'll go get you some stuff later, or you can wear one of my ties. You know you like my ties."

"Nope. No more love for you."

"You know you're wrong. You felt good before. Now that I'm hitting it raw, it's even better. You're all wet, and I feel *my* pussy tightening around my dick. That's why I had to tear it up. Look, you have me all hard now."

I'm horny but sore. Do I or don't I?

"Braxton in a bed; we do it everywhere but in the bed, and be gentle. No more marks."

Braxton picked me up and threw me over his shoulder and tapped my ass while carrying me to the bedroom. "*That's* what I'm talking about."

Once there, he threw me down.

"Be gentle."

He kissed me and slowly pulled his T-shirt off. Then he gently kissed my breasts, making his way to my stomach, and used his hands to spread my legs apart to take a nibble. Afterward, he climbed on top, entering me slowly.

"I love you, Braxton," I moaned.

He took his time, making love to my body. His strokes and kisses were so soft and gentle, yet firm. My baby listened and knows my body. What a beautiful feeling. I didn't know when they started, but I felt hot tears running down my face. I was falling deeper in love.

8
Caged Bird

T hings were going very well with Braxton and me. He still does things to surprise me. Consistently, he puts a smile on my face. It's the little things. My favorite movie is *Love Jones*, so the other day, he took me to a Love Jones-type lounge. Later that night, he reenacted Larenz Tate's poem from the movie. Then, I was complaining about my computer. I needed an upgrade, but I hadn't had a chance to take it to the shop. He bought me a new one. He listened to me and constantly encouraged me. He always calls me beautiful, but he also makes me feel beautiful. And for the first time in my life, I'm beginning to think I am.

Thanksgiving was in a couple of days. Things were indeed serious. Braxton wanted me to meet his parents, which I was nervous about. If they didn't like me it could be the end of our relationship. I wasn't sure what they would think about me or what to expect. Well, I know they won't be like Derrick's crazy-ass family. The thing that really had me nervous is he wants to meet my parents. My parents aren't the friendliest. They barely deal with me. Now that I think about it, I haven't seen my parents since graduation. I was on my way over there hoping for compassion. Maybe they're in the holiday mood. Yeah, right. I've only talked to my mother twice since then. Maybe it won't be too bad I tried to convince myself as I drove to the dreaded destination.

To be honest, I didn't know if either one of them will even be there. My father still worked for MTA, and my mother worked as a secretary, but I don't know their schedules.

My parents live in a nice middle-class suburb. The houses on the block are all of decent size, ranging from

Ranchers to Colonials, Ramblers to Cape Cods, with various arrays of flowers, ponds, and cobblestones. My parents' house, a split foyer, sat on a corner lot. Appraising the other houses, I have to say their home was one of the best landscaped. Driving through, like many, you would assess that there was a lot of love and care in this neighborhood. From my personal experience, however, it is clear the outside picture does not dictate the true story.

When I pulled up to the curb, I saw that all the cars were there. *This should be fun,* I thought. I deal with my mother better than my father. Like an uninvited guest, I walked to door and rang the doorbell.

My father answered shortly after.

"Hi, Daddy," I said jubilantly.

"Hey," he said unenthused. "Your mother is in the kitchen."

I walked in the kitchen to see my mother and sister. They were always so close. Truthfully, my sister is close with both Daddy and Mommy. Envy described my feelings toward their relationship, not jealousy. I just wanted either parent to show some interest in me, say they were proud, or at least give me a hug occasionally. With my sister, their love and affection were given openly.

"Hey, Ma, Ashley," I said.

"Hey, Yasmin," my mother said with the same enthusiasm as my father.

"Hey, Yas, what have you been up to?" Ashley asked.

I took a seat at the kitchen table. "Nothing much. Working and hanging out."

"You still hang with crazy Landon?" Ashley asked.

"Yeah, that's my girl," I responded.

"Hmm," my mother grunted.

My mother never liked Landon. She thought she was spoiled, bourgeois, and a bad influence. I was surprised at her reaction because she never really cared what I did or who I hung out with. She always said there was something about her she didn't like. At first, it bothered me, but now, I'm at the point where I just have to say *whatever*. Landon treats me more like family than they do. Her parents were even more compassionate toward me. For my graduation, they gave me a nice present and a card that wished me good luck on all my future endeavors. My mother and sister only stayed briefly at the ceremony. We didn't even go out to celebrate afterward.

"So what brings you over here, Yasmin?" Mom asked.

I took a deep breath. "I wanted to know what you were doing for Thanksgiving. I want to bring my boyfriend over to meet you."

"Yasmin, you have a boyfriend now? Where did you meet him? What's his name?" Ashley drilled.

I looked at her and smiled. "His name is Braxton, and I met him at a club. Well, actually, I first met him at a club, but we didn't really hook up until I met him at work."

My mother sucked her teeth. "A club? What good man can you meet at a club? At least he has a job, but it's inappropriate to date someone you work with. It's stupid. What happens if you break up? I'll tell you what, you'll look stupid. I hope he's not your boss. Please tell me you're not having sex with your boss. I raised you better than that."

Just then, my father walked in. "What's going on in here?"

"Nothing," my mother quickly said.

But daddy's girl, Ashley, added her two cents. "Yasmin's new boyfriend is her boss, and she wants us to meet him."

Daddy looked at me like he was disgusted. This is why I hate dealing with them. They always twist stuff around and assume the worst.

I spoke up before it went any further. "Braxton is not my boss. He works at BET. I'm handling an account with them. We work for two different companies."

"It's still inappropriate," Mom threw in.

Changing the subject I asked, "What are you doing for Thanksgiving? Will dinner be here or over at Aunt Patti's?"

Aunt Patti was my mother's sister and has always been nice to me. The only other person who made me feel love and accepted was my maternal grandmother. My grandmother would always tell me she loved me and how pretty I was. I missed most her hugs. She was the one who encouraged me and told me it would be OK. Aunt Patti was nice too, but she had a family of her own. She also lived in Virginia, which was about an hour away, so I rarely saw her.

"Dinner will be at my mother's house this year. We're driving to Philly tomorrow," Daddy said.

I was upset, hurt. When were they planning to tell me? Once again I was left out.

"That's sounds like fun," I lied. "Give Grandmother a hug for me."

My other grandmother loved and adored Ashley. She had pictures of Ashley all throughout her house, and when she had company she would brag about Ashley. She was cordial to my mother, but I could tell there was tension even though she never said any hurtful things to her.

My mom was a shade darker than me, but she had brown eyes. You would think it would bring us closer, but it didn't. In actuality, it seemed liked Mom ignored me more when my grandmother was around. I always thought my dad's mother didn't like us because of our complexion and learned to deal with it.

Now toward me, my father's mother was a witch. The meanest woman I've ever met. It seemed like she goes out of her way to be mean to me and make me feel unwanted and unloved. She would always give me chores, and then complain that I took too long or wasn't doing it right. She would always say,   "Can you do *anything* right? Why are you so slow? You think people are going to give you your way all the time because of your green eyes? Well, they're not. Those green eyes are evil. Evil, monstrous eyes; ugly, really ugly. All they will ever cause you is trouble.

Men will tell you how pretty they are because they're fascinated by the color, but that'll wear off. They don't want you. They never will want you for nothing more than a fling. You're good for nothing, just a waste of time. Nobody wants you now and never will. You'll have bad luck. I'll give you some advice: don't fall in love; all you will ever have is heartache."

I still remember those words. Every time a guy comments about my eyes, I hear her hurtful words, except with Braxton. When I first met Braxton, truthfully, I didn't think he noticed them; he noticed me. It doesn't hurt that his eyes are also different, but it's more than that. He called *me* beautiful, not my eyes. But again, it's more than the eyes. With Braxton, we have this physical, mental, spiritual deep connection. Before he ever told me he loved me I could feel it in his touch, when he held me or kissed me, and I feel it now when he looks at me.

"Ashley, how will you survive that long ride?" I asked just to make conversation.

"I'll be fun. Daniel is coming with me," she smiled.

"Daniel? Who is he?" I asked clueless.

"Daniel is her boyfriend. Such a respectful young man, and he is very handsome. He attends Howard. He's going to be a pediatrician," my mother beamed.

"That's good, Ashley. How long have you been together?"

"Six months."

"What are you guys doing for Christmas? I want you to meet Braxton. I think you'll like him."

Uninterestedly my mother responded, "We'll be in Jamaica for Christmas."

Damn, do they tell me anything? I thought. "When were you planning to tell me about Thanksgiving and Christmas?" I asked, even more hurt.

"What do you mean, when were we going to tell you? You're the child. You're not the parent. We're telling you now," Daddy responded.

Pissed, I was done. I couldn't take anymore. I gathered my stuff and stood up. "Well, Happy Thanksgiving and Merry Christmas," I said as I walked to the door.

"With that attitude you need to go. Matter of fact, don't step back in my house until you get it adjusted. And you owe all of us an apology," my mother called out behind me.

Once I got in my car, I drove off as fast as I could. I was in the car for only five minutes before I had to pull over to let the tears fall.

"Why do they hate me so much? Why? What did I do? I honestly don't know. Whatever it was I'm sorry. Why? This is so typical of them. They never include me. I'm mad at myself for allowing them to upset me like this. When I graduated I promised myself to get it together, take care of Yasmin. Yet here I am, crying over something that will never change."

I sat there for another fifteen minutes before my cell phone rang. It was Landon, just who I need to get me out of this funky mood.

"Hey, Landon," I said sniffling.

"Yas, what's the matter? It better not be that Braxton. Is he acting up? Do I need to send one of my men over there to handle him?"

I laughed. Landon was always there trying to make me feel better.

"No, Landon, I just left my parents' house, and I let them upset me again."

I rehashed to Landon what happened. She knew and had seen how callous my relationship with my parents could be.

"I'm sorry, Yas. It will be OK, and you have me. I love you, girl. Don't let them upset you. Let's go out and have a drink. You can spend Thanksgiving with me and my parents."

Although Landon's parents are sincere and welcoming, I always felt uncomfortable. Especially with her father. I get this crazy vibe. I don't like the way he looks at me. On several occasions I've caught him staring at me. He's never actually tried anything, but I'm not giving him the opportunity so I rarely go with Landon when she visits. "Thanks, but I'll be all right."

"You're sure? Afterward, you can go with me over to Eric's, but you have to be gone by midnight. Landon needs some loving. If you want, I'll get Eric to set you up with one of his friends."

"Landon, you know I'm with Braxton. Don't play," I laughed.

"You're with him, but you're not married. He's nothing but a bunch of games anyway, thinking he's a pimp," she slyly remarked.

Landon was still obviously jealous over the amount of time I spent with Braxton. I admit I didn't help her claim. I mentioned the way he reacts when other men look at me. That was all the initiative she needed to start the *get rid of Braxton* campaign. She said I can do better and he's too controlling. I told her he's gotten better since we're committed, but it fell on deaf ears.

"Landon, please don't start on Braxton. I'm having a bad day. Thanks, but no thanks on your offer. Braxton actually wants me to meet his parents. I'm spending the holiday with him."

Landon sighed like she was defeated. "Yas, I'll admit he seems to be stepping it up. So, because you like Braxton and you're happy, I'll be nice, but that doesn't mean I like him. I still think you can do better. But who am I, other than Landon, your *best* friend, the one who will tell you no wrong? Truthfully, I think you should be with Kevin. Kevin is making a lot of money, and he's sincere."

"Kevin is like a brother, and again, I'm with Braxton."

"All right, all right, all right, enough about Braxton. Let's go to Pearl."

"OK, I'm on my way, and Landon, thank you for making me feel better," I laughed.

"You're my girl. I always have your back. You're the sister I never had. When you marry Kevin, he'll be like a brother I never had, and we can be one big happy family," she said before quickly hanging up.

Times such as this make me appreciate Landon. She irks me the majority of the time, but when I need her, she's there. Just like the time my parents forgot my eighteenth birthday. Coincidently, Ashley was in cheerleading competition out of town. So my parents were in California cheering their baby on. Landon went out of her way to make sure I had a good birthday. She would not let me sit around and mope over my parents. We had a minishopping spree courtesy of her parents. Her parents rented us a limo. We had a hotel suite that included our own personal masseuse and manicurist. It was a weekend event that included lots of fun. Her parents even had a birthday cake made for me. Unfortunately, even though they went far and beyond to make me feel special, the sting of my parents returning with no mention of my birthday confirmed to me that I didn't matter to them.

9
Trippin' (That's the Way Love Goes)

Thanksgiving arrived, and I was nervous as hell about meeting Braxton's parents. I'd already changed my outfit three times. Finally I decided on a pair of auburn-colored slacks and a cream knitted, button-down shirt. I sprayed my Issey Miyake, put my jewelry on, and brown Nine West boots. With my hair pulled up in a loose ponytail I began doing anything to keep busy.

At 1:45, my doorbell rang. It had to be Kevin. The other night when I hooked up with Landon she neglected to tell me she invited Kevin along. Kevin ended up driving, and I left my cell phone in his car. He was dropping it off before he went to his parents. After his parents, he was meeting Nicole. It must be serious. I met Nicole a few times, but I didn't really have an opinion on her just yet. I checked the peephole expecting Kevin, but there was my baby. Braxton was early, which was a surprise. I wasn't expecting him until three o'clock.

"You're early. This is a first. You said you'd be here at three o'clock. I wasn't expecting you until three thirty or four o'clock," I joked.

"Ha-ha. I'm getting better. Why? You not happy to see me?" he said, kissing me on my lips, and then stepping into my apartment.

"I'm always happy to see you, but why are you here early?"

"I missed you, and I wanted to get some of your loving," he said, unbuttoning my shirt and kissing my neck.

"Uh-uh. Nope. Maybe later. I spent too much time getting ready. I can't look crazy when I meet your parents."

"It's been awhile. I need to relieve some tension," he said, taking off my shirt, then bra. A moan escaped when I felt his tongue on my nipples. Sugar Daddy was jumping, ready to be stroked.

"Boy, please, you just left here at eleven. Chill."

"I keep telling you, I'm not a boy. I'm going to show who's a boy. You know you have some good pussy." He unbuttoned my pants. Just as he was about to pull them down, my doorbell rang.

I quickly buttoned my pants, threw on my shirt, and attempted to button it up. "One minute," I yelled.

I opened the door, and there was Kevin. He was dressed in Sean John. Looking very good, and smelling just as good wearing Burberry cologne.

"Hey, Ms. Y.E.S. Yes," he said, giving me a hug.

"Hey, Kev."

"Look at you. You're that happy to see me. Do you need help buttoning your shirt? You know I don't mind."

I looked down to see my shirt.

He lifted his hands to button it.

"Naw, man, I'll take care of her," Braxton said walking up to me, wrapping his arms around my waist and pulling me close.

"Hey, man. I didn't see you over there," Kevin said, startled. "Well, I just came to give Yasmin back her phone. You two have a good holiday." Kevin handed me the phone.

"Yeah, we will," Braxton replied.

"See you later, Kev," I said, closing the door.

Braxton was cool. I'm impressed.

I turned around and began to unbutton Braxton's pants, but he stopped me.

"What's up with that?" he barked.

"What's up with what?" I asked, giving him the same crazy look he was giving me.

"You and Kevin. What's the Y.E.S. about?"

"Are you bipolar? I'm tired of you flipping the script on me. You get jealous of every man that talks to me. Kevin is like my big brother." I pushed my way past him and began to fix my clothes.

"What's the Y.E.S.? Did the two of you ever go out? He's definitely not looking at you like a sister. You see the way he tried to button your shirt. You even smell like him now."

"I do not. He was just playing."

"Playing? Yeah, right. He looks at you like he wants you. How long did you date and did you have sex?"

"What?"

"Don't *what* me. Answer the question."

I decided to be honest. "We went out a couple of times, there was no chemistry. No sex. The end."

"No chemistry? I'm a man. I know he wants you, and I don't like it."

"Well, he knows I'm with you, and he has a girlfriend."

"Whatever. What's the Y.E.S. about?"

"Think about it. You went to Columbia. You're a smart man, figure it out."

"Yasmin, stop with the guessing games."

I smirked. I decided to take my clothes off because I did smell like Burberry. "Are you ready, Mr. Bipolar?"

"No, Ms. Y.E.S. Why are you changing your clothes?"

"My shirt is wrinkled," I lied.

"Whatever."

He was really irking me. "Look, Braxton, I understand what you're saying, but this jealousy thing you have going on needs to stop. I don't cheat. I never gave you any indication that I have or would. How can I? Your dick is always up in my pussy. Look at you now. You left at eleven last night, and your dick is back knocking on my pussy door."

He chuckled. "Cute."

I looked at him and shook my head. "My name is Yasmin Elaine Sinclair."

"I know that, smart-ass," he replied.

"I'm going to tell your mama she needs a refund check from Columbia. YYYasmin EEEEEEElaine SSSSinclair. *Y.E.S.*"

Braxton walked up to me. "I was overreacting as usual, and I apologize."

"Yeah, whatever," I said. Leaving him standing there I went into my bedroom to pick out a new outfit. This time I put on an auburn and brown wraparound.

*

We arrived at Braxton's parents' around four. The outside of the large three-story Victorian home was beautiful. The circular driveway, ponds, waterfall, and cobblestone were all welcoming, yet intimidating at the same time. Apprehension was present, my stomach in knots. I took deep breaths to try to calm my nerves. I hoped I was prepared for dinner with the Simms.

Braxton, who was being extra nice after our little argument, especially since I put the kitty kat on lock, grabbed my hand and led me up the walkway. When we walked in I was even more overwhelmed. I wasn't expecting so many people. There had to be at least fifty people there. For some reason I didn't consider anyone else being there besides Braxton's three brothers and significant others. I knew some things about Braxton, such as he's the youngest, which I concluded is why he's so difficult and used to getting his way. His father is an anesthesiologist, his mother was a nurse, but once the kids came, she chose to be a stay-at-home mom. As my mind began running rapid, a woman approached.

"Hey, Ma," Braxton said, hugging a woman who resembled Diahann Carroll.

"Hey, baby," she said returning his hug. She then turned to me.

"Yasmin, aren't you beautiful. My son told me you were, and he wasn't lying. I'm so glad to meet to you," she said hugging me warmly.

Immediately, I like her. In that quick moment, her demeanor came off as loving and kind. She made me feel so welcomed.

"Thank you, Mrs. Simms. I'm glad to meet to you as well."

"Jeff, come here. Come meet, Yasmin." She winked at Braxton. "I know I'm going to like her."

I laughed.

Braxton was the splitting image of his father. He had his father's height, complexion, and those grey eyes.

The remaining introductions I received from Braxton's entire family were warm. They all were friendly, accepting, and seemed truly genuine. I only wished my family was a quarter of this accepting of me.

Braxton took our coats and went to get us something to drink. I sat on the couch and prepared for Twenty-One Questions.

"Yasmin, I know your parents must be proud of you. Braxton told me you're handling the BET account," Mr. Simms commented.

I nodded and smiled, hoping he would change the subject concerning my parents.

"Yasmin, what did you do to Mr. Bang! Bang! Bang!? The boy ain't never brought a girl home. He was out there as you young people say, freaking. But you sure are pretty," Braxton's uncle commented.

His uncle reminded me of John Witherspoon in *Boomerang*. He was direct and funny, but he dressed in current fashion trends.

I laughed.

"If he acts up, call me. Braxton don't have anything on me. I'm single now. I think I like you for myself. I even have the perfect name for you, Sweet Thing." His uncle grinned.

He was a nice-looking older man, who, I found out, recently retired from the army. Six foot, mocha-colored skin, wavy salt-and-pepper hair, and he looked to be in good shape.

I just laughed. I didn't know how to respond. Thankfully, Mrs. Simms saved me temporarily.

"Charles, leave her alone," she ordered.

"Calm down, Beverly," he shot back.

"So, Sweet Thing, tell me what you did to my nephew."

"I didn't do anything, Mr. Simms," I smiled.

"Call me Uncle Charles, Sweet Thing."

This night should be interesting.

I met Braxton's three other brothers, Jeffrey Jr., Horace, and Vincent.

Jeffrey AKA JR was the oldest at thirty-one; he looked just like their father as well. He was 6 foot 6, the tallest of them all, and had the same caramel skin, grey eyes, and wavy hair. He and his wife, Patrice, a teacher, have been married two years, but no kids yet. She was nice, but plain, reminding me of Olive Oil from Popeye. Very tall, about 6 foot 1, butterscotch skin, black hair pulled into a bun, and very, very skinny. Jeff JR, a lawyer, worked not too far from Landon's parents' firm.

"JR, what type of law do you practice?" I inquired.

"I practice family law."

"OK, my best friend's parents' firm is not too far from where you work. Are you familiar with Taylor and Taylor?"

"Yes, I've worked with them before; very prestigious. Matter of fact, I was co-counsel with one of their attorneys, Kevin Anderson. He's very sharp. Do you know him?"

I smiled. "Yes, I know Kevin very well."

"Yeah, she knows him a little *too* well," Braxton said a little irritated as he took a seat next to me.

"I see Braxton needs to borrow those green eyes of hers. Look at the steam coming out of his ears. Somebody's jealous," Uncle Charles instigated.

Everyone seemed to get quiet and wanted to know the 411.

I felt so embarrassed. If I could, I would have slapped him and left. I hated attention. I didn't know his parents, and he was making it seem as if Kevin and I were more than just friends.

"Well, JR, yes, Kevin is like a big brother to me. I told the baby over here that, but we all know how babies are. They always have to be the center of attention. I saw Kevin earlier. He was on the way to his girlfriend's house for dinner. Kevin calls me Ms. Yes, Y.E.S., and Braxton couldn't make the connection. My name is Yasmin Elaine Sinclair, Y.E.S. Just a little joke. And this baby had a tantrum."

Everyone got a laugh out of me calling Braxton a baby except him, of course.

"I see she's time enough for you, Mr. Freaky Freak," Uncle Charles instigated.

Braxton just sat looking stupid. I ignored him for the most part, taking the opportunity to meet his two other brothers.

Horace, a thirty-year-old cardiologist resembling Mrs. Simms, seemed nice. His 6 foot 2 demeanor was definitely laid-back.

Vincent, twenty-nine, also resembled their mom. He was attached, no kids. He worked in the entertainment industry. Doing what I don't know. His girlfriend looked like a straight-up gold-digging video vixen. Yup. Slut. Ho. Tramp. Hated to be mean, but it is what it is. She wore a skintight tiger bodysuit, very inappropriate for the dinner. She had teeth too big for her narrow face and poppy eyes. She wore a long blond weave, had very light skin, was petite, and reminded me of Seabiscut, the horse.

I caught Braxton looking her over, studying her body like she was the book and he was the student preparing to take the exam. He saw me peeping him out, so he put his hand on the small of my back and rubbed it a little.

Uncle Charles, not missing a beat, said, "Mr. Smooth not smooth anymore. I'm going to have me another wife by the end of the night. Mr. Freak has two strikes now."

Braxton, in a little funky mood, asked, "Is dinner ready yet?"

"No, Braxton," Mrs. Simms said. "Let me finish up."

"Can I help, Mrs. Simms?" I gave her a look that said *please let me help before I hurt your baby boy.*

"Sure, honey," she smiled.

I followed her into the kitchen, and she cleared it out so we could talk.

I hope she's not going to reprimand me about her son. He's the baby not me.

"So tell me about yourself and your family."

The smile went away.

"What's wrong, baby?" she asked.

I don't know why, but I felt I could talk to her. I was honest. I told her how I felt like a black sheep growing up, the incident a couple of days ago, and about my grandmothers. I was truthful about everything.

She hugged me and with tears in her own eyes told me I was beautiful and I am loved. She assured me anything we discussed was between us and any time I wanted to talk, I could call her. She also insisted I call her Ma. That definitely surprised me. I just met this woman, but I really appreciated her compassion.

"My son loves you. I never thought I'd see the day."

Again, I was caught off guard that she was frank, but I was relieved. I breathed. "I love Braxton too."

"I can see that. I know you'll be good for him. Put him in check."

I helped her finish up, made the potato salad, a quick peach cobbler, and rice and gravy.

When dinner was ready, I, along with the rest of the aunts, helped Mrs. Simms bring out the food.

I didn't want to sit next to Braxton so I quickly took a seat next to Uncle Charles. Braxton's brother, Horace, sat on the opposite side.

Braxton was left to sit next to Vincent's gold-digger girlfriend, who, I found out, was named Keisha.

"Well, look who's sitting next to me. I told y'all Uncle still got it. Sweet Thing, will you marry me?" Uncle Charles joked.

"Braxton, what's going on at BET?" his father asked.

Braxton, still is irritated, curtly replied, "Nothing."

Nosy Uncle Charles inquired about Keisha. "So, Keisha, what type of work you do?"

"I model," she said proudly.

"What type of modeling have you done?" Mr. Simms asked.

"I did a couple of music videos. Vincent said he's going to have me audition for some acting roles soon."

She's clueless, I thought.

"Good luck," Braxton's dad said and focused on his food.

We sat and ate. The turkey was moist, the macaroni and cheese, yams, and greens were so good. Everyone was too busy enjoying the good food to talk. Well, everyone except Uncle Charles.

"Umm umm umm, this food sure is good. Beverly, the turkey and greens is good as usual."

Everyone agreed.

Uncle Charles, not done yet, had to add two more cents. "Yeah, Bev, this some good potato salad and the rice and gravy make me think I'm in South Cackilackey."

"Thank you, Charles, but I can't take credit. Yasmin cooked the rice and gravy and fixed the potato salad."

"Yasmin, you cook too? The food is very good. Braxton, she's definitely a keeper, but Uncle Charles is stepping on your toes, boy," Mr. Simms teased.

"Step on his toes, Jeff, I then stepped. My, my, my, put on your red dress tonight and your high heels," Uncle Charles sang.

Uncle Charles is a fool.

Braxton didn't say anything.

"What else you make me, Sweet Thing?"

"Just peach cobbler."

"My favorite. She's going home with me to tonight. I didn't know Mr. Smooth could be so quiet."

Uncle Charles whispered in my ear, "I like you. Don't hurt my nephew too bad. But go ahead and laugh. I've never seen him like this. He usually will talk your head off. You made my night. I'm going to tease him a little bit more, and then I'll give you back to him. I know, don't cry, but you can't keep up with this old man."

I burst out laughing. "You are so right, Uncle Charles."

After dinner, everyone went into the media room to watch *Soul Food*, but that was cut for football.

I helped Mrs. Simms clean up and could hear Braxton whooping and hollering like he's at one of the games.

While everyone was occupied I called Landon to wish her as well as her family a Happy Thanksgiving. Her new plans included hooking up with Will at some party. She asked me to go, but I declined. On my way to the media room, I saw Braxton and gold digger Keisha. She was leaning on him like she was sick and needed him for support. I bet she did. One arm wrapped around his back, her arm and weave on his chest. If we weren't at his parents' house I would have blacked out on him. Especially since he had the nerve to get jealous over Kevin, but I had to respect his parents' home.

Pissed, I turned around and bumped into Mrs. Simms and Uncle Charles.

"What's the matter, Sweet Thing?"

"Nothing," I lied.

They looked past my shoulder and saw Braxton with Keisha.

"Braxton, I need some help, now," his mother called out.

Before he came I excused myself and went into the bathroom. I stayed in there and calmed my nerves before I hurt Braxton. I really didn't feel like dealing with him tonight.

I made my way to the media room and saw Keisha hugged up with Vincent. She looked at me and gave me a look that said, "I can have your man anytime."

I gave her a look back that yelled, "Try me!"

I sat there for twenty minutes debating if I wanted to take Landon up on her offer. It was tempting. But no, I had to tell this fool off.

My cell rang. It was Kevin.

"Hey," I said.

"I know you doing the family, relationship thing like me, but I have to talk to you about a couple of things," he said.

"What's that?"

"First thing, I apologize about earlier. I was just playing. I didn't realize he was there. I didn't mean any disrespect."

"I know. Everything's cool," I lied.

"My second issue, are you feeling overwhelmed? I just got finished getting interrogated. I'm usually doing the interrogating; very uncomfortable when you're on the receiving end. Everyone is nice, but all eyes are on me."

I laughed. "I know exactly."

He sighed. "I'm glad it's not only me. I snuck out. Said I had to check on something. I've been gone too long. So I'll talk to you later, Ms. Y.E.S."

"All right, Kev, talk to you later."

I closed my phone and saw Braxton staring me in my face. I ignored him and focused on the TV.

"Yasmin, can I talk to you for a minute?" he asked.

"I'm really into this game. Can we talk later?" I lied.

"You weren't too busy to talk to Kevin," he said, taking a seat next to me.

My phone rang again. This time it's Landon. Perfect timing.

"Yes, Diva?" I got up to give myself some privacy.

"Can you please come with me? I don't want to go by myself."

"How long?"

"Just a few hours. It's eight now. You'll be home by three."

"No way."

"Please."

"OK, but you will owe me, and twelve—one tops."

I found Mrs. Simms.

"Mrs. Simms?"

"I told you call me Ma."

"Ma, it was so nice to meet you, but I'm going to leave."

"No, don't go. Just ignore Braxton. You said it yourself; he is a baby. Anyway he drove, didn't he?"

"He did, but my best friend is going to pick me up. She needs company tonight. I need some air anyway. I promise we'll meet up again."

"Aww, but I don't want you to go."

"I'm sorry, I already committed to her."

"Remember, you just promised me we'll meet up. I will hold you to it."

"Of course."

She was understanding and gave Landon directions. Even though she wanted me to stay, she understood. I went into the bathroom to pull my hair down and freshen up.

Landon was there fifteen minutes later.

"Tell your friend to come in and say hi."

I went to get Landon. She was in a tight black dress that showed off her slender model 5 foot 9 figure that I knew would drive the men crazy. The black spiked four-inch boots screamed *I'm sexy and I know it!*

"Ma, this is my friend Landon."

We briefly made small talk.

"Nice to meet you, Landon," Mrs. Simms said.

"Same to you."

"Well, you girls have fun; be safe."

She gave me a hug and whispered she knew Braxton was wrong but be nice and don't stay mad at him too long.

Landon and I went into the media room to say good-bye to everyone.

"Well, I'll be. Look at my Sweet Thing. She let her hair down. If only I was a little younger. She brought a friend too. Look at you two. My, where are you two Sweet Things going? Y'all looking real good."

Landon pointed to the screen. "To the after party. My friend plays for the Steelers."

I introduced everyone to Landon. Then I gave Uncle Charles a hug, and the rest of the family.

Braxton pulled me aside. "Where do you think you're going?"

"I don't *think* I'm going anywhere. I *am* going out. See you whenever; have fun with Keisha."

He took a deep breath. "We need to talk."

"We'll talk later," I said and walked away.

"Bye-bye, Braxton, so long," Landon threw in.

When we got into the car I filled Landon in on the issue with Braxton and me. I left out the Keisha part.

She laughed. "He's jealous of you and Kevin. I told you Kevin is more your speed. He even knows it, and that's why he mad."

"No, Landon. I'm staying with Braxton. I just need to teach him he needs to calm down. His mother and family are so nice."

"Oh God, I give up. Yeah, yeah, I see you're calling her Ma already. Enough of the Braxton song. Let's go party."

Despite Braxton being an ass, overall, I had a good time. It was nice feeling welcomed.

10
Oops! (There Goes My Shirt)

I wish I would have stayed at Braxton's mother's
house and just ignored him. This party is too
much for me. It was definitely alive, but I was
not in the mood. Landon was off somewhere having a ball,
but I was ready to go. She didn't need me. I was at the bar
sipping on a Malibu Paradise trying to be alone.
Unfortunately, a lot of the players keep approaching me,
even though I sounded like a broken record saying, "I'm not
interested"; yet, they pursued. I've ignored them for the most
part, but it only enticed them more. I finally gave up and
took some numbers and danced.

I had a nice little buzz going on until I felt
someone's hands on my body. My back was turned so I
couldn't see who it was. He wasn't touching me offensively,
so I continued to dance. Everything was cool until I feel his
dick getting hard.

I tried to break away, but he held me tightly. "I see
Braxton's not handling his business. My door is open. Let
me show you how a man feels."

"In order to show me what a man feels like, you
must first be one."

"Only one way to find out," he countered back.

"No need. My man, Braxton, is handling everything
lovely. You won't be handling SHIT this way."

I walked off and looked for Landon. She was
preoccupied with some guy, but I was ready.

"Diva, can I go home, please?"

"Yas, give me thirty and I'll be ready."

"OK, thirty." I went back to the bar and drank some
more. Thirty minutes turned into an hour and a half.

When we finally got to the car, I told Diva off. "You said thirty minutes, not ninety. You dragged me out to this party, for what? I saw you when we first stepped in, and that was it. I was on my own. Then I had to cuss out the nasty-ass Javon feeling all up on me. I'm not doing any more parties with you! You can just tell me about them."

"Look, Yas, don't take your frustrations out on me. Take that back to Braxton."

"Whatever, Landon. No more parties."

"Anyway, I'm going to drop you off and hook back up with Will."

"Goddamn, do you let you cat-trap take a rest?"

"Don't even go there. I practice safe sex, and I fuck just as much as you. In fact, you probably have me beat. You have live-in dick. I just have a variety. For the record, though, I don't sleep with a lot of men. I do flirt, but I've only had sex with Eric and Will for this last year. You had sex with Derek this year, right? And now Braxton, so I'd say we're even. Don't get mad at me because you won't be getting any dick tonight."

"Touché. You got me this time but don't count me out. I have a vibrator, Mr. Rubber."

"Vibrator, ha! Please, poor Yas, drunk and horny."

"You think you're so funny."

"I am. I hope Mr. Rubber can make you have multiple orgasms tonight," she laughed.

"Mr. Rubber and I will be all right. All I need is a couple more drinks," I laughed.

"If you say so but give me the word and I can make a call for you. Some things just can't be substituted. A dick is one."

"Like your ass doesn't have one."

"I didn't say that, Yassy, but you're frustrated, mad. You need the real thing that can flip you over, tap that ass, and break the back. A vibrator won't be doing that."

"Enough with the jokes, Diva."

"Aww, I'm sorry. Did I hurt your feelings?" she laughed.

Once I was home Landon asked if I needed her to walk me up. I told her I was all right. When I got into the apartment I blinked the light to let her know I was in.

I was so horny. Damn, Braxton got me addicted to his dick like a drug addict to heroin, and I needed my fix.

I began walking, stripping, and throwing clothes everywhere. I bumped my foot on my chair. "Shit." Drunk and a little disoriented, I sang some rendition of Toni Braxton "I Love Me Some Him."

I love me some him
Another man will never do
But tonight they will
Mr. Rubber, where are you?

I went into my closet and pulled out my vibrator. "Hey, Mr. Rubber, I'm so horny, and Braxton is an ass, so tonight you'll do."

I started singing again.

I love me some Braxton
Another asshole won't do.

I switched songs. Now I was singing "Oops," by Tweet. I lay across my bed, spread my legs, and started to please myself. My eyes closed, I listened to the vibrator hum. I moved the vibrator in and out of my pussy nice and slow. I took my free hand and started to play with my nipples. My hips began to move up and down as I twirled the vibrator around, shoving it deeper and harder into my pussy.

"*Mmm*," I moaned.

Soon, I could feel the juices flowing from my pussy. It was feeling good but not as good as Braxton's dick. No matter how I moved, I couldn't get to that next level. I moved my hips and thought of the way Braxton fucked me.

"Braxton," I whispered. I needed Sugar Daddy inside of me to take me to the orgasmic place.

"Braxton, I need some dick. I love that dick."

I shoved it in harder and harder, but I couldn't get there. My hands and wrist were working vigorously. In fact, my hand was cramping as I continued to rotate the vibrator. I closed my eyes tighter and imagined Braxton's body on mine. "Braxton, I need my Sugar Daddy." I envisioned his lips kissing mine, his hands grabbing my ass, and my legs wrapped around his waist. My hallucination felt so real. I could actually feel Braxton's body. It felt too real, and then, I felt hands removing my vibrator.

Shook, I opened my eyes prepared to scream. I was shocked. Staring back at me was Braxton. Before I could speak, he placed his mouth on mine and kissed me hard. I accepted it. He moved his mouth from my lips, down to my neck, then my breasts. I felt like I was floating. He made his way back to my mouth and spread my legs wide, plunging his dick in me so hard he took my breath. "*Uhhhh*," I moaned.

He pumped long and hard strokes, continuing to push up on my cervix. The pain felt so good. He couldn't get deep enough.

"You love this dick?" he asked.

"*Mmm-hmm*" was all I could get out as he took me to ecstasy.

"I can't hear you. Who do you love?" He stopped.

"I love you. I love this dick. Give me this dick. Give it to me."

He rammed his dick in and just held it there. My kitty kat pulsated. He pushed his dick farther in my pussy like was trying to make a new hole. Talk about feel it in my back.

"*Ahh*," I screamed.

He kept pushing farther and farther. Then he pumped me hard. Each time he did he hit my G-spot. The way he was sucking on my neck, I knew I'd be bruised, but I didn't care. I needed this dick. I could barely talk. All I could do was scream out my pleasure. He was pumping so hard, so hard that his balls were slapping against my ass.

I was so close to coming. Suddenly, he stopped.

"Give it to me. Fuck me," I begged.

Now he pumped real slow, too slow. I moved my hips in an effort to try to get him to fuck hard again, but he kept teasing me.

"Fuck me, *mmmm*," I panted. "Fuck me. Please fuck me real good. This is your pussy, so fuck me. It's yours! Fuck me," I cried.

He ignored me, continuing to take slow strides. So I wrapped my legs around his waist. I pulled him close, wrapped my arms around his neck, and kissed him hard. I started squeezing my vagina walls as tight as I could.

"Shit, damn, *aargh*," he moaned.

I started pumping, and this time he pumped back. We were fighting to see who was going to cum harder, faster, first. Sweat was forming on his head, his breathing intensified. He was about to cum. I squeezed my muscles again. I could feel his dick jerking. I have him, or so I thought.

He got himself together and lifted my hips and pumped.

"Oh shit! *Ahhhh*," I screamed.

I squeezed my vaginal walls again, and he started jerking, and I was out. I literally saw stars and colors. I was in la-la land. I couldn't see or talk for what seemed like forever, but in reality, only a minute . . . or several. My alcohol has been worked off. Braxton lay beside me trying to catch his breath. And we just lay there for about twenty minutes listening to each other breathe.

I was mad at myself for sexing him, but at the same time, happy I did. No one has ever loved me as good as Braxton. The sex just got better. I tried not to smile, but the sex was just so damn good. I shivered just thinking about it. I quickly recalled earlier events and gave him attitude.

"What are you doing here? How did you get in?"

"You gave me keys a while back, remember?"

"Now you decide you want to use them."

"Well, you weren't complaining a few minutes ago."

"That's not the point."

"You know you're glad I was here. Mr. Rubber wasn't doing the job," he chuckled.

I sat up and hit him. "How long were you here?"

"I saw you when you came in." He sat up too.

"Why didn't you say something? You shouldn't sneak up on me like that."

"I was enjoying the show."

"Well, I was scared."

"You were calling out my name. I had to give you some Braxton."

I only vaguely remembered all the details, but I remembered enough. "Get out, Braxton!"

He laughed. "Don't be embarrassed. You were very entertaining. I'm an ass, huh?"

"Yes, you are."

"Don't be mad."

"You had the nerve to get upset over Kevin, but you were all in gold digger's face."

"Hey, that's my brother's girlfriend. I wasn't looking at her like that."

"Whatever. But you really showed your ass when you made that comment about Kevin, insinuating we were more than friends. That was my first time meeting your family. Everyone was looking at me like I was sleeping with both of you. That was real fucked up. Then you disrespected me by looking at that phony gold-digging bitch. I saw the way she was all hugged up on you."

"No one thinks you sleep around. My mother already gave me an earful. As far as me and Keisha, that's nothing. I was taking her to a room to lie down."

"No one thinks that now, but I had to explain that. I shouldn't have had to do that. As far as Keisha, I know you're not that dumb to fall for the damsel-in-distress act. You could have called your brother. That's who she was there with, right?"

"I was coming out of the bathroom, and I saw her. She looked like she was about to fall. I just caught her before she fell."

I rolled my eyes. "You have served your purpose. Now you're irritating me. Please leave."

"Oh, so you're putting me out three o'clock in the morning?"

"Did I stutter?"

"Girl, stop playing. You know you want some more dick." He pulled me down and got on top of me. His dick was hard, but I was sober and not feeling him.

"Get off me and get out."

He tried to kiss me, but I turned away.

"So, it's like that?"

"Yeah."

He got up and left the room.

Good, I thought. *I don't feel like being bothered anymore. I have a headache all of a sudden. I need some sleep.*

I rolled on my stomach, closed my eyes, and tried to go to sleep.

"What the hell is this?" Braxton barked.

I turned around to see him partially dressed. He had some cards and paper in his hand.

"Paper," I said.

"So you get mad and go out and get phone numbers. Who were you going to call when I left?"

Shit, I forgot about those. I meant to throw them away. "Don't come in here trying to flip the script on me. You were an ass all day. You had gold digger in your face. You said it yourself, I'm a pretty girl. Of course, I'm going to get offers. It's what I do with them. You can throw them away if want. I really don't care. Your jealous ass is going to think what you want to anyway. I came home to be by myself, at least, I thought I did. What are you now, a stalker? You shouldn't be invading my privacy. Did you sniff my underwear too, freak?"

"You and that smart-ass mouth. You gave me the key; you came in all drunk. If you would have paid attention, you would have seen me. You know you should always pay attention to your surroundings."

"Are you going to give me another safety tip or tell me why you were spying on me in my house?"

"Are you going to tell me why you have other men's numbers?"

"First stalking, now snooping. How do you know what I have?"

"I'm not stalking you. I have claimed that pussy. You claimed it for me. I'm not here and you still calling out my name. Smart-ass, when you first came in, you started stripping. You think I was going to interrupt that? Hell no. Then you were playing with yourself. I watched the show. Next thing you calling out my name saying you needed some of this dick. So I gave you what you wanted."

"You had the lights out. How could I see you? But why were you snooping in my stuff?"

"I was asleep on the couch. When you bumped your foot you woke me up. Oh yeah, I like your song about how I'm an ass."

"Get out! You still shouldn't be looking through my stuff. I don't invade your privacy, so don't invade mine." I got up, grabbed a shirt, and walked toward the living room to put him out.

"Nobody was looking through your stuff. Like I said before, you stripped and your clothes are all over the living room. Remember, you kicked me out. I picked up my clothes, and I see some clown's number on it. I looked at the floor, and numbers everywhere. Do you collect numbers from every man at the party?" Braxton said, following behind me.

Damn. Nobody told his ass to come here anyway.

"That smart-ass mouth of yours is speechless now."

"Well, if you weren't all up in Keisha's face I wouldn't have gotten those numbers."

Braxton walked up on me. "Last time you took that clown's number I let that slide. Technically, we weren't together. You and I are together now. Don't do that shit no more. Don't disrespect me by taking numbers from other men. Especially men at a football afterparty. They only want one thing. You're right, you're a pretty girl, but you're mine. I've always been honest with you from day one. I have no reason to lie. Keisha is my brother's girlfriend. Even if she wasn't, I wouldn't want her. Yeah, I was looking at her, but not because I wanted her but because she looked a damn mess. I was wondering what my brother was thinking bringing her there."

"I don't like Kevin in a sexual way. He's more like a brother. You shouldn't have made that comment about me and Kevin. I didn't want to go to the party, but I didn't want to be around you either. I didn't take any numbers to piss you off. But you know how you men do. The more you're ignored the more you want us."

"The numbers should have been in the trash."

"You're right."

"I know I am. I admit I was wrong to make the comment about Kevin. I apologize, but I'm not wrong about Kevin. He wants you, and I don't trust him. But I'll trust you, and I'll be nice to Kevin."

I shook my head.

"Don't shake your head. I told you I'll be nice, but I don't trust him. I'll be watching his slick ass. Come here," he demanded. "You know you're so sexy when you mad."

"No."

"Why do you have to be so difficult?"

"Why do *you* have to be so difficult?" I countered.

Shaking his head, he said, "Whoa, you're going to drive me crazy."

"Well, you've already accomplished that with me."

Laughing, he said, "Always got a comeback."

"Of course."

"That's my girl, now stop playing and come here."

I walked over this time. "What do you want, Braxton?"

"You know what I want."

"I don't read minds."

"So you want to keep playing games?"

"Who said I was playing? What do you want?"

"You."

"Me? I don't know. You're too much of an ass. You have to prove yourself," I said, continuing to mess with his head.

"Prove myself?"

"Yup."

"You're a trip. How am I supposed to do that?"

"Well, I've showed you a lot of my skills. As you know, I'm very talented. What talents do *you* possess?" I asked cockily.

"Look who's cocky now. You know I got skills. I just gave you a little sample. I thought I was in church for a minute with the way you were calling on God."

I busted out laughing.

"Don't laugh. I thought you had the Holy Ghost when you starting speaking in tongues," he laughed.

"I see you've gotten a lot laughs off of me tonight."

"Aww, is my beautiful Yasmin embarrassed?"

I gave him a puppy dog look.

Braxton cleared his throat and started singing. "You are so beautiful to me." He sounded like one of the *American Idol* rejects that they have on the best of the worst shows. I had to laugh.

"Now you're laughing at me," he said real serious and giving me a funny look.

I couldn't stop laughing.

Braxton grabbed me and picked me up, throwing me over his shoulder like I was Jane and he was Tarzan. He took me to my bedroom and threw me on the bed before jumping on me and tickling me.

"Heh, heh, heh, heh, heh, AHH. Stop tickling me."

"Say mercy."

"Mercy, mercy mercy."

"Where is that smart mouth now?" he teased.

"It's not my fault you sound like an *Idol* reject," I managed to get out while he was tickling me.

"Mercy, I was playing. You got skills."

He stopped. "I know I do." He then pinned me down to the mattress and kissed me. After a couple of minutes he let me free.

"You're wrong for that."

"What, you want more?"

"All right, you win."

"I know I did. I have you, don't I?" he said, sincerely.

I got on top of him and kissed him.

"Dang, girl, you think I'm a sex machine, don't you? You want some more dick?"

I hit him on the shoulder. "No."

He pushed me off of him and grabbed me from behind. "Good, because you aren't getting any. I'm going to sleep."

He grabbed the covers, covered us, wrapped his arms around me, and went to sleep. I lay there for a while just listening to him breathe. Yeah, he has a temper and can be on the jealous side, but I love him.

11
He Loves Me

I am loving life and loving my baby. After our Thanksgiving argument we've been straight; no more fights. A couple of days before Christmas Braxton did meet my parents. I stopped over to drop off some gifts and brought him along. My parents were surprisingly friendly. My father talked to Braxton about work and sports, my mother even invited him back. Ashley and her boyfriend Daniel were there as well. We stayed only an hour. I couldn't take any more of the façade. Afterward, Braxton saw I was a little tense and asked what was wrong. I didn't elaborate. I just said I was in shock over the visit; my parents weren't usually that friendly. He joked and said that's because I have such a smart mouth. I just played off the comment. I wasn't ready to reveal that part of my life to Braxton.

Christmas was spent with the Simms. Everyone was glad to see me. They were worried I dropped Braxton after his temper tantrum. I thought it was funny; of course, he didn't. My buddy Uncle Charles was there, but he had company this time. He brought an attractive middle-aged woman with him. She was about 5 foot 5, had short hair, and was petite. She definitely loved herself some Uncle Charles. She laughed at everything he said, not like that was hard. Uncle Charles is comical. I sat next to Braxton this go-around. It was really nice. His brother Vincent had a new date. This one had more class. She was actually dressed decent in a pair of slacks and a blouse. His two other brothers didn't make it.

For Christmas I bought Braxton a Kenneth Cole watch and some cologne. I bought his mother and father fragrances as well. He bought me a charm bracelet from Tiffany's. His mother bought me a nice necklace.

New Year's was a blast. We ended up at some party Landon hosted at the Renaissance. At the stroke of midnight I was having an orgasm with Braxton.

Today, January 8th, 2003, my birthday. I'd just received a bouquet of flowers from Braxton. It's Friday. Just got paid and everything is cool. Almost everything, that is. My monthly visitor decided it wanted to come early, an unwanted birthday gift. Talk about bad timing. Tonight I was celebrating with Braxton, Landon, and Kevin. I hoped Braxton would be nice to Kevin like he promised. They haven't seen each other since Thanksgiving so I haven't had any issues with Braxton's jealousy.

I was sitting in my office daydreaming when I heard the phone ring.

"Yasmin Sinclair."

"Hey, Beautiful, Happy Birthday!"

"Hey, you, thank you and thanks for the flowers."

"You're more than welcome. I can't talk long. I was calling because I'm not going to be able to make it later. I have an emergency meeting in NY. I won't be back until late."

I would be lying if I said I wasn't disappointed. But after thinking for a second I remember I couldn't have sex and Braxton not near Kevin may not be too bad. "I'm going to miss you. I haven't seen you in a couple of days. They're keeping you busy, but I'll survive. You owe me."

"I'll definitely make it up to you. I have to go. Love you, Beautiful."

"Love you, babe."

I sat at my desk trying to get some work done, but I wasn't feeling it. I decided to take the rest of the day off to pamper myself. I went to Georgetown and bought myself an outfit. I settled on a black one-piece pants suit that hid the bloating in my stomach and then some around my waist. I got a facial, manicure, pedicure, and colored my hair to a spiced cognac.

After my pampering I went home to get ready for the night. Once I bathed I decided on Romance fragrance. By the time six arrived, I was lounging on the chair flipping through the channels.

Kevin and Landon came knocking on my door like they were the police. I opened the door to see many Happy Birthday Balloons, flowers, a card, and presents.

"Happy Birthday!" they yelled in unison.

"Thank you. It is so good to be loved," I beamed.

"Look at you! Aren't you looking sexy," Kevin commented.

"Yes, Yas, I couldn't have picked out a better outfit. Very good. I'm so proud."

"Thank you, you two looking good too."

Landon had on cream pants with a cream sweater, and Kevin, black slacks with a cream sweater.

"Are we ready to go? Never mind, I see Braxton isn't here. I see he still can't tell time."

"Braxton had an emergency meeting in NY so he won't be able to make it."

"Aww, isn't that a shame? I had a feeling this was going to be a good day."

"Where're we going?" I asked, ignoring Landon. I grabbed my coat and locked the door.

"Let's go to the harbor in Baltimore. I want to go to Phillips, and then we can come back to D.C. Yasmin, you can sit in the front since it's your day," Landon suggested.

"Ah, thank you, Your Majesty."

"Well, this is your day."

We got into Kevin's new Cadillac Escalade and headed for Baltimore. When we got there, the wait was long. The wait wouldn't have been that bad if Landon hadn't complained so much.

After dinner, we headed to H20 in D.C., but Landon had a late date so we dropped her off.

Kevin walked me back to my apartment. I invited him in and we talked a little. I put in my Hidden Beach jazz unwrapped CD; listened to Jeff Bradshaw play his tune, and we drank Merlot.

I looked at the clock; it blinked 1:05 back. "My birthday is over."

"I didn't realize it was so late. I need to go. I'm supposed to take Nicole out to brunch tomorrow. I need some sleep."

"Are you sure you're OK to drive?"

"Yeah, I'll be OK."

I got up to walk Kevin to the door. I opened the door and gave him a hug. I didn't see Braxton approach.

"Hey, man," Kevin said.

"Hey," Braxton answered.

Looking at his face I could tell he was a little irritated. His voice, however, was cordial.

Kevin stepped out. "Well, I was just leaving, I'll see you later."

"See you later, Kevin. Drive safely."

"All right, Yassy, Braxton."

I closed the door and turned to Braxton. "Aren't you a pleasant surprise?"

"I thought you were going out with Kevin *and* Landon."

"I did, but Landon made other plans and ditched us."

He looked around at my apartment, then picked up Kevin's card. "Nice card."

"So I don't get any love now? No hug or kiss?"

He walked over and gave me a weak hug.

"How did the meeting go? I wasn't expecting to see you until tomorrow."

"I was expecting you to be in bed."

"Nope, I was just hanging out. I didn't realize it was so late," I said yawning.

"Just you and Kevin kicking it like old times?" he said even more irritated.

"Yes, why? Is there a problem?"

Braxton walked over and sat on the couch. "Did I say there was?"

"Well, actions speak louder than words."

"And your point?"

"Nothing. Just continue your attitude."

"I don't have an attitude."

"What do you have then?"

"I don't like the fact that at one in the morning Kevin is leaving your apartment."

"Well, Kevin had a lot to drink, and I wasn't going to let him leave until he was sober. Why are you still on this thing with Kevin? I told you we're just friends. I thought you trusted me."

"I do trust you. I told you I don't trust him. He didn't look drunk to me. He wanted you drunk so he could dull your senses. You know how horny you are when you drink."

"So now I'm a drunk? Do I look drunk to you?"

"No, but the outfit is very enticing, and as a man, I know if I were hanging with you, I would want that body all over me."

"Kevin is not a freak like you; he has self-control."

"Yeah, whatever."

"Kevin has never stepped over the line."

"Yasmin, I keep telling you, I'm a man; I see the way he looks at you, and I don't like it."

"Kevin is my friend, so you're just going to have to deal with it."

"I'll deal with it. Kevin just better continue to watch his boundaries."

"Anyway, I had a good day and how was yours?"

"That's why I'm here. I had a meeting in New York today because I had to discuss my new position."

"New position?"

"Yeah, your man is now a junior VP with BET."

"Aww, congratulations!" I screamed, jumping on his lap and kissing him.

"So that means I get some congratulatory loving."

"Sorry, it's that time. No loving for you."

"Ahh." He scrunched his face.

"We can cuddle."

"Nah, that's OK. I'm going home. See you in five to seven days. Isn't that how long it takes?" he said pretending to get up.

I grabbed a pillow and hit him in his head. "Oh, it's like that. You just like me for the sex."

"Yeah, you got some good-ass pussy," he teased.

"That's not all I have. My tongue isn't so bad," I said giving him a kiss.

"You ain't ever lied."

I took the pillow I used to throw at him and put it on the floor. Then I got on my knees and positioned myself in front of him. I unzipped his pants and pulled out my Sugar Daddy.

Braxton looked at me as if to say, "Do you know what you're doing? Can you handle big boy?"

I licked my lips. His dick was already semihard from my touch. I placed my moist, hot mouth on the tip of his dick, circling it with my tongue; I then sucked the tip, holding the tip with my tongue. I sucked for several minutes, then I added an inch more and sucked a little more.

"Umm," he moaned. His dick was completely hard now.

I took in four of his nine and a half inches going up and down, adding suction as I sucked.

Braxton grabbed my head, urging me to take in more. I did, taking in another inch. I teased him with my tongue.

"Ahh!"

I began to lick up and down Sugar Daddy like it was the actual candy. I suctioned five inches in and held it at the top of my mouth. I could hear his breathing increasing, and his body tensing. I knew he was about to cum. I let his dick fall out of my mouth.

He panted.

I positioned my head, licked up and down his shaft, teasing him more. I then took one of his balls in mouth and played with it, rubbing it with my tongue. I switched to the other one. When I knew he couldn't take any more I stopped.

I positioned myself and dove in, giving him my best deep throat. I took in all of him this time.

"*Ah ooooooo . . .*"

Braxton started squirming, and I quickly pulled out. Then he started shooting cum everywhere.

"Watch it!" I yelled.

It took him a few minutes to get himself together. "Damn, Beautiful, you know how to please your baby, don't you?"

"Of course, although you almost choked me."

"How I do that?"

"Squirming. As long as you keep still I'm straight. But I know you're haven't had anyone of my caliber before."

"Cocky now."

"I'm just speaking the truth. You know no one can love you like Yasmin."

"Beautiful, you're so right." He grabbed me and kissed me.

"Now can we cuddle?"

"Almost," he said, handing me two gift boxes and a note.

The first gift was a charm for my bracelet. The note said I was his lucky charm, and the second box contained tickets for a show in New York.

"Because of this new position I can't take you this month, but next month you and I will have all week. I'm going to lock you up for days."

"Please don't sing, Maxwell, don't ruin the mood."

"Remember what happened last time you talked about my singing?"

"I ain't scared."

He stared at me and smiled.

"What?"

"I can't just look at you now."

"No?"

"I love you, Beautiful."

"I love you too, sexy."

12
Spend My Life with You

New York was fun. We were staying at the Waldorf Astoria, which, in itself, was a treat. We did manage to go out and see a couple of shows. I visited my favorite store, Carol's Daughter, and spent way too much money. It was worth it, though; quite a few of the items would be used tonight.

Braxton was annoyed and irritable. I could tell he wasn't enjoying the shopping portion of the trip. I always was one for a bargain. I told him he could have stayed in the hotel, but he chose to come, so, oh well.

"You buy enough yet?"

"No. Let's walk through Harlem."

"How do you know New York better than Maryland?"

"Landon and I used to come here twice a month."

"Well, I'll buy both of you tickets or provide the sedan. You can shop till you drop together. Let's go."

"I told you to stay at the hotel. I know you're not complaining. You have just as much stuff as I do in your closet, and we stopped at some of your stores."

"Uh-uh. Don't try it. We stopped at two stores and were in and out in an hour. You keep backtracking. Besides, I have enough stuff to carry."

We'd parked a good distance, and I had to admit, his arms were full. "Let's go, crybaby."

"I'll show you a crybaby later."

We went to the hotel to drop off my items and were supposed to go back out to get some lunch. However, Braxton lay on the bed and ordered room service.

"I thought we were going back out."

"We are, after lunch."

However, after lunch, Braxton went to sleep. I knew his butt was going to do that. I knew some of New York but was not familiar with this part, so I was stuck and mad. What was supposed to be a thirty-minute nap turned out to be two hours. He still wasn't up by the time three rolled around, so I left him a note telling him I went to the spa.

Just as I was finishing up at the spa, Braxton met me nice and refreshed. He took me to see *A Raisin in the Sun,* which was excellent. Afterward, we had dinner at Justin's. Following dinner, we took a stroll around New York, Upper Manhattan.

"Yasmin, you flipped the script on me. When I first met you I knew you were special. I didn't expect to fall for you like I have."

"What you trying to say?"

"Well, you just shut that smart mouth for a minute and let me finish."

I zipped my lips.

"I told you prior to meeting you I never wanted to get serious with anyone. I basically was with whomever for the moment and would easily get annoyed. I enjoyed being a bachelor."

"I—"

He took his finger to *shh* me. "But then I met you. I like being around you. You have me all jealous, and I don't want anyone else with you. I miss you when you're not with me. You have me saying I love you, which is something I never thought I'd say to another woman besides my mother." He pulled me close and stared at me for what felt like an eternity, but in actuality, was a minute. "I love you, Yasmin. No one has, or can, make me feel the way you do. Will you marry me?"

My mouth dropped open. I couldn't believe it. I couldn't speak.

"You can talk now."

My body was shaking. I was so elated. "Yyyyes!" I covered my mouth and started to cry.

"Who's the crybaby now?" he teased.

Still barely able to talk, I hit him.

"Don't you want to put on the ring?"

My mouth, still uncooperative, I never even noticed the ring. I nodded my head yes.

He placed the ring on and kissed me.

I looked down to see my engagement ring. It had to be at least a three karat princess cut platinum ring. No words could describe my feelings, but I knew this is who and what I've been searching for all my life. Finally I let go of my insecurities; I had no doubt that his love would always be here. I found love.

13
Someone to Love

It's been two months since our engagement.
Braxton and I decided on a wedding October 7,
2003. His family, of course, was excited; even
my parents. Who'd have thought that? Kevin congratulated
me, but I could tell he was a hurt. He was still with Nicole,
but I think Braxton was right. Kevin still hoped there was a
chance for me and him. Landon was surprisingly happy, but
told me I better not act brand-new. She also made me
promise to still to hang out and not turn into Suzie
homemaker.

I lay in Braxton's bed debating if I was working
today. It's that time of year when everyone gets sick, and I
thought I might have caught the stomach virus.

"You're looking nice and crazy."

"Well, next time I want your opinion I'll ask. Until
then, keep your opinion to yourself."

"OK, I don't feel like arguing this morning. It must
be close to that time of the month."

I ignored him.

Braxton got up to get ready for work. Before he left,
he came in. "Are you going to work today?"

"I'm still deciding. I don't feel like it. I'm still
sleepy."

"You have a meeting at BET today, don't you?"

"Damn, I forgot. So that means I have to go, but
afterward, I'm going home."

"You're not staying with me tonight?"

"You don't let me sleep."

"I will tonight. I promise."

"Yeah, right."

"After your meeting do you want to get some lunch
with me?"

"Oh no. We work together. Not professional at all."

"Remember I got a promotion. We don't work together anymore."

"That's right. I won't see you. Does this mean I'm stuck with Sean and the bitch?"

"Be nice."

"Matter of fact, I have a complaint against Ms. Stevens, Mr. VP; put her on notice. She irritates the hell out of me. If you don't reprimand her, I will have no other choice but to hurt her feelings."

He laughed. "Are you going to have lunch with me?"

"Nah, let's keep the personal separate for now."

"Your loss. I was going to treat you good today," he teased.

"I bet."

He walked over to kiss me good-bye.

I start gagging. "What the hell do you have on? It stinks."

"Are you OK? I don't stink. I've worn this before. You've never had any complaints."

"Get away, it stinks."

"Are you OK?"

"Yeah, I'll be OK once you leave with your stinky cologne."

"You sure?"

"Yes. It's that time of the year. Colds, stomach viruses, and other stuff are going around. I'll be fine. I have the seventy-two-hour bug."

"Why don't you just get Bob to handle the meeting? Stay here and get some rest. I'll leave work early, come back to take care of you."

"No, I'm fine," I lied. "Go ahead. I'll call if I need you. I'm getting up now."

He blew me a kiss and left.

I went into the bathroom and still smelled his cologne. Barely making it, I threw up in the bowl.

Unfortunately, it didn't make me feel better but worse. In actuality, when I thought about it, I've been nauseated for more than a couple of days. I haven't been regularly taking my birth control pills and was fucking Braxton two to three times a day. Duh, my ass is pregnant.

I showered, dressed, put on a pants suit, and rushed for the office. I wanted to go to CVS and pick up a test, but I was running too late. I let Bob know I wasn't feeling well, advising him after the meeting I was going home. He called me a trooper for working and told me to please get some rest. I must have really looked bad because he insisted on going in my place. In fact, he encouraged me to go home. I lied again and told him I would be fine once I drank some water. I walked into my office, grabbed the BET stuff, and rushed over there.

On my way, I prayed the bitch didn't try me today. I was not one to be fooled with. Before I got out of my car, I fixed my face and tried to cover up all signs of my sickness. *How did I miss this?* I thought. I have felt a little sick, but assumed it was a bug. I had the signs. I just assumed it was my period coming. But in thinking back, I missed two periods. And now that I realized I may be pregnant, the nausea has intensified.

How was Braxton going to feel about a baby? How do *I* feel about a baby? Well, I can't worry about that now. I have to get through this meeting.

I walked into BET and felt overwhelmed by all the scents. I practically ran to the receptionist.

"Kim, where's the bathroom please?"

Kim was here when I had my first meeting at BET. She and I were cool. We started talking one day when I was waiting, and we were now on a first-name basis. I would often talk to her before meetings. Kim was in her early thirties, very attractive with rich dark skin, high cheekbones, was tall with a medium build. She had her hair cut in a short do that complimented her face, and was married with three kids. She always hinted that she knew something was up between me and Braxton, but I never confirmed.

She pointed. I put my stuff down and ran in the bathroom and threw up in the first stall. How was I going to get through this? I kept getting sick.

"Yasmin?" I heard Kim whisper.

"Kim, over here." I opened the stall.

"Oh, you look a mess. Take this," she said, handing me a coffee bag. "This helped me when I was pregnant."

I took the bag and sniffed. "Is it that obvious?"

"Yes. You may want to try sipping on coke and eating saltine crackers to settle your stomach too."

I walked over to the faucet, splashed some water on my face, and rinsed my mouth out. I looked myself in the mirror. I did look a mess. I pulled out my purse and tried to work my magic. I pulled my hair from a bun and let it hang. I figured my hair could hide some of my face.

Kim gave me a try-again look.

I just pulled it back in a bun this time.

"Congratulations," Kim said.

"Congratulations?"

"Yes, on the engagement and pregnancy. Beautiful ring." She grabbed my hand and examined the ring.

"Thank you," I smiled.

"Now I know why Braxton has been happy and extra nice."

"Kim, what are you talking about?"

"Yasmin, really; level with me."

"Really, Kim, I don't know what you're talking about."

"Yasmin, this will be just between you and me."

"OK, Kim; please, this is between us. Yes, Braxton and I are engaged. However, no one knows from my office or this office that we were even dating. We're keeping it professional for now."

"How long can you keep a baby hidden? You're wearing his ring."

"I'm wearing a ring, but people don't have to know whom I'm engaged to. As far as the baby, definitely don't say anything to Braxton. He doesn't even know."

"What?"

"I just realized it today. When I leave here I'm going to take a test. I just have to get through this meeting with Sean and Ms. Bitch Stevens."

"You got it right the first time. I would love to see her face when she finds out you're engaged to Braxton, and then having his baby."

"I thought she was married."

"She is, but she still wants your man."

I knew that bitch did, I thought. *I will definitely be watching her.*

"Kim, does anyone else think Braxton and I are dating?"

"You know how people in the office talk. Braxton is very handsome and in demand. Females are always checking him out and are very observant. Right now, they think Braxton has a thing for you, but don't think you're actually dating."

"Good, so this ring will throw them off."

"Yeah, everyone but me," she smiled. "I can't stay in here long. I was only supposed to be gone five minutes. But sniff on the coffee and that should help."

"Kim, remember, this is between us."

"Yes, Yasmin."

She's going to run her mouth, I thought.

Kim left, and I attempted to get it together, and then I headed for the meeting.

The meeting went well. Less than an hour, and Lisa didn't have too many questions. I think it was the ring. Her face was screwed up until she saw the ring. Like Kim said, she assumed I was engaged to someone other than Braxton. She congratulated me and wished me well.

After the meeting, I went to thank Kim. As I was leaving, I bumped into Braxton.

"You don't look good at all."

"I know." I sniffed the bag.

"What's that?"

"Tissue," I lied. "My nose is running a little. You better get away before you get sick."

"Let me go get my keys. I'll take you to my house and get you better."

"I'll be fine. I drove. I'm going home now."

"Nope. I want you to go to my place. I'll be there in an hour."

Braxton was making me sick, literally, and the coffee wasn't helping. I started feeling lightheaded and felt my body sway.

Braxton saw me disoriented and grabbed me. "Yasmin, that's it! We're going to the doctor. You almost passed out."

I looked over at Kim like, *help me!*

Kim walked over. "Mr. Simms, I'll get her some water. I'll make sure she gets home safely."

"Thank you, Kim. Braxton, I'll be fine. Nice seeing you again," I said, trying to give him a hint.

Before he could speak Ms. Stevens approached gloating like she was about to drop a bomb. "Braxton, did Yasmin tell you her good news? She's engaged. Isn't that just wonderful? Yasmin, you must send me an invite to your joyous occasion."

"Sure," I said, trying to get her to move on. But she just had to keep on gloating.

"Yasmin, I can't wait. When is the wedding?"

Braxton brushed her off. "Thank you, Lisa. We'll make sure you get an invite. But would you excuse me? I need to talk to my fiancée for a minute."

Any other time, I would have added a smart remark or two to her humiliation, but right now, I only wanted out. I could hardly breathe.

"Fiancée?"

"Congratulations," Kim beamed.

"Yes, congratulations," Lisa said, swallowing hard, then walked away.

Well, there goes privacy.

"Yasmin, let's go to my office."

I followed Braxton to his office trying to think of a way to get out as quickly as possible.

He shut the door and wasted no time grilling me. "Yasmin, why do I have the feeling you're lying to me?"

"Lying? About what?" I asked, innocently.

"Yasmin, we're engaged. I've been honest with you since day one, and I assume you've been honest with me. What's going on?"

I sniffed. I sniffed. I sniffed. I sniffed my coffee bag. It didn't help. "I have to use the bathroom, where is it?"

"Why, so you can sneak out of here?"

I sniffed again. "I really have to go."

"I have one over there."

I ran to the bathroom and let it flow.

"Ugh," I heard Braxton say.

"Braxton, get away. You are making me sick."

"No, not until you tell me what's going on with you."

"OK, OK, OK, you win, just step back."

He stepped back and looked at me like, *spit it out.*

I had to tell him the truth. I stood there for a minute thinking how to say it.

"Today!"

"Braxton, I think . . ."

"Yasmin?"

". . . I'm pregnant."

He looked at me, took in a deep breath, and smiled.

"So, you're having my baby. Why didn't you tell me?"

"It hasn't been confirmed. I was on my way to the store, before I bumped into you."

He walked over and tried to hug me.

I pushed him away and gagged.

"I'm sorry. Let's go get the test."

"That's OK. I'm going to get the test. I'll meet you at your house in an hour. Please take a shower and don't put on any cologne or oil."

Laughing, he said, "OK, one hour. Don't have me waiting too long."

"I won't. Now go stand on that side so I can leave."

"All right, Beautiful."

I walked over to open the door and quickly left BET.

Once I got outside I felt much better. I took out my cell phone to call Landon.

"Landon?"

"What's going on, Yassy?"

"Are you sitting?"

"Yas, are you OK?"

"I'm pregnant."

"You're scaring me. What?"

"You're going to be a godmommy."

"I'm too young."

"Land, I didn't say grandmother, I said godmother."

"I heard you. I guess that means we can't have a drink tonight. I'm just joking. He's making sure your ass won't be going out. He knocked you up. His jealous, possessive ass probably did it on purpose."

"Diva, be nice."

"I'm joking. Congrats. I can't wait to shop."

"Thank you. I haven't taken the test, but I have all the symptoms."

"When are you telling Braxton?"

"He found out this morning." I explained the story.

Landon laughed. "I wish I could have seen that bitch's face. Well, congrats, again. Let me know if you need anything."

"I do."

"Damn, Yas, I just said it because it sounded nice. I wasn't expecting you to take me up on it. What?"

"Help me tell Kevin. He looked hurt when I told him about the engagement. Now the baby. We never were serious, but he does still have feelings."

"My poor, poor Kevin. I can't do that."

"Land, come on."

"All right, but you will be there to. I have to go. We'll do it later this week. Tootles." She hung up.

I went into CVS and purchased the test. When I returned to Braxton's he was waiting, opening the door before I reached it.

"Have you showered?"

"Yes, come on take the test and see what it says."

"Can I put my stuff down first?" I put my purse down and grabbed the test. I went into the bathroom and when I tried to close the door Braxton was there.

"Braxton, you haven't been going to the bathroom with me. You don't need to start now."

"Sorry."

I sat on the toilet and peed on the stick. Before I could wipe myself and pull my pants up, Braxton was in there. "*Excuse* you?"

"I've seen and sampled everything." He picked up the test, examining it like it was written in Chinese. "With this pregnancy test, how can you tell if you are?"

"We have to wait ten minutes. If there are two lines, I am."

Braxton looked at the test. "Ten minutes, huh?"

"Yeah, nine minutes to go."

"Well, I see two lines now." He turned the test around revealing the results to me.

I was pregnant. Braxton and I are having a baby. We are forever connected.

Braxton walked up to me, hugged me, then kissed me on the cheek. "You keep on surprising me, making me happy, Beautiful."

"I love you, baby."

"I know I love you. I touched this test after you peed on it," he joked.

"I didn't pee on that part," I said, sticking my tongue out. "So, how do you feel about being a daddy?"

"I don't know. I never really thought about it. I told you I was going to be a bachelor for life. I was going to leave that up to my brothers. You flipped the script."

"So?"

"I'm glad you did. I'm happy being with you. I'm happy you're in my life and having my baby."

14
Make It Like It Was

"G ood morning, Beautiful," Braxton said, kissing me on my lips.
                "Hey you, good morning."
"Hello, son." Braxton kissed my stomach.
"How do you know it's a boy?"
"I can feel it."
"We'll see."
Braxton got up to get ready for work. "Are you working today?"
"Yes, I'm trying to get up. But I'm so sleepy," I yawned.
"Stay home. You and Bryan can get some rest."
I was now technically almost twenty-two weeks pregnant. We played around with our names trying to come up with baby names. We didn't come up with any girl names, but we decided if it was a boy, we would name him Bryan. Bryan Joseph Simms. Joseph was Braxton's middle name. Br from Braxton and Ya from Yasmin. Nicknaming him BJ for short, deep down I knew it was a boy too.
"Nah, I have to get some work done. But you can help me up."
Braxton came over and pulled me up. "My mother called. She wants to know what day you want to go shopping."
"I don't know if I can hang with Ma. She's so excited about the baby. She'll probably buy the store."
"I know she will. That's why it's just you and her. I went shopping with you in NY, and that was enough. You can take my wallet and have fun."
"Ha-ha. It was not that bad shopping with me."
"Humph. So, when do you plan on moving the rest of your stuff?"

"My lease is up in October."

"The baby is due in November. You're not working me at the last minute."

"I'm not. I'll gradually move my stuff in. It's July now. By the time September comes, 90 percent of my stuff will be here. I already have a lot here already."

"Yeah, I do see that. I used to be able to walk in my closet. Well, it's getting late. I have to get to work. See you later, Beautiful. See you, Bryan," he said, kissing me, then rubbing my belly.

The baby kicked.

"That's my boy."

The baby has been kicking for the last couple of weeks now. Each time he kicks I still get a little emotional. For once in my life things are good. I am happy, someone loves me, for me, not my eyes.

"Pregnancy hormones," he teased as he walked out the door.

I finally got dressed and headed out the door too. In the car, I put on my Floetry CD and drove off. I was sitting at the light waiting for the light to turn. The last thing I remember is listening to "Sunshine," grooving to the music. Next, I heard a loud bang, my head hit the steering wheel, and everything went black.

*

"Yasmin!"

"Yasmin, can you hear me?"

"Yasmin!"

I saw a bright light. There was a lot of commotion around me.

"Her pressure is dropping, Doctor."

"Yasmin, stay with me."

I thought I recognized the voice. I tried to open my eyes, but I couldn't. I tried to talk, but my mouth was dry and nothing came out. I tried to take a deep breath but felt a tube. It hurt. My head was spinning, my stomach cramping, and the pain paralyzing.

"Yasmin!" I heard Braxton call out.
"Braxton, where are you?"
"You're going to have to leave now."
"I'm not leaving her!" he yelled.
Why is he yelling? What's going on? I felt like I was floating, yet I was so tired. I'm sleepy. Brax—
"We're losing her!"
I heard more commotion, and then a long beep. Things went black again.

"Her pressure is coming back."
Again it was black.

"Yasmin, can you hear me?"
This time when I breathed I didn't feel the tube. I tried to talk but my throat was still very dry. I still struggled to open my eyes. I felt someone holding my hand. It was Braxton. I would recognize his touch anywhere.
"Yas?"
I finally opened my eyes and looked around. I saw Landon and Kevin. Landon just looked at me and started crying. Kevin looked at me with sorrow and pity in his eyes. I saw Mr. and Mrs. Simms. I finally looked over at Braxton. His eyes were bloodshot; he was crying.
Suddenly, I felt this wave of emptiness. *Please, God, no. Please, God, no. Please, God, no,* I prayed. I felt the tears running down my face. Slowly I took my free hand and felt my stomach.
"Nooo," I coughed out. I couldn't breathe. Everything was spinning again.
"Calm down, Yasmin. Listen or I'm going to have to sedate you. Please calm down."

I couldn't. "No, I want my baby," I coughed out. Breathing was difficult.

"Everyone out."

The nurses came in to restrain me. I felt cool water run through my veins, and everything went black again.

I woke up immediately grabbing my stomach. My baby was gone. It isn't a dream. I began crying.

Braxton got up, climbed into the bed with me, and held me. I could feel his tears. I needed to know what happened.

"What happened?"

"You were in an accident." He took a deep breath. "When you got here they had to do a D&E."

Before I could ask any more questions the nurse came in to check my vitals.

"Do you know your name?"

I nodded my head yes.

"Do you know what day it is?"

I shook my head no.

The nurse called in the doctor. He did another exam and explained to me what happened in more detail.

I had been unconscious for five days. I was involved in an accident on Thursday when a drunk driver hit me from behind. This made me hit the vehicle in front of me. Basically, I was sandwiched in. My body jerked forward, and I hit my head, losing consciousness immediately. The impact from the air bag hit my stomach causing trauma to the baby. When I came in I was in active premature labor. My water had broken and basically the baby was too small to survive.

*

I stayed in the hospital for three more days. I was so numb. Braxton barely left my side. Landon and Kevin, along with Braxton's family, came daily, everyone except my parents. I just wanted everyone to leave me alone. My heart ached for my baby. I was scared to sleep because every time I did, I heard baby cries. I would search for my baby. *Mommy's coming,* but I could never find him. I'd then wake up crying hysterically.

15
How Can I Ease the Pain?

My baby was going to love me. Love me because I was Mommy. Love me because I loved him, and he was made from love. Not because of my green eyes. Now all I felt was a big void. My heart hurt more with each passing second. I didn't know how to ease it or what to do. I keep reliving that day; even worse was the day I found out that I was having a boy.

Before leaving the hospital I was given discharge papers. In with those papers was a death certificate for a boy baby. Well, needless to say, that's when I really lost it. The realization hit me, I never would get a chance to hold my son or see him smile at me. I would never hear him cry or hear him call me Mommy. I never even would get a chance to see him if just for a second. I know I only carried him for five short months, but we had a bond. When I would talk or sing to him he would kick. He loved me, I know he did, but now, I will never get a chance to tell him how much I loved him. This pain is too much.

Landon has come by, but she didn't know what to do. She's never been hurt or had to deal with a loss. She always has her parents for support. She kept saying she's sorry and I'll have other kids one day. She just doesn't get it. I don't want other kids. I want my son.

I was trying to get it together, but I couldn't. Every time I think I'm finally getting together, I get a reminder of what I lost. I turn on the TV, I see a baby. I go out, and I see a baby. I hate to go to sleep because when I do, I still hear baby cries. I know it's my baby. He needs me, but I can't find him. I feel like I've abandoned him. I'm in so much pain. I don't know how much more I can take. Some days, I just feel like checking into an asylum and giving up.

The doctors reassured me that I didn't do anything wrong, but I can't help but think differently. I feel like it's my fault. I should have protected my baby. I should have been more cautious. I kept replaying in my head things I should have done, or could have done. I should have listened to Braxton and stayed home. No one understands how I feel.

It's been two and a half months since my miscarriage. I should try to get up, but I just can't move. I was looking at the walls. No music, no TV, no sunlight. Just me, and that's the way I wanted it.

Braxton and I haven't been communicating. He tries to talk to me, but I can't. The only thing I want to do is lie in bed. Braxton's mother has been here for me. She keeps telling me to cry, let it out, but I know if I do I won't stop.

One day, I decided to call my mother. "Hey, Ma."

"Yasmin, hey."

"Mommy, I feel so lost. Why did I have to lose my baby?"

"Yasmin, sometimes things happen for the best. You weren't married. You didn't need to be having kids out of wedlock anyway. You're engaged, not married. You shouldn't be giving the cow away for free. Think about it. You're having sex and giving up everything. What could you offer once you're married? At least you didn't have a hysterectomy. Once you're married, you can have other kids, then it'll be a blessing."

"OK, Ma."

"Yasmin, I know you don't want to hear this, but it's the truth. Well, I have to go. Your father and I are going out with Ashley and Daniel. Aren't they such a cute couple? Daniel is such a gentleman. Bye." Then she hung up.

More stupidity on my part. What did I expect—compassion? She didn't even visit me when I was in the hospital. What kind of shit was that? I just lost my baby. She's gloating about Ashley. My family has said things and done things to hurt me, but none of that compared to the hurt I felt now. I said it before, but this time I'm done with them. Fuck them and their judgment.

I swear I'm cursed. It's not meant for me to be happy. I keep hearing my grandmother's words. She was right. All I have is bad luck. I know it's just a matter of time before Braxton leaves.

God, what I did to deserve this hurt? Why can't I just be happy? Why did you take Bryan from me? I can't let go of this pain. I'm scared. If I let go of the pain, then I'll be letting go of my son. God, please help me.

I heard the door opening. Braxton was here.

"Hey, Beautiful." He came over and lay beside me.

I didn't respond.

"Yasmin, you need to get up today."

I still didn't respond.

"Yasmin, I know it hurts, but you have to get up. You can't lie in bed forever."

He tried to hold me, but I couldn't let him. Instead, I pushed him away. I couldn't let him touch me.

"Stop, don't touch me! Just leave me alone!" I yelled.

"No, Yasmin, you've been like this too long. You have to move on. This isn't good for you. You can't stay like this forever."

"You don't know what I feel. It hurts. I lost my baby," I finally cried.

He looks at me sincerely. "Yasmin, he was my baby too. My son died too."

Now Braxton was sitting up in the bed and I saw the tears falling down his face. I know I should have wrapped my arms around him and cried with him, but I couldn't.

"Yasmin, I love you, and I loved our son. But we have to move on. You can't, we can't mourn forever. We can't stop living. We can do something to honor him."

I got up and looked at him like he was crazy. "What the hell do you mean I can't mourn my son? I carried him. I felt him kick. He was my baby. I loved him, and now he's gone. What, am I supposed to forget about him like he never existed? Just leave and don't come back," I cried.

I could see his patience wearing thin. "He was my baby too. I didn't say forget about him. He was my son too, and I loved him. I was there when we made him, and I was there when he died."

I just stood there and acted like his words didn't faze me, when they did. In reality, I was sorry for him. I felt like I was to blame, and he needed to just leave me alone. Rather than showing any emotion, I choose to scrutinize my apartment.

Looking around, I saw bare walls, dust, missing furniture that either was sold or taken to Braxton's. I used to feel at peace when I was home. It was my haven. My apartment now lacks. It's dull, cold, and missing a life, literally, like me.

I looked at Braxton. He too has the worn look. He too was in pain, and I really was sorry for him. I just couldn't deal with him right now. I needed him to leave me alone. Frustrated, I yelled, "Braxton, just leave me alone."

He looked at me with sorrow. "Yasmin, I'm trying. Losing our son was the hardest thing I ever had to deal with. I know you're hurt, but I'm hurt too. I was there. I had to sign his death certificate. Do you know how much that hurt? It did. It still hurts. I don't know what to do. I told you I've never been with anybody this long. How can I make it better? Just talk to me. Let me in. Let me love you. Let me hold you. What do you want me to do?"

"You don't get it. You can't make it better. I want you to just leave me the fuck alone. Just leave!" I yelled.

"Fuck it." Braxton stood up and left. I heard the door slam.

I looked outside to see him pulling off. Once I was sure he was gone I let go. I cried a little at first, but soon I was hysterical. I just kept yelling *why?*

I sat there and cried for hours. I finally let it out. While it still hurt, I did feel better. Afterward, I got up, cleaned, bathed, and actually ate. I missed Braxton, but at the same time, I was grateful he gave me this time. He's been in my face every day for the last two and a half months.

I felt terrible about the way I disregarded his feelings. He did lose his son too. I knew I was wrong to treat him this way, but I just needed my privacy and space. I had to grieve my own way.

*

Three days later, three days since I'd seen Braxton, I wanted to call, but I just couldn't. I didn't know what to say. I kept seeing the hurt in his eyes. I hope he doesn't leave me. I hope he understands. I do love him, I just needed space. I hope he knows I do need him. I already lost our son, and I don't want to lose him. I prayed that I didn't push him away. I lay in bed once again and cried. I prayed Psalm 23.

The LORD is my shepherd, I lack nothing.
He makes me lie down in green pastures,
he leads me beside quiet waters,
he refreshes my soul.
He guides me along the right paths
for his name's sake.
Even though I walk
through the darkest valley,
I will fear no evil,
for you are with me;
your rod and your staff,
they comfort me.

God, please help me be strong. God, help me, please. Help me, please. I didn't know when he came, but when I awoke, Braxton was there.

I looked at him. "Braxton, I love you and I apo—"

He stopped me. He placed his index finger on my lips to quiet me. He then got into the bed with me, wrapped his arms around me, and held me. He just held me, and we cried together.

16
Stranger in My House

"Good morning," I said to no one in particular.

"Good morning, Yasmin, you look nice today."

"Thank you, Greg."

"Would you like to go out for lunch?"

"No, Greg."

"I'm going to get you one day."

I just laughed at him.

Greg was still Greg, the office gigolo ho.

I've been back to work now for a couple of months. My car was, of course, totaled. I upgraded to a SUV, a Nissan Armada. Big truck, but I was not trying to get sandwiched anymore. Truthfully, I now have a phobia about riding in smaller cars.

Work was very difficult at first. People were coming by giving me their condolences and asking if I needed anything. Although it was nice and I appreciated their concern I would have preferred to be left alone. My boss Bob was really kind. He asked if I was OK and offered me additional time off, but I declined. He was surprisingly, understanding, about Braxton. He had a hunch that we were dating, said we had good chemistry, but never said anything because my work performance was always exceptional. Things at work were starting to get normal again.

However, Braxton and I were a different story. Braxton has been really tense. I guess losing our son affected him more than I thought. He was now distant at times, and it seems like he's struggling with something. I asked if he wanted to talk, but he brushed me off. So now I gave him some space.

Besides, I was having issues of my own. I still blamed myself for losing the baby. The rare times that Braxton and I have been intimate I'm there physically, but mentally, my mind wasn't. I kept thinking about the baby. Now I'm extracautious about birth control, making sure I take the pills, and I requested he use a condom. I could not deal with losing another baby.

I called Landon to see what was going on with her. Ever since my miscarriage she's been distant. It's very awkward when I talked to her. It's like she struggling to find the right words to say. I understood her apprehensiveness. She's never had to deal with death. I do miss hanging with the diva. The boisterous, free-spirited one who says what's on her mind. Landon makes me laugh, so I picked up the phone to call her.

"Hello, this is Landon Taylor. How may I assist you today?" she answered.

"Hey, girl, what's going on? I haven't hung out with my girl in a while, and I miss you. Are you trying to go out tonight and get a drink? My treat. We can go to Pearl and get your favorite, a Victoria Secret."

"Hey, Yasmin, I can't. I'm going to have to take a rain check."

"What? Are you sick? Landon Taylor turning down a drink and going out? So what, or should I say, who, do you have tonight?"

"No one. I'm tired, and I'm going home to rest," she replied uneasily.

"Landon, I'm really concerned now. Are you sick? What's going on?" I asked alarmed.

Landon took a deep breath. "Yasmin, I don't know how to tell you this, but I'm pregnant."

I swallowed hard. "Pregnant?"

"Yeah, I'm pregnant, imagine that."

"How far along are you?"

"I'm almost four months."

"Four months and you're just telling me? You're my best friend. Why did you keep it from me so long?" I asked hurt.

"Yasmin, believe me, I wasn't trying to hurt you. You've been struggling with . . . you know the . . . The timing wasn't right."

"The miscarriage . . ." I finished her sentence. "Landon, you're still my girl. I admit I am still dealing with losing my son. I always will, but I'm still here for you."

It sounded like Landon was crying. "Thank you, Yas, I appreciate it."

"You're really surprising me today. Are you OK? Now you're crying? You *are* keeping the baby, right? You're almost four months."

"Yes. I'm fine, it's just my hormones."

"Landon, how do you feel? Are you happy? Are you ready to be a mommy?
What about the father?"

"If you want to know who the father is, it's Eric," Landon chuckled.

Good, I thought because I had no idea who the father was. "Is Eric excited, and I thought you used condoms?"

"Yes, Eric is excited. I know he purposely got me pregnant. He has been trying to get me to commit, and I told him I was not ready. But you know how freaky I like to get. He used it to his advantage."

"How did he do that?"

"One night we were in the hot tub, and he bet me he could eat my pussy underwater, then make me cum in less than two minutes. If he won, I had to commit, and if I didn't cum, there was no commitment. Plus, he promised me a car. You know I couldn't pass up on that deal. Shit, I didn't think he could hold his breath that long. Of course, I took the challenge. Well, needless to say, thirty seconds later, I was screaming. By the time, he reached one minute, I was talking in tongues, and when he reached two minutes, his dick was in me raw and feeling oh so good. Oh, and I have a new truck too. Mercedes, of course."

I just laughed at her. *Now that's my Landon,* I thought. "So not only did he get you pregnant, but he got you to commit. I knooooooow Landon is not committing. If so, the world must be coming to an end."

"Ha-ha, I'm committed. Seriously, I admire you and Braxton. I saw how he was there for you during the miscarriage, and it got me thinking. Commitment isn't that bad. When you're going through a difficult time, I mean, if you have someone who loves you, it definitely helps. I know I gave you a hard time about him in the past, but Braxton is a good man. He's good for you."

My mouth just dropped open. She gave my Braxton a compliment. "What did you just say? Are you talking about my man, Braxton Simms? Pregnancy has really changed you. I'm scared. I'm not use to you being so sincere."

"I know, I know I said it, but don't ask me to repeat myself. And if you ever mention this to anyone, I will deny it. Moving on along, have you talked to Kevin?"

"Mood swing I see. You gave Braxton a compliment, now you're asking me about Kevin."

"I don't know what you're referring to. I just asked if you talked to Kevin. I haven't seen him in a while," Landon laughed.

"No, I haven't. Let's call him. We should all hook up for dinner," I suggested.

"That'll be fun. I'll call him and call you back."

I hung up and called Braxton to let him know I was going out.

"Hey, baby, how's your day going?" I asked.

"Hey, Beautiful, it's going. I have a lot of work, so I won't be coming over there tonight. I need to go home and get some things together anyway."

Hearing him call me Beautiful today still makes me smile like it did when we first met. "No problem. I was actually calling you to let you know I'm hanging out with Landon and Kevin."

"What are you getting into tonight? Don't drink a lot. You know how drinking makes you horny. I'm not going to be there to take care of you."

"I won't. We're just getting something to eat. We probably will just end up at Cheesecake Factory. Landon will be restricted for a while," I said.

"Landon restricted?" he asked.

"Yes, restricted. She's pregnant."

"Landon's pregnant?" he asked sounding shocked.

"I know. I can't believe it myself. Seeing is believing, though. She said she's almost four months so I will see tonight."

"Almost four months? That far along?"

"Yeah, she said she didn't know how to tell me because of our miscarriage."

Braxton took a deep breath. I knew it hurt to hear me mention the baby. A tear rolled down my face as I thought of Bryan. He would have been here now. I looked at the calendar. My baby, our son was supposed to be born two months ago. I should be home nursing our baby.

"Yasmin, are you still there?" Braxton asked bringing me out of my trance.

"I'm sorry, baby, my mind was elsewhere."

"I know. Mine was too. Landon say anything else shocking?"

I thought about the compliment she gave him. "No, oh yes, she did." I remembered she was committing. "She said she and Eric were in a relationship and were having this baby."

"Oh, well, Beautiful, you have a good time. Call me later to let me know you got home safely."

"I will, I love you, baby," I said.

"Love you back," he said hanging up the phone.

*

Landon, Kevin, and I ended up at the Cheesecake Factory. I didn't realize how much I missed my friends.

Landon's pregnancy proved I had no idea what was going on in their lives.

"So, Kev, what's going on with you?" I asked.

"Are you still with Nicole?" Landon threw in.

"I'm doing good, and how about you, Ms. Y.E.S.?"

"I'm doing OK," I replied.

"I'm glad to hear that. You look good," he said.

When I finally got out of my depression I started working out. I had a bulge due to the baby. I thought I still looked pregnant, and I didn't want anyone asking questions. I've been working out four times a week, and it has helped with a lot of my tension. My stomach looked normal, and I was in a size 9/10 now.

"Thank you. Thank you and Nicole for the card and flowers," I said giving him a hug.

"How is Nicole?"

"Nicole is fine. We just came from the Bahamas."

"Hello? Did you two forget I'm sitting over here? You two are having this boring conversation. Kevin, I haven't had a chance to tell you my news."

Kevin looked at Landon bracing himself for bad news.

"Landon, before you tell me what it is, answer these two questions. Do I have to lie to your parents? Does it involve any illegal activity?"

Landon looked at him and laughed. "No and no."

"Well, do you need me to represent you? This doesn't involve any altercations?" he asked.

"Kevin, I'm not that bad. I was just going to tell you I'm pregnant."

"You what? All right, Landon, you're not bad. What type of legal trouble are you in?"

Landon stood up and revealed her stomach to Kevin. She was actually pregnant. I could see a little bump on her usually flat stomach. It was real. I'd be lying if I said I wasn't envious, but I just said a quick prayer that her baby would be healthy.

"I've already discussed this with Eric, so I'm telling you. You and Yasmin are the godparents. That means you will have the baby every other weekend and have to change the dirty diapers. And as godparents, you're also responsible now for making sure I'm fed and my feet are rubbed—basically, taken care of. You're going to have to cook and clean. I can't do anything strenuous."

"Landon, I see pregnancy has caused you to lose your damn mind. Have you told your parents?"

"Good question, Kevin," I instigated.

"No, and that's where you come in. Daddy loves you like a son. So tomorrow when you two have breakfast, tell him, big brother. I set breakfast for 9:30."

Kevin and I looked at each other. The next five months were going to be HELL—a diva pregnant. Mercy mercy mercy.

*

By the time I made it home, I was exhausted. Landon had already started with crazy demands. After we left the Cheesecake Factory she decided she wanted a Frappuccino from Starbucks. She gave us a guilt trip so we caved in. After she got it, she didn't like how it tasted. She said the girl who made it didn't know what she was doing and claimed it didn't taste right. So we had someone else make it over. The second one she said was better, but after three sips, she didn't want it anymore. Then Diva wanted us to help rearrange furniture. That request wasn't fulfilled. I think I may change my number tomorrow. I tried to call Braxton, but all I got was his machine. I figured he was asleep. I guess I'd talk to him tomorrow.

17
Love Don't Love You

"**B**raxton."

"Braxton," I gave him a nudge.

"Braxton," I gave him another nudge.

"What?"

"It's time to get up."

I got up and started getting ready for work. I spent the night with Braxton, which was rare for me these days. I should have stayed home. Sex for us now was like a chore. It lacked the passion and creativity. We both came, but the thrill and the sincerity was gone. I didn't even feel safe the rare times Braxton held me. I walked into Braxton's closet looking for something to wear. There wasn't much to choose from. Prior to the miscarriage I was moving things in, but now when I got my clothes dry cleaned, they ended up back at my place. We no longer discussed moving in together or marriage. I believe we both needed our space.

Braxton has been so moody and even more distant. I see him maybe once a week. Every time I attempt to see him, he makes an excuse. Usually he tells me he's busy at work. It doesn't bother me that he's working. I'm happy. He has an important position, but I know it's an excuse. Women's intuition was telling me it's something else.

Landon, unfortunately, is keeping me occupied. It's been a month since her pregnancy announcement, and things were crazy. Landon has really gone into diva mode. She actually thinks I'm supposed to be her personal servant. Sad thing is, usually I am since I'm not spending quality time with Braxton any longer.

"Braxton, you're going to be late."

He didn't budge.

I went over to shake him. "Braxton, get up."

He finally got up and looked at the clock. "Why did you let me sleep so long?" he asked irritated.

"I didn't let you do anything. I tried waking you up, but you just lay there."

"That's exactly why you should have stayed home."

"*Excuse* you?"

"You heard me. I told you I had to get up early, but you came over messing with me."

"When I came over, you started with me. I couldn't get in the door before you started stripping me."

"Yeah, whatever," he said going to the bathroom. He tripped over my shoe. I laughed.

"That shit wasn't funny. Your shoes are all over my place. Look at this bathroom. Your stuff is everywhere."

"I know you're not complaining with your sloppy self. Dirty clothes thrown on the floor, dirty dishes. Whatever. I'm going to work. See you later."

*

For the past couple of weeks I've just been in denial. I know losing the baby really hurt him. I'm scared it has him scared of commitment. The few times I see him we fight about stupid stuff. Like now. It's been four days since our last argument, and we haven't talked at all.

So I swallowed my pride and decided it was time we talk. I called Braxton, but his secretary said he was in a meeting. I thought she was covering, so I called again, two hours later. Same thing. I decided then to go to his house. So when I got off, that's what I did. We were going to talk.

When I got there I didn't know whether to knock or use my key. I figure if he's up to something why give him the opportunity to cover up? Go in, that's why he gave me the key.

When I walked in I heard some jazz playing and saw an open bottle of Chardonnay. Sounds like Kim Waters. Oh shit, don't tell me he has some bitch in his house. My heartbeat quickened. I walked in the living room and breathed a sigh of relief. There he was, alone, fully dressed, sitting on the sofa. He didn't see me, but I could see a look of anguish on his face. I saw him place his head in his hands.

I walked over and placed my hand on his back.

"Braxton, baby, are you OK?"

He looked startled to see me. "Yasmin! What are you doing here?"

"Baby, you've been really tense, and I wanted to do something special for you. Give you a massage, some love," I smiled.

"I'm busy; maybe another time." He then picked up his papers.

I took the papers from him. "Braxton, you've been upset and stressed for a long time. I love you. Let me take care of you for once."

"Yasmin, what do you want? You want to go out? Let's go." He got up and grabbed his coat. "Let's go."

I thought maybe a change of scenery could help, but this is deeper and we needed to talk.

"No, Braxton, talk to me; tell me what's going on with you. I want to make us better. I miss you. I don't want to fight."

He looked at me sincerely. I could tell he wanted to talk to me, but he just brushed me off. He went into the kitchen, staying at least twenty minutes. Finally, he came back still tense with some wine.

"Still here?" he said, annoyed.

"Do you want me to leave?"

"Yasmin, I'm going through some things, and I need some space."

I walked over to him and hugged him. He let me. Braxton actually held me. He held me so tight I didn't think he would let go. It felt so good. I thought this is finally the breakthrough we needed.

I kissed him. "Braxton, I love you so much. These past months have been very hard for us. I think about our son every day. I lost him, and I don't want to lose us." By now I was crying.

Braxton just pulled me close into another hug. "Yasmin, I'm sorry for the way I've been acting the past couple months. I've had a lot on my mind. I'm dealing with some things."

"Braxton, I know it's been very difficult. I'm still going through the emotions. I'm just trying to keep busy. Each day is different. I have my good days, and I have my bad. It's been very hard this last month with Landon. Her being pregnant is harder than I expected."

Braxton took a deep breath and walked away. He sat on the couch. "Yasmin, come here."

I sat down instantly feeling his uneasiness. "What is it?"

Braxton took another deep breath. "Yasmin, I do love you." He sighed.

I tensed up. My heart was beating so loud I could hear it. I began to rock. He continued. "Ever since we lost the baby it seems like things have been going crazy."

I agreed.

"When I first met you I told you I'd never been in a serious relationship. I realize now it's a lot. Yasmin, to be honest, it's too much."

I stopped breathing for a minute, and then asked, "What are you trying to say, Braxton?"

He looked at me regretfully. "Things were a lot simpler before. I miss being free. I feel closed in, pressured, like I'm in bondage. I can't commit to you anymore."

"What?" I rose up and walked to the window. "So after all that we've been through, that's it? You just want to be what friends? Buddies?"

"I'm so sorry, Yasmin. I don't want to hurt you. I can't give you what you need or want right now."

Devastation described what I was feeling at this moment. I felt my heart being ripped from my chest. I wanted to smack the shit out of him. I wanted to cry, scream. I wanted to just drop down on the floor, cry, and beg him not to leave me. But somehow I remained strong and put on my *fuck you then* face. "OK, Braxton, I can respect that. I appreciate your honesty."

Braxton walked over to me. *Don't touch me. If he touches me, I will lose it.* Unfortunately, right now I was torn. It could go either two ways. Either I kirks out, or I just beg him not to leave. Either way it'll be humiliating on my part. I can't lose control—I won't lose control.

"Yasmin, you deserve better. I don't want to hurt you. That's why I'm doing this. I want to see other people. I'm just trying to be honest. I respect you too much to cheat or lie to you, so I think we should go our separate ways."

What the FUCK did he just say? I wish he'd just shut the FUCK up. I hear you loud and clear. He's trying to rub it in. Damn, why won't he just SHUT UP, let me recover from these blows? Instead, he continues to throw combination after combination that are literally knocking the wind out of me.

"Believe me, I didn't mean to hurt you. You know lately we haven't had a relationship. We've been forcing it too much. I don't want to hurt you anymore than I already have. You understand?"

Damn. Let me catch my breath, hold my composure. Why is he antagonizing me? Stay strong, Yasmin. Keep that FUCK YOU face on. I have to get out of here.

My voice quivered, but I was able to speak. "Well, Braxton, again, I truly appreciate your honesty. OK. What you're saying is fine. I think you're right. I'll just grab some of my things and leave you to your work."

I took his key off the key ring and gave it to him. I took a deep, silent breath and slid the engagement ring off my finger. It left a mark, yet another reminder of Braxton.

"Yasmin, I really didn't want to hurt you. But you deserve more. You're so beautiful with those pretty green eyes."

I thought of my grandmother. I couldn't help but hear her words. "Those evil monstrous green eyes—you're only good for a fling."

Definitely time to go. "OK, Braxton, later. No hard feelings." I got to his door and remembered this asshole has my key. I turned around, tightened up my *fuck you, bitch* face and strutted like I was Eva the Diva.

"Braxton, can I have my key, please? I'll have your stuff delivered to you."

He went to retrieve my key. As he was handing it to me he decided he wanted to talk some more. *Please just shut up.* I thought, *He purposely is trying to get me to break down. I don't understand why he is doing this.*

"Yasmin, I'm so sorry. Are you OK?"

With all the strength I had, I smiled. "Braxton, no hard feelings. We're still cool. It's fine. You're right. We've been through a lot, and sometimes things just don't work out. We need a break. I think we need to meet other people." I then gave him a *who cares* shrug. "I respect you're honesty. You said it yourself, I'm a beautiful woman. There's somebody out there for me. Don't worry about me. You remember how you used to get jealous of other men looking at me? I won't be single for long. OK?"

I could see his jaw tighten by the mention of other men. His whole body seemed to tense. *Isn't this some shit? Did he expect me to stay single and cry and wait for him to come back? He has a lot of nerve.* Truthfully, that's what I wanted to do, but I had my dignity.

I walked over, gave him a hug, and kissed him on the cheek. "OK, you. It's been good. I'll see you around." I wiped the lipstick off his cheek and strutted out his door.

I couldn't get home fast enough. It seemed like every light was red. Everyone was going ten miles slower than the speed limit, and everything was in slow mode. I couldn't take it. I wanted to yell, scream, run over all of these people in my way. I finally made it to my apartment. As soon as the door closed, I collapsed on the floor and let it out.

How could he do this to me? I went there thinking I was getting us back on track, I opened my heart out, and he does this to me? They say there's a thin line between love and hate, right? Right now, I agreed because I hate him.

"*AARGHHHHHHHHHHHHHH!*"

I lay on the floor for hours just crying, praying that he would come knocking on my door saying he made a mistake. I prayed he would love me again. I couldn't move. I wanted him. I couldn't believe he left me. My mind was alternating between blaming him and blaming me. I put too much pressure on him. I needed him. Who's going to love me now?

I didn't know what to do. I loved him. I gave him my heart. I let my guard down. He told me he'd always love me and be there. He looked me in the eyes and promised, but he lied. I was just a fling. That's all he wanted me for. He got bored and threw me away like I was trash. My grandmother was right, that's all I'm good for. I cried myself to sleep that night and the remainder of the week.

*

The week after it still hurt, but I stood tall up and I was in fuck him mode. I gathered his stuff and placed it in boxes. He had about two boxes' worth of stuff. I called FedEx and requested they pick it up. They were coming in the morning. The other stuff from him was destroyed. I shred or bleached whatever I found from him. I threw out all the cards, clothes, anything—jewelry, even my charm bracelet, except my autographed Jill Scott CD. I loved my Jill. She was one of the good times and simply was staying with me to sing me through.

After all of that I was tired and I still hurt like hell. I cried myself to sleep that night, still cursing Braxton.

18
Pretty Baby

It was definitely over with Braxton and me. We've had no communication at all in the last couple of months. It's been hard. I never loved someone as much as I loved Braxton. I let myself trust him, gave him my all, and then some. I loved Braxton more than I loved myself, and I was feeling really stupid. I kept wondering what I did, what I could have done. I'd picked up the phone so many times since we broke up to call, but I never went through with it. Thank God I didn't add humiliation to my list of dismay.

Loving Braxton has caused me to lose it. Seriously, I've had to seek counseling. Talk about crazy love. Yes, I did see a counselor. She helped me start the healing process. Writing in journals, taking a Tae Kwon Do class to relieve some tension, she served her purpose, but I dropped her after my fifth visit. Psychiatrists have a tendency to keep you medicated so you keep coming back. I definitely had issues, but I was not about to be dependent on a drug.

I've had one date since the breakup. I went out with this guy, Wayne, I met a while back. I ran into him one day leaving the bank. I was vulnerable, he asked, I accepted. We ended up at some party. The entire time I felt like I was on display. He kept calling me over making comments like,

"Didn't I tell you she was pretty?"

"You see the eyes? They're real."

"Show them the dress, baby."

"She's all that, isn't she?"

Disgusted I was. Needless to say I drank a lot, and when the party was over, I was good and horny. I figured I would use him and kick him out. I know I was wrong. I didn't really like him. But again, I was vulnerable and horny. It had been some months. I know toward the end of Braxton and my relationship it wasn't the best sex we'd had, but I came. I was used to having it on a regular. After all, we were together almost two years.

When we arrived at my place Wayne started kissing me. I wasn't feeling that so I turned my head. He tried again, and I turned my head once more, then he moved to my neck. Good, he got the point. He slobbered on my neck so bad I thought he really was a dog in heat. I was immediately turned off, but he was getting turned on. I felt his dick getting hard, and it felt like a good size. But I wasn't feeling him. I could just use him for the night, but why bother? Anyway, he assumed he was going to sex me tonight. Um . . . no, not happening, fool.

Wayne, ever so anxious, started stripping. He winked at me. I thought, *What the fuck was that for? You're REALLY turning me off now.* His body was all right, but what I saw next I was not prepared for. I gagged. I saw the ugliest freaking thing I've ever seen in my life. It looked like a rotten, peeled banana that has been sitting for a months. It looked stank, deformed. I gagged some more and turned my head. *What the . . . An uncircumcised dick.* I had to get him out. Some women like that, but not me. It looked like an infection. My facial expression signaled something was very wrong.

"Are you PK?" he asked, looking at me like I was crazy.

"I had too much alcohol. I feel real nauseated all of the sudden."

I added some gagging, hoping to kill his mood. All I had to do was look at that rotten dick. Ugh, ooh, that shit looked nasty.

"I think you better leave," I said in between gags.

"Are you sure?"

"Yeah, I'm going to lie down, my stomach," more gagging.

He got the hint and left.

I cleaned myself up after that episode and got more depressed, which initiated the therapy sessions. That episode also made me limit my alcohol intake. I realized drinking while I was depressed like that could have led me into trouble.

Landon has been somewhat supportive. She told me she knows Braxton loves me but has issues he needed to deal with. She thought time apart is what we needed and thought we'd get back together. The next minute she, of course, was throwing insults at him, but what else would you expect from her?

I was envious. Landon and Eric are now married. They had a large, intimate ceremony in Cancun. It was gorgeous. She had the best. Preston Bailey coordinated the event. What else would you expect from the diva? Kevin, along with Nicole, came. I was the only odd ball. Everyone was happy in love except for me. Landon is living the life I wanted, and I'm living an undesired single life.

I've been keeping myself busy with work and preparing for my godchild's arrival. Landon's baby shower was today. She's having a little boy. I'm just trying to get out of bed, but it just was not happening.

My CDs of choice are Vivian Green, "A love Story," Mary J. Blige, "My Life," Me'Shell N'Degéocello, "Fool of Me," all, of which, keep me functional. Today, the CD of choice was Me'Schell N'Degéocello, "Fool of Me." I lay in bed thinking of how things would have been different if hadn't lost my son. But I guess it wasn't in God's will. I knew I had to move on, and I will, just not today.

An hour later, I got up and called Kevin.

"Hello."

Great, Nicole. She seems nice, but she was a little too reserved for Kevin in my opinion.

"Hello, Nicole, how are you today?"

"Fine."

"Good, I was just calling to see if Kevin was ready for this shower. You are coming, right?"

"No, I have a prior engagement, but you two have fun. Let me get Kevin for you."

Good, I thought. Kevin and I talked for a while. I had all of the decorations so he said he would meet me at the hall. It was ten now, and the shower was at three. It was a Jack and Jill type shower so there would be plenty of men.

It took me two hours to decorate. Landon had a Winnie the Pooh theme, and I purchased her a cake from Cake Plus in Laurel, who makes the best cakes.

I stood back and looked at the place real good. I outdid myself. Well, really, Landon did. She told me where and how she wanted everything. It was a quarter to two when Kevin finally showed up.

"What's up, Kev? Are you ready for the diva and the baby?"

"You get the baby the first week," he teased.

"Cool, you tend to the diva."

He laughed. "Ms. Y.E.S. What's going on? How are you doing?"

"One day at a time, but I'm OK."

"You know if you ever need me, I'll be there," he said grabbing my hand.

"Thanks."

"Are we interrupting?"

I turned to see Landon's parents.

"No, hello, Mr. & Mrs. Taylor," I said walking over.

"Hello, Yasmin, Kevin," they both said.

"You two really did a good job decorating," Mrs. Taylor complimented.

"Landon picked everything out. She just told me what she wanted."

"Yasmin, thank you for doing this for Landon. You're always there for her." Mrs. Taylor gave me a hug.

"Yes, Yasmin, Landon is always talking about you. Yasmin, we're also sorry about your loss," Mr. Taylor said sincerely.

"Thank you," I said clearing my throat. *Please, no pity for me today.*

Kevin sensed my weakness. "How was your vacation?"

"Wonderful, relaxing. Martha's Vineyard was just what we needed."

"Good for you," I said.

Soon, other guests started to arrive. There were a lot of Wizard players and other NBA players. I wasn't sure if they were there for Eric or Landon. My girl is definitely loved. One guest that could have stayed away was Javon Edwards.

Javon approached. "How you doing, Miss Yasmin?"

"Fine, thanks," I said trying to brush him off. I started messing with decorations on the table.

"I know Braxton's not taking care of you these days. He has a new flavor. She's not as sexy as you, but that's his problem. Stop playing, let's hook up." He handed me his card.

I took it to shut him up, but I had no intention of calling. In fact, first chance I get, it's going in the trash.

"That's what I'm talking about. Damn, you look better each time I see you. Holla later."

I smiled, and he walked away.

Braxton has a new friend. He didn't waste any time. What should I expect? He said he wanted to see other people. He probably called her as soon as I left. I can't stand Braxton or Javon. Two of a kind. *Ugh . . . ass. I know he said that shit to piss me off. Damn, it's working. OK, get it together for your girl.*

Landon made a diva entrance arriving at four with a speech. She had the pregnancy glow and was so pretty in her white baby doll dress. The way she complained you would have thought she gained one hundred pounds, but she only gained fifteen. Eric looked so happy. I'm glad at least someone is.

Landon fanned herself, flashing her seven karat princess, or should I say, *queen* cut diamond. "Thank you all for coming to my shower."

"*Our* shower," Eric interrupted.

"Sorry, baby, *our* shower. I especially want to thank my best friends who are our baby's godparents, Kevin and Yasmin."

We waved.

"Don't they look cute together? I know they will be standing here one day. I want to thank you guys for always having my back. I love you. Be prepared later, though. I need a massage. Fellas, you see my girl Yas? She's single and needs some love. Show her some, but the finances better be correct. Give them a hand now, everyone, and let's party and open gifts." Landon signaled the DJ to play music.

No, that bitch did not just say that.

The shower was fun. I had a good time. Landon collected thousands of dollars worth of gifts and about ten thousand in cash. She had more than enough things for the baby. As godparents, Kevin and I had to help her take that stuff home. Both of us had big SUVs so it only took one trip, but afterward, I was tired. When I got home I was exhausted. I collapsed on my bed. I wasn't asleep for long when the phone rang. I started not to answer, but thought it could be Landon. She was due in three weeks, but babies had their own schedule.

"Hello," I answer groggily.

"Yasmin, I'm sorry. Did I wake you?"

"Who's this?"

"My bad. My name's Chauncey. Your friend Landon gave me your number."

Landon. I was going to hurt her. "Yeah?"

"I was calling to see what's up with you?"

"So were you at the shower today?"

"Yeah, I was."

"So you know what I look like, but I'm clueless about who you are."

"Yes, I definitely know you're a PYT (pretty young thing), but you don't have to be clueless. Let me take you out."

My phone beeped.

"Can you hold on, Cha?"

"Chauncey," he finished. "You're not going to forget me, are you?"

"No."

"Hello," I said when I clicked over.

"Yas, don't be mad, but I gave your number to a guy named Chauncey. Very cute 6 foot 7, light skin, curly hair. He's cut. Some guys have a six-pack he has a twelve-. Be nice when he calls. Oh, he plays for Miami."

"Too late, Diva, he's on the other line now."

"He didn't waste any time. He did say he was feeling you."

"Diva, I'm going to curse you out later for giving out my number."

"Blah, blah. Go talk to sexy Chauncey."

"Well, bye." I clicked over.

"Sorry, Chauncey."

"You remembered me. I'm just going to get right to the point. I want to take you out. Is that possible?"

Why not? I had nothing better to do with my time. "OK."

We exchanged info, and I agreed to go out with him the following week.

Afterward, I lay in bed yet another day thinking about Braxton. It was time to move on let him and the past go.

19
All I Need

"How are you feeling?" I asked Landon.
It was the first week in July, and the doctors were saying any day.

"Ready. I'll be glad to drop this load. I miss my bikinis in the summer. This boy already is restricting Mama."

"I know. It'll be over soon, and you will have a baby boy. Landon, you're blessed."

"I'm sorry, Yas, you're right. You're still going to be in the delivery room with me, right? I don't know what to do."

"You know I will. I don't know what to do either. Remember, I was knocked out."

"Yas, don't chicken out on me. Is your cell charged?"

"Yes, Land."

I was getting ready for my date. I've talked to Chauncey a few times. He seems like a nice guy. I still don't remember him from the shower, but I'll finally meet him tonight, and I'm looking forward to it. Hopefully, I'll have some restraint because I was horny as hell. I almost invited Derek over when he called yesterday, but I came to my senses. I rummaged through my closet, looking for an outfit. I still didn't have any idea where Chauncey was taking me. But I decided on a spaghetti strap, multicolored dress. It was ninety degrees out.

"You look good."

"Thanks, Diva. I still don't remember him though."

"You need to watch more sports. He's one of Miami's best players. He's in the paper a lot."

"Uh-oh, you know I hate publicity and attention."

"You'll be fine. He gets good publicity."

my doorbell rang.

"I hope that's not him. He's not supposed to get here until six. It's 5:30."

"I knew I liked him. Unlike your *ex,* he can tell time. He's early. This means, he couldn't wait to see you and doesn't believe in having a woman wait."

I opened the door and was blown away. He is definitely seeexxxy. When I looked at him I did recognize him from TV. Chauncey is extremely tall with smooth butter skin, sexy big brown eyes with long eyelashes, curly hair, and definitely muscular. I immediately felt an attraction.

"Come on in, Chauncey."

He handed me a dozen purple passion flowers. "Rare and beautiful, like you."

Landon was there front and center. "Hello, Chauncey, you look nice in your outfit."

He was dressed casually in khakis and a Polo shirt.

"Hey, Landon, how is it going? I see you're still pregnant."

"Yeah, any day."

"Chauncey, are you ready? Landon, are you going to be OK?"

"Yes, Yassy, I'm leaving with you."

Landon got her stuff, and I locked up. When we went outside we both looked at each other. Chauncey was making a good first impression. He held the door open to his Bentley for me to get in.

"Chauncey, I'll be right over. I have to help Landon in the car."

I walked Landon over to her Mercedes truck. "Landon, a Bentley?"

"All right, he really likes you. Go ahead. If I wasn't pregnant—"

"If you wasn't pregnant *nothing.* Eric is running the show now."

"Since your date is waiting I won't tell you off, but no one runs Diva."

I walked over to the car. Chauncey, being the gentleman he is, helped me in and closed the door. I leaned over and opened the door for him.

"Yasmin, tell me about yourself."

I gave him the nice, edited version: Graduated, got job, oldest child, single.

"And yourself," I asked.

He is the oldest of three kids. He's from Baltimore but got a scholarship to play ball in California. He was drafted to play for Miami and is 27.

"Have you ever been in love?"

"*Excuse* me? You're direct."

"I just like to get straight to the point."

OK, I am definitely feeling him. "Yes, but he wasn't ready. He wanted to have fun. So I told him I appreciated his honesty, and I moved on."

"His lost will be my gain."

"You think so?"

"I know so."

I liked his style. "What about you?"

"I was, but I fucked it up. When I first was drafted to the NBA I had a girlfriend, but the groupies were coming. I cheated, she wasn't having it, and left me. I definitely learned my lesson."

"Sorry to hear that. How has dating been?"

"It's hard finding someone that's not trying to get with me because of money."

"How do you know I'm different?"

"I've been watching you for a while, and I don't get that vibe from you. You seem to be independent."

"Don't tell me you're a stalker?"

"No, nothing like that. I saw you a couple of times with Landon. I like how you handle yourself. I saw other dudes approach you that had more money than me. But you still turned them away. I know you were dating some dude. But Landon told me that was definitely over. So I jumped at the opportunity."

"Landon just put all my business out there?"

He laughed.

We talked some more, and he took me to a restaurant outside of D.C. Chauncey shut the place down. It was just me and him. I definitely had a good vibe from him. After dinner, we talked some more, and I'm not going to lie. I wanted to sex him, but I wasn't doing that again.

"So what would you like to do tonight, Ms. Lady?"

"I thought *you* were taking me out. You should have had this planned."

He stood up and walked over.

I followed his cue and stood.

Once in front of me he kissed me lightly on my lips. "Well, pretty lady, will you let me take you for a ride?"

"OK, but it depends where you're going to take me."

"Just to my place."

I was definitely horny, but I'm not having sex with him. I hope he doesn't think I'm one of his groupies that would be impressed over dinner and ready to drop the drawers, because Ms. Yasmin is not the one. "If I wanted to sit in a house I would have stayed home."

"You don't have to sit."

"Well, I'm not lying or standing."

He chuckled. "I'm not going to try anything."

I give him a *yeah, right* look.

"I'm serious."

I knew I shouldn't have gone. Sleeping with Braxton on the first date was one thing, but with another person? Especially an NBA player. That's a straight groupie move.

When we got to his place I was in awe but didn't show it. His house looked like it belonged in a magazine. It was decorated in deep chocolate browns, creams, and burgundies. He had mahogany wood, marble, and plush furniture throughout, even fountains; a very mature, sleek look.

I took a seat on his couch crossing my legs. Chauncey came over sitting right next to me. He wasted no time and started kissing me. I kissed him back. When I felt his hands go up my dress I stopped him. "Chauncey, you have me at your place. Are you the only entertainment?"

"No, Yasmin, I have other things. You want to watch a movie?"

"That'll work."

He got up and put in *Trois: Pandora's Box*.

I laughed at him. I know I just said I wasn't going to do a groupie move, but I've had a change of heart. Truthfully, I like Chauncey, but really, I could care less right now if he calls me tomorrow. I'm just trying to have fun. I decided to fuck with him.

"What's so funny?"

"You trying to seduce me. You're sending me a subliminal message, the movie. You want sex; just say it."

"I'm feeling you. I told you I've been watching you for a while. Your style, you can hold a conversation, your smile. You're wifey material."

"Hold it, now you're starting to sound like a song. Boy, please. You've been out with me three hours. We're adults. I'm not one of the groupies you usually deal with. You started out getting straight to the point. I like that, so cut the bullshit. Let me help you out. If I were to give you some of this sweet stuff I possess, will it be worth it? I hear you're a good player on the court. Honestly, I haven't seen your skills. If you're that good on the court, then I think other skills may be lacking."

"See, now you're challenging me. I have skills." He smiled, showing his pretty white teeth.

"Well, like I said, cut the bullshit. Come on," I said, licking my lips.

Chauncey walked over to me and grabbed me right off the sofa. He kissed me forcefully. His kisses were on the sloppy side but not bad enough to turn you off. This time when I felt his hands go up my dress I didn't stop him. He tugged at my panties, but they weren't coming off easily; therefore, he ripped them off. Oh, he is paying for those. His dick was getting hard so I decided to help him out by unbuckling his pants. They fell right on the floor. I pulled away from the kiss to check his dick out. After my last experience I had to make sure his ass was circumcised, and it was. Good length, pretty, and smooth. I hope he knows how to use it.

Chauncey pulled me close, lifting my dress over my head. Once it was off, he threw it somewhere across the room. I did the same to him with his shirt. Now all I had on was my bra. He quickly unsnapped that. My nipples were erect and ready for attention. Chauncey read my mind. They were now getting attention. I let him lower me to the floor. Once we were there he took his thumb to play with my clit. When his tongue hit my spot, my neck, I was ready.

My cell started ringing. I ignored it. Before Chauncey could focus back on my clit his cell started to go off. He turned it off. Mine started again, so I picked it up to turn it off. I saw LANDON and quickly answered. "Land—"

"Yas, my water broke. I need you. Meet me at the hospital."

"OK, Land, I'm on my way." I hung up and saw Chauncey with a sad puppy dog look.

"Sorry. You heard. I have to go to the hospital."

"I understand, but we will finish this after the baby is born."

"Of course." I walked over and kissed him.

He started putting on his clothes. I was halfway dressed, looking for my bra and underwear.

"Looking for something?" he said holding up my underwear and bra.

"Yes, can I have them so we can go?"

"No, this is my mine to keep. I might give it back when you return."

I laughed. "You can't have me in the cold hospital without panties and a bra."

"I'll keep you warm." He threw the bra but kept the panties. "Remember, I ripped them?"

"Chauncey, come on. Landon will kill me and you if I'm not there."

"Nope, the panties are mine. Are you ready?"

"I guess I have no other choice. You owe me a pair of panties."

We left his house, but this time we took his Suburban. It had dark tinted windows to keep out unwanted attention. He got us to the hospital in twenty minutes. I ran in with Chauncey right behind me and headed straight to receptionist to give her my info. The girl was instantly starstruck with Chauncey.

"Oh my God, Chauncey Smith, can I have your autograph? I can't believe this. Another NBA player is in here."

I had no patience. "No, you cannot. Where is Landon Taylor-Ayers's room?"

She ignored me. "Chauncey, I love you."

"Where is your supervisor?"

Chauncey spoke up. "Shorty, we need to know where Landon Taylor-Ayers's room is."

I was irritated with the receptionist. I looked up and saw Braxton's brother, Horace. I hated to call him over, but this chick was plucking my last nerve. "Horace?"

He looked up at me and smiled. "Yasmin."

"Hey, Horace, my friend is in labor, and I need to find out where she is. Your staff seems to be incompetent."

Chauncey walked over rubbing my shoulders trying to calm me down. "You can be a feisty one, I see. I like that."

I smiled at him.

Horace looked at us. I could tell he wanted to say something but didn't. He gave me Landon's info and showed me to her room.

We walked in and saw Landon relaxing.

"You're looking good, Diva. You've seen the anesthesiologist already?"

"No, so far I just have mild pains. My water broke, but I am only four centimeters. I'm feeling good."

I walked over and gave her a hug, then Eric. "You ready, Eric?"

"Definitely."

"Where are your parents and Kevin?"

"Parents are on the way. Kevin is out of town."

"I know Kevin did not leave me with you."

"What's that supposed to mean?" she asked a little hurt.

"Pregnancy hormones. I'm sorry, Land."

Eric shook his head. "This is what I've been going through. I'll be glad when this baby gets here."

"I know, man. Females are the worst when they're pregnant. I remember those days," Chauncey laughed.

Hold up. He has a child? Yasmin, wake up. You almost had sex with a man that has a child. It's not the fact that he has a child, it's that I didn't know. You are too vulnerable. You need to slow down before you catch something. Thank you, God, for having Landon go into labor.

"You have a child?" Landon asked.

"Yeah, well, two kids."

"Same mother?" she grilled.

"Nope."

The doctor came in to check Landon so Chauncey and I left.

He pulled me to the side. "Do you have a problem with me having kids?"

"No, I just was caught off guard. We almost . . . you know. Anyway, I should have asked you that. I assume the mothers are your ex and the girl you fucked up with."

"Yup."

"It's cool. Anything else I should know?"

"Nah, but I want to know if I can kiss you."

"No, because my ass is cold, and I don't have any underwear on," I teased.

"You mean these?" He pulled out my panties.

"Put that away," I said embarrassed.

"Can I have a kiss?"

"Will you put it away?"

"Maybe."

I blew him a kiss.

He laughed.

"You didn't say what kind of kiss."

He put my underwear in his pocket.

The doctor came out and told us we could go back in.

Landon said she was still only four centimeters. The doctor thought her labor was at a standstill so he was going to start her on Pitocin. The nurse came in to start the solution. After about an hour the drug started working, and that's when Landon got ugly.

I had Chauncey go out into the hall. "Landon is getting irritable, and it looks like it'll be a long night. You can go home. I'll call you when the baby gets here."

"You sure? I don't mind staying here with you."

"Thanks, but you know you want to go. Go ahead, I'm straight. I'm about to take a nap anyway."

He laughed. "OK, call me, though. You need a ride home."

"I will."

He bent down and kissed me. "See you later."

I watched him walk away, so sexy. When I turned around, there was Horace.

"Yasmin."

"Hey, how's it going?"

"Fine. Yasmin . . ." Horace shifted to his other foot.

"Yes?"

"Can I talk to you for a minute?"

"Sure, what's up?"

"I know you and Braxton broke up, and that it's none of my business. But you are like a sister."

"OK."

"Be careful. Don't rush into anything."

"Horace, I appreciate your concern, but I know what I'm doing."

"Braxton—"

I stopped him. I wasn't interested. "Horace, please, I need to check on my friend." I walked away not giving him a chance to respond.

"*Owwwwww,*" Landon screamed. "Where the hell is the doctor at? I need an epidural. Damn you, Eric. You'll pay for this."

"Landon, calm down. Breathe," Eric suggested.

"No, *you* calm down."

"Diva, be nice."

"Listen, neither one of you knows how I feel, so shut the fuck up. This shit hurts."

"*Owwww,*" Eric screamed.

"What's wrong with you?" I asked.

"She has her nails digging in my skin," he whined.

Landon's OB and anesthesiologist came in. The doctor checked Landon, and she was 7 centimeters, but the baby's heart rate was dropping.

I prayed for Landon and her baby. It felt like déjà vu, and I started crying, reliving my ordeal. Landon's parents were there. Eric and Landon's mother comforted her while her father walked over and gave me a hug.

They ended up taking Landon back for an emergency C-section. Only two people were allowed. Eric and her mother went back. I sat waiting with her father, praying both my friend and godson were healthy.

Thirty minutes later Eric came out looking worn. "He's here. A big 8 pounds 1 ounce."

I ran up to Eric and hugged him. "When can we see the baby?"

"They're setting up everything now. I'm not sure."

An hour later I sat in the room with Landon and family holding my godson. He was so cute. He had a little bit of hair and big grey eyes. He had Landon's and my complexion for now, but looking at Eric, I was sure he was going to darken up.

Eric took the baby from me and kissed Landon. He had his son. I know he and I will be fighting over this baby. I'll let him hold him for now and get that bond going.

"How are feeling, Diva?"

"Tired. No more kids for me. Mommy, now I know why I'm an only child. I'm sorry for asking for a sister."

Eric and I laughed.

"That doctor better have given me my bikini cut."

"So is the baby a junior?" I asked.

Landon looked at Eric "Not quite."

Confused, I asked. "What do you mean, not quite?"

"Yasmin, I know you've been through a lot. I want to honor your son. It wasn't until I became pregnant that I could understand the bond. The baby's name is Eric Bryan Ayers."

I was speechless. All I could do is cry. "Thank you," I said, in between sniffles. I hugged Landon and cried some more.

She was crying. "I just had surgery. You're hurting Diva."

"I'm sorry."

I said a prayer for my baby, and then took my godson from Eric. This baby will always be special to me.

20
Sweet Misery

It's Friday night, and I'm babysitting. The baby now five months, is getting so big and even cuter. We're in the mall Christmas shopping. It is a madhouse, but I have nothing else to do. The NBA season was about to start, so I rarely saw Chauncey, which also was a good thing. It gave me time to spend with myself. Time alone gave me the opportunity to focus on my needs and wants and issues. Every day was a struggle, but I was making a point to look me in the mirror each day, at least fifteen minutes, and talk.

"Waaaaaaaaaa!"

"What's matter, big boy?" I said rocking the baby.

Taking a seat in the eatery, I took out his bottle and began feeding him. "Is that what you wanted?"

"Yasmin?"

I lay the baby down in his stroller and stood up. "Ma, Mrs. Simms. How are you doing?"

"You got it right the first time," she said, hugging me.

"How have you been?"

"OK, considering."

"Is everything OK?" I asked, concerned.

"My heart has been broken since you and that stubborn child of mine broke up."

Here we go. How to respond? "It was for the best. We needed space."

"Well, you've had enough space. I want you to come over for Christmas."

"I don't think that'll be a good idea."

"I know Braxton loves you; he's just being stubborn. He's not good with expressing himself."

"Mrs. Simms, with all due respect, Braxton can express himself when he has to. I can't stop my life because he still needs to grow up. I can't and will not wait around."

"I told you to call me Ma, but I apologize; you're right. You can't be mad at me because I want you with my son."

"You're right. How about we compromise and I call you Ms. Beverly?"

"That'll work for now, but I've already told you, you will be my daughter-in-law."

I shook my head and gave up.

"I have a question."

"Yes?"

"Are you and that guy Chauncey dating, or it that a fabrication?" she inquired.

"How did you know about that?"

"Horace."

I smiled.

"Never mind, I don't want to know. You *are* going to be my daughter-in-law. I've already told Braxton you're the only one he can bring to my house. Even though you two are taking a break you can still call. Promise me you will."

"Waaaaaa waaaaaaa!"

I bent down and picked up Eric. "What's the matter with auntie's baby?"

Mrs. Simms smiled.

"Would you like to hold him?"

"May I?"

I placed the baby in her arms. "Isn't he adorable?"

"Yes, he is."

"He reminds me of Braxton when he was a baby. What's his name?" she commented.

I smiled. "Landon honored our son. This is Eric Bryan Ayers."

"That's beautiful."

"It is. I wonder a lot what he would look like. I think about him every day."

"I know; it's hard. You have a special guardian angel."

"That I do. I just wish I could have held him just once to tell him how much I loved him. I lost a lot when he died." I felt the tears coming, but I managed to stop them.

Mrs. Simms came around to comfort me. I was mad at myself for getting emotional, but at the same time, I had to admit I am still hurt.

"You know, Yasmin, I'm always there for you, no matter what happens between you and Braxton. I will always consider you my daughter."

"Thank you, I really appreciate that. How is my favorite uncle?"

She laughed. "Charles misses his Sweet Thing."

"Tell him, tell everyone I said hello and give them my best."

"You know you can do that. The invitation is still open."

"Thanks, but no thanks."

"What are you doing for Christmas?"

"No definite plans. I'll probably be with this big boy."

"You're not going to your parents?"

My parents and I were still were distant. I've purposely avoided them since my miscarriage. Accidentally, I mentioned Braxton and I broke up. Mom gave me the same lecture about giving the cow away for free. Then to add more insult, she added I couldn't even walk away with dignity. I did see them once at Ashley's birthday party. I said hello, dropped off a gift, and kept it moving. My mother called rarely. The conversations were always forced. I just make up an excuse to get off the phone. They depress me more, and I wasn't going to torture myself any longer.

"No," I said through misty eyes.

"Yasmin, please reconsider. Come for me."

"I'm sorry I can't."

I could tell she's hurt, but I have to do what is best for me. Seeing Braxton is not. I was finally moving forward, and I have to keep moving.

She gave me back the baby. "Will you keep in touch?"

"I will." I gave her my number, and she walked away.

I felt bad for turning Mrs. Simms down. I almost called her back, but I came to my senses. I will always appreciate everything she's done, but she was part of my past.

21
Whatever You Want

I wanted to see Chauncey. He is good company. He's corny but funny, and I was horny. I like how he greets me with a song hook or uses some when we speak. But I know he has some games and business to tend to, so I'd have to wait. We've been seeing each other for the last couple of months. I definitely am attracted to him. However, I did have a few issues, such as he sweated too damn much, and if he's on top, that crap fell on me. He also thought he was the best when it came to sex, but you know how an anorexic looks in the mirror; thinks she's fat when really she's not. Well, Chauncey thinks his dick is big, but it's really not. I'm not saying it's the smallest; it's a decent size, but I wouldn't be bragging. And he only wanted to do it his way. I tried to get him to let me take control, but that wasn't an option. With Braxton, he was always open and willing, but here we go again with Braxton. Back to Chauncey, I know he likes me, but I also know he has other female companions; condoms were definitely a must. I like him, but I can't say I was in love.

Today has been a long day. It feels about ten degrees outside, and all I want to do is get in my bed, wrap up in my blankets, and read a book. I really needed a vacation but haven't figured out where I want to go.

When I got home I saw flowers everywhere. I reached the top level of my apartment building and see Chauncey with the biggest bouquet of flowers I've ever seen. They were beautiful. He was such a sweetheart.

"Sweet Lady, won't you be mine?"

"Hello," I smiled and gave him a hug.

"Come take a ride with me."

"How long have you been waiting?"

"I just got here. Are you going to ride with me?"

"Let me put this in the house and I'll be right down."

I went in and dropped my stuff off. When I came out, Chauncey was waiting to escort me to his car. We ended up at the airport.

"I want you to take a trip with me."

Since I wasn't doing anything and I just said I needed a break, I went along. "How long?"

"Just a week."

"Don't you have a couple of games?"

"Yes, just two more in Miami, then I have a little break. I was thinking about you. While I'm at practice you can go shopping, go to the spa, relax, do whatever you want. At night you can come watch me play and afterward, it's just me and you."

"You know you had me until you told me I had to watch you play. I want to have fun, not sit there bored."

He laughed. "That's why I like you. You don't just tell me anything, but I am nowhere near boring."

"You're not, but I don't have any clothes. Why didn't you let me grab some things?"

"I got you. You don't need anything."

"OK."

We got on a private jet and headed to Miami. The ride was nice. Between the plane ride and the ride to the hotel Chauncey tried to school me on the game. He had reserved a suite for me. It was late, a little after eleven when we made it to the hotel. I was tired. I just wanted to lie down, but Chauncey had other plans. What did I expect? He came to Maryland to get my ass, but surprisingly, he let me take control for once. I made sure I put it on him. He and I both went to bed with a smile.

The phone woke me up at ten. It was the hotel giving Chauncey a wake-up call for his practice at twelve. "Chaunce, that was your wake-up call. Time to get up."

He was knocked out, so I started playing with his dick. That got him up. He grabbed me and pulled me on top of him. He was trying to stick it in, but that wasn't happening. I grabbed a condom off the nightstand. After he slipped it on I rode him like he was a mechanical bull. Fifteen minutes later he was busting a nut.

"Damn, you have me not wanting to go to practice. I want to stay in you all day."

"Sorry, that's not an option." I got up and handed him a towel.

"Well, take a shower with me."

"Nope, because then you'll be late. I'll give you some attention tonight."

He smiled, got up, and started getting ready for practice. After his shower, I jumped in. Since I had a couple of hours to myself I decided to go shopping. I forgot I had work clothes from yesterday. I wrapped myself up in a robe and went out to see Chauncey before he left.

"Now you're teasing me." He walked over to kiss me.

"No, I'm not. I don't have any clothes, remember?"

"Glad you said something." He went in his wallet and handed me a credit card.

"Thanks, Chauncey, but I can buy my own clothes."

"No, you can't. I told you I got you here. Just don't clean me out," he joked.

I took it, but I wasn't going to go overboard. "I'm not."

Chauncey ordered some room service, stayed another fifteen minutes, then ran off to practice. He told me the car would be here at 6:30 to pick me up. After I ate, I went on a minishopping spree. I bought some jeans, shoes, tops, jewelry, a little of everything. I even bought Chauncey some things. I was only planning on spending $1,000, but ended up at $7,000. I hoped Chauncey wasn't upset. I looked at the time. It was 5:30. Time flies when you're spending other people's money. I understood now how Landon spent so much money.

Since it was a game I decided on a pair of my new 7 jeans that hugged my ass just right. A black fitted top and black pumps finished the ensemble. I let my hair hang out with loose curls.

I was a little nervous at first. I wished Landon was here to help me unwind. I was in the box with the wives and the girlfriends. The wives had their own little clique. It was obvious the girlfriends got no respect. The wives just looked at us like we were a fling and didn't feel the need to be bothered with us. Frankly, I could care less. I didn't want any phony females in my face anyway. I ignored all of the females looking at me like *who are you?* Instead, I focused on the game.

Seeing the game is definitely more exciting than hearing about it. Chauncey looked good. He scored twenty-one points the first half. Very impressive. He looked up at me giving me a wink, along with a smile as he made his way to the locker room for halftime.

"Who are you here for?" one of the females asked.

I gave her a once-over. She was cute. Smooth chocolate skin, high cheekbones. She had a long weave, but it looked good on her.

"Chauncey," I replied.

She looked me up and down. "Um, I wouldn't get too comfortable if I were you."

I looked at her and laughed. "That's your problem."

She rolled her eyes and got up to leave.

"Hey, I'm Tanya," one of the wives said.

"Hey, Yasmin."

"That's April. She has a thing for Chauncey. She's been trying to get with him since last year."

"I figured as much."

"Are you and Chauncey serious?"

I thought she was a little too nosy but decided to answer. "No, we're just dating. We're taking our time. I know he's very busy."

"Well, don't take too much time. Someone else is always waiting to take your place. How did you hook up with him?"

She was asking too many questions, but I answered. "My best friend Landon hooked us up. She's married to Eric Ayers."

"I know Landon. She very . . ."

"Outspoken," I finished.

"Yes."

"That's my girl."

She seemed to lighten up after that. We talked throughout the second half. After the game she gave me another heads-up. "Well, watch these bitches, especially *her*." She nodded to April. "She wants him bad."

Chauncey had a good game. They won. Chauncey scored thirty-five points of the ninety-two points that night. There was a party after the game. Of course, Chauncey was the man of the hour. There was some media so Chauncey had to do his job. Since I was his date, I ended up in a couple of the photos. I didn't like that, especially the ones with him kissing on me. But overall, it was a good night. Chauncey was very attentive, making me feel special.

"You look pretty."

"Thank you. You bought it. Speaking, of which, I got a little carried away."

"Uhh, that bad?"

"Depends what you consider bad."

"Well, you're going to have to work it off. How bad is it?" He made a face like he was bracing himself for bad news.

"I will. I did buy you something too."

"Don't try to butter me up."

"Okay, I spent seven thousand."

"That's it? I thought you did some damage."

"*Excuse* me, Mr. Money ain't a thang."

"Well, I'm thankful you didn't break my pockets."

I met a couple of the other players, and they were cool. Of course, the groupies were out, but Chauncey was into me. After two hours of partying, we were ready to go back to the hotel.

"Are you ready to work off what you spent?"

"Chaunce, are *you* ready? Like you handled it on the court, I'm going to handle you tonight."

He nodded his head, then gave me a wink. He couldn't get the door open fast enough.

When we walked in, a naked girl sitting on the fucking chair waiting with her legs spread wide open greeted our eyes. This was not a pretty sight. The girl was light skinned, about 5 foot 7 with a medium build, and big sagging breasts. That, with a 24 inch long blond track that reached her butt, and an earring pierced to her clit finished the look. Her face wasn't even cute, with too much packed on foundation that didn't match her complexion.

Chauncey went off. "Get the fuck out of my room, you nasty bitch. How the fuck did you get in here anyway?"

The girl looked embarrassed, but she did it to herself. She tried to grab her clothes, but Chauncey stopped her.

"Fuck that! Leave that shit and get the hell out, nasty bitch. Bitch, is you fucking crazy? You got my damn room smelling like shit. You need to go soak in some douche or whatever the hell y'all use."

"Please, I'm sorry. I need to get my clothes."

"You dumb-ass bitch. You should have thought of that before you did this dumb shit." He picked up the phone to call security.

The girl started crying. "Please, don't call. I can't lose my job. I'll leave."

Chauncey ignored her and made the call anyway.

I wondered if I wasn't there if Chauncey would have fucked her. It wasn't like we were in a committed relationship. But looking at the girl again, I would say no. She was a straight-up ho that looked like she had been run through too many times. I now knew what Doug Christie's wife meant when she said these hoochies were ruthless. She gets criticized a lot for following her husband, but you have to. Bitches have no respect and are always concocting a plan to get yours. I have nothing but respect for her.

Security and the manager arrived, apologizing for the incident. Chauncey demanded another room. Of course, it was granted, and free of charge. The girl was escorted out the door.

Chauncey took a seat on the couch in our new room. "Sorry about that," he said pulling me into his lap.

"It's not your fault."

"I know, but I told you, I've been thinking about you a lot. I want to spend some time with you. I'm feeling you."

"I'm feeling you too."

"You don't act like it."

"I'm just going with the flow. I'm not trying to rush into anything. You're a busy, popular man. I know earlier was just a glimpse of what it's like being with you."

"Damn nasty ho. I'm not going to lie. What happened earlier is common, but I been there and done that. I want something more."

"You're talking a good game, but you and I both know I'm not the only chick you're fucking. Before you lie or sugarcoat it, I'm not mad. We never discussed a relationship. We've just been enjoying each other's company. As far as a relationship, we'll see. Being with you comes with a lot of publicity. I like my privacy."

"I can respect that, but I want you to be my girl. You know I like you. I just want to be with you. I gave you my credit card. I want you to meet my kids. Let's take it to the next level."

I had to laugh. "All right, Chauncey. I'll give it a try."

22
In My Mind

C hauncey and I were serious. I've met the kids and one of the baby mamas. We took the kids to an amusement park and had a ball. His kids are cute, and we got along. I enjoy spending quality time with them. I'm impressed too. Chauncey really is a good father, very attentive and aware of everything going on in his kids' lives.

When we came back from our personal trip without the kids things started getting crazy. I knew Chauncey was one of the star players, but I didn't think he was so popular in the media.

He has a charity for young boys. A couple of weeks ago he hosted a sports day for the kids in Baltimore. He wanted me to go. I knew it would be fun, and I'm glad I did. The kids were so funny. There were plenty of groupies. I even saw Derek's mother there looking a hot-ass mess. Her color theme that day was red. She wore a red tube that stopped above her navel. Of course, her navel was pierced. She tried to use body glitter to cover up her stretch marks. It didn't work. Her hair was in a short style this time, tapered on the sides with a flip on the top. It still would have been cute if every other flip was red. Her jean skirt stopped right under her ass. The red thong was definitely in full view. Mama Shenaynay wouldn't have been complete without her four-inch acrylic nails and tongue ring. I checked her feet to see she was wearing stilettos that were too small. Her feet were hanging out on both ends, with her fake toenails scrapping the ground. When Chauncey was occupied, Derek approached me.

"Hey, Yas."

I was speechless, but managed to offer a smile.

"You can't speak now that you hangin' with ballas."

"Hello, Derek."

"Can I get some love? You with ole boy now, but you'll be back."

"Bye, Derek."

"Oh, you too good now."

"What do you want?"

"Damn, girl, I just wanna talk."

Before I could cuss him out, Mama Shenaynay came with two little boys. Looking at them I would guess their age ranged from three to seven.

"Derek, get these kids. I told you, I'm not babysitting their asses. Here, Mama trying to hook up with sexy Chauncey." She then looked me up and down. She remembered me then and tried to act like we're best friends.

"Hey, girl, how you doin'? Yeah, girl, I ain't see you in a long time. You and Derek getting back together? Y'all should. These kids need a stepmuva. Shit, all three of his baby mamas are trifling. Anyway, girl, you know Chauncey. You think you can hook me up?"

I told her I'd see and walked away. Those two were definitely entertaining. I expected a large turnout but not the media. You had the local news, newspapers, even BET. BET was doing some Sports Edition, and I wondered if Braxton would be checking out this footage.

Now that it's the playoff time, things have gotten worse. I went to a couple of games. I was cheering for my man, so the paper listed me as Chauncey's "main girl." I didn't like that. People at work were asking me for tickets on the sly, but I'm not the one. One day we went to the jewelry store to pick up a ring for his mother. Now it's being reported I have a ring and we're secretly engaged. Landon called me on that one and asked if it was true.

She told me ignore it. In fact, she told me to wear a ring to really start something, but I didn't. She loves the attention. I told her she could have it. In fact, I'm reconsidering this relationship.

For instance, today I'm in the store looking for some stockings for the Espy's tonight, a black tie event, which I don't mind since Landon and Eric are going. On my way to check out, I saw a magazine with Chauncey's picture on the cover. I picked it up and flipped through it. Here I am listed as his fiancée again. It's a very good picture, I admit, but I like my privacy. I picked up another magazine. There we are again. When I flipped through this one, I saw pictures of us on our minivacation with a friend, Geester. Geester is popular rapper who is doing movies. He's considered one of the people to watch in the next year. Not to take anything from Chauncey's popularity, I think they were there more for Geester. Regardless of whom, they were there invading my privacy. It's crazy because you had no idea where the paparazzi were. I never saw them. I'm glad we didn't get intimate in public, but the pictures told another story. You saw pictures of us holding hands, swimming, him piggybacking me, him on top of me, kissing me. They even had one of us in the house. I saw pictures of me by the window straddling Chauncey with a towel wrapped around me. This was ridiculous.

Flabbergasted, I just grabbed my stockings and headed to Landon's to get ready. I couldn't wait to get into my dress. It's cranberry in color with unique embroidery throughout and stopped at my feet. There was a split that went midthigh. Earlier, I went to the hairdresser to get my hair cut in layers. I added color with highlights to bring out my eyes. That's right, I am not ashamed of my eyes anymore. I love the new do. My hair is still a good length past my shoulders, stopping at my upper back. I couldn't wait till the diva saw it.

Before I could ring the doorbell, Landon swung the door open. "Yassy, is that you?" she teased. "I love your hair. Chauncey and the media are going to be on you."

"Thanks, Diva, but I don't want any more publicity."

"Here we go again. It's not that bad. Most of the pictures are taken during the season, or if the players get into any legal trouble."

"You like attention. I don't, but anyway, where's my baby?"

"With my parents."

"Aww, I wanted to see him."

"You don't have time. Let's get ready. Chauncey will be here soon."

Landon and I hurried upstairs to get ready. Her hair was styled in a short fly do as usual. Looks like we both had similar highlights. I laughed.

"What's so funny?"

"I've been around you too long. You're finally rubbing off on me. Our hair color is the same. We really look alike now."

"You're right. You're finally taking my fashion tips."

"Where's Big Eric?"

Landon sighed. "He went to get his tux."

"What wrong, Land?" I asked taking a seat on her bed.

"Eric thinks because we're married I'm supposed to be a housewife. Thinks I shouldn't party or go out unless I'm with him. We both know I like doing my own thing. Diva is not staying in anyone's house. He wants me to come to his games and cheer him on, then we can party.

"First off, I don't like being cooped up in a box with a whole bunch of bitches. You know how they are. I'm not the one to sit in your face acting phony. I'll go to some for support but I need to do Landon. One of the reasons I married him was because I knew he would be away a lot, giving me some breathing room. Truthfully, all of this smothering has made me want to call old acquaintances."

"Landon, don't do it. Eric will kill you."

"I like my freedom."

Before I could respond Eric came in. "Hey, sweetheart." He gave Landon a kiss on her cheek.

When his back was turned I saw Landon roll her eyes. I just shook my head.

"Hey, Ms. Yasmin."

"Hey, Eric, how's it going?"

"Cool, but your friend always has an attitude."

"Eric, Yas asked you how *you* were doing, not about me. Get out so we can get dressed," Landon demanded.

He listened.

"Landon, you are so mean," I instigated.

"Yas, don't start. Help me get into my dress."

"It must be tight."

She gave me her famous, devious smile.

It was. The dress fit Landon like a snug glove. Her stomach was flat as a board. Landon being a C cup was a good thing because the dress required no bra. Her breasts were still perky; no evidence she had a baby at all. The dress was gold and complemented her complexion.

I let Landon do my makeup. I must admit, I like a lot. We did a quick check before heading downstairs. We looked good. When Chauncey saw me, his eyes lit up and he gave me an approving nod.

Eric, however, did not look pleased. "Land, sweetheart, that's a little tight, isn't it?"

"Eric, calm down. I'm going with you. You will be the envy of all other men."

Chauncey and I looked at each other and had a private laugh.

Eric didn't press the issue. We took an Escalade limo to the ceremony. There were so many people there, media, of course, and athletes from every field. Landon smiled for the camera like she was the star. Eric smiled, but we knew he didn't like his wife getting attention.

Chauncey, like Landon, loved attention. He was poised like he was going to cover *GQ*. I only opted to take a couple of pictures with him.

We mingled a little before the ceremony began. I saw some of the players' wives I'd met. Landon was doing Landon with Eric following her around like a lost puppy dog.

Chauncey made sure I didn't wonder off by holding my hand. Every time I drifted too far he was pulling me close. "I didn't tell you how good you look tonight. *Real* good. I can't wait to take that dress off of you." He slapped me on my ass surprising me.

"Chauncey, are you crazy? Remember, we're in public."

"Unwind, Yasmin. Don't be so uptight. Have some fun."

"I am."

"OK, then, you won't be mad if I do this." He leaned down, grabbed my waist, and kissed me.

"*Excuse* me? Hello! Do you two need to get a room?"

I opened my eyes to see Landon breaking us up.

"Hey, Landon," Chauncey said.

"Calm down, Chauncey. I need to borrow Yas for a minute."

I could tell Chauncey wanted to object, but Landon gave him a look.

Once we walked away she pulled me to the side. "I see you're having a good time."

"Were we that bad?" I asked, embarrassed.

"You had a couple of stares, but you weren't that bad. That's not the reason I pulled you over though."

"Good," I said embarrassed. I then looked up to see Braxton staring right at me. Our eyes locked, and my heart skipped beats. All of these feelings came rushing back to me.

"Yas, get it together. I was trying to warn you. Remember Chauncey. Sexy Chauncey, Chauncey that has the sexy body who is feeling you, Chauncey your man. Don't let Braxton get to you. Braxton broke your heart. Look, he has a date."

That snapped me back into reality. His date was repulsive. The chick must have sensed something because she was staring me up and down. Then she had the nerve to grab Braxton's arm. She doesn't know; been there done that. She needed to realize even though he's with her he'll be thinking about me. Braxton and I will always have a connection.

Back to his date, she was tacky. I could tell from where I was standing she had a weave. *Damn, Braxton, at least you could have picked a chick that had a decent weave.* She was about my complexion, 5 foot 7. Her face was not cute. Something in the eyes, nose, and mouth wasn't right, like it was too close together. She had a puss face, not at all attractive. Her dress was black, plain, and ugly. It didn't even fit her right. Neither her shoes nor jewelry did anything to complement her or the dress.

"I'm cool. I'm just shocked Braxton brought her tacky bad weave-wearing ass. He could have done better than that. Look at her face. She looks like a puss face. Ugh."

"You becoming more and more like me every day. You make me so proud," Landon proclaimed.

We got a good laugh off of Braxton and his date. "She is a sight. Look at that outfit," I instigated.

I felt strong arms wrap themselves around me. "Are you ready to go in? Landon, Eric's waiting for you by the door," Chauncey stated.

Landon walked off, annoyed to meet Eric.

Chauncey leaned down, brushed my hair to the side, and whispered in my ear. "You two look like you're starting trouble." His breath on my neck made me shiver.

"What's wrong? I got you hot and bothered?" he teased.

"Yes, you do. But let's go in. I just might have to be nice to you later. I hope you're ready. Can you handle this?" I teased, then started to walk off, but Chauncey pulled me back, kissing me on my collarbone, cheek, and finally lips.

"Yas, you have my dick hard. I need you to be my cover."

"You started this. Follow my lead." I glanced over at Braxton. I could see the vein popping out of his neck. He was jealous. Good for him. I am his loss.

The ceremony was long, but we managed to have fun at the table. Every now and then I sneaked glances at Braxton. He was always staring back. I know I was wrong, but it was like he had this hold over me. I wanted to be over him so badly, but I still felt a connection. Landon kept kicking me on the sly. I know I have to get over Braxton. I think of the hurt he caused and focused my attention back to Chauncey.

After the ceremony, Chauncey and I went back to his place. I blocked out Braxton. I made Chauncey believe, and tried to make me believe, it was all about him. It probably would have worked if Chauncey wouldn't have taken control. He had me when he was licking my clit. He licked my clit and my insides like a lollipop. I was calling for mercy. We were in doggy-style position when he penetrated me. It was cool, but Chauncey sweated profusely, and it was dripping on me, in my hair. Ugh. I knew I was more annoyed because I had seen Braxton earlier. Finally, I did block it out and was able to get some pleasure.

Afterward, I just lay in his bed unable to sleep, thinking about my past, Braxton.

23
Still in My Heart

Chauncey's team made the playoffs, so I rarely got a chance to see him. I did make a couple of the games. It was cool because I needed some space. I was really trying to get over my unresolved feelings for Braxton.

Especially today since I was on my way to BET to fix some glitch they're having with our new software. I took programming as a minor and told them I'd look into it. Then I had to give updates. I pray I don't see Braxton. I don't know how I'll react seeing him up close and personal. Nonetheless, I made sure to look my best, choosing a mid-thigh olive green dress work appropriate but screams, "Damn!"

I walked in, went to the receptionist, and gave her my info, then waited for them to call me in. I was hoping to see Kim. I haven't seen her in a while, and I miss talking to her.

"Yasmin."

I turned around and saw my girl Kim. I gave her a hug.

"Yasmin, you look good. Look at you. You let you hair grow out."

My hair was now at the middle of my back with more highlights.

"Thank you. I was wondering where you were. I was about to ask for you."

"Yeah, I got a promotion."

"Congrats, you deserve it. How's your new boss?"

"A pain in the ass."

"You're not working for Ms. Stevens, are you?" I teased.

"No, Mr. Simms."

"He's that bad?"

"He definitely has his moments. He hasn't been right since you broke up. If there is a picture or story about you, I know to stay away. By the way, Chauncey is definitely sexy. I wouldn't mind waking up with him every day. I see why you look so good. When you break up you definitely move up."

"Thank you, Kim. Chauncey is cool. He's definitely a lot of fun."

"So when is the wedding?"

I laughed.

"So this means you and Braxton are definitely over? I'd be lying if I didn't say I hope you two work it out. He's such a better person when you're around."

Before I could respond, I felt him walk up behind me. I smelled his Acqua Di Gio cologne and a shiver ran through my body.

"Excuse me, Kim. I need to see you."

Poor Kim, she looks miserable.

Braxton really sounded like he's an ass. I felt bad for my girl. I breathed, folded my arms, spun around, and smiled. "Braxton, it's nice to see you again."

I could tell by the look in his eyes he was surprised to see me. "Yasmin. Hello, how are you?"

"Lovely, thanks," I said showing my pearly whites.

"Mr. Simms, I'll be in your office," Kim said, walking off, giving us a little privacy.

"Glad to hear that. You look good." I noticed him trying to look at my ring finger. My arms were crossed so he couldn't see it was ringless.

"Thanks. You know you should try being nicer to Kim."

"What?"

"You heard me. I feel sorry for her. I would hate to work for you."

"I'm not that bad."

"I can't tell."

He laughed. "Only you would come to my office with a smart-ass mouth, giving me demands on how to treat people."

"It's the truth. You should work on your communication skills. Communication is not one of your better qualities."

"Is that so?"

"Yes, you need to work on that, as well as your temper."

He stared at me while he tried to get his thoughts together.

"Anyway, how have you been? How's the family?"

"Everyone's good, Beau—Yasmin?"

I thought he better not go there. *Don't call me Beautiful. My name is Yasmin to you now.* "Yes?"

"I—"

Before he could finish the receptionist interrupted. "Ms. Sinclair, they're ready for you."

"Braxton, I have to go. Maybe I'll see you around." I strutted off before he could respond. I looked back to see him staring at me with desire.

The meeting went well. Since it was a programming issue I didn't have to deal with Ms. Stevens. I was grateful. I was there longer than I would have liked, three hours, but it was OK.

I saw Braxton on my way out. He was tied up in a conversation. I could tell he wanted me to wait, but I smiled and walked out.

I thought I handled myself well. I was proud of myself, but I know now I definitely still love Braxton, and that's a big problem.

Once I was in my car I hit track 14 and let Vivian Green tell my story.

> *It's been a long long time now*
> *And I'm still trying to get you out*
> *of my head, of my heart, of my whole damn*
> *soul*

This love is still lingering it's getting old
But it ain't dying it's not even trying
And I can't fight it
I just bury it at the bottom hoping you might
find
You were my love, you were my first
And now this love is just a curse
Oh, yeah

*

After seeing Braxton, I also realized I was being unfair to Chauncey. Chauncey has been attentive and sweet when he is around. I'm far from in love with him, but I thought I should at least give the relationship a chance. We are together. I checked his schedule and saw that he'll be back today. I figured I'd do something nice, unexpected.

I've talked to him a few times, but I never told him I was planning on surprising him with a treat—me. I just told him I would stop by that evening. Chauncey always had bras and panties delivered to me weekly, along with flowers and other gifts. This was his way of paying me back for ripping my panties the night Landon had Eric. I have a lovely collection going on too. I decide on the black, white, and red corset with thong to symbolize Miami colors. I added thigh-high boots and a black trench coat. I pulled my hair in a ponytail, applied my MAC lip gloss, and headed to the door.

Before ringing the bell I decided I have to play the part. I stood leaning with one hand on the wall, the other on my hip, one leg crossed over the other, exposing my thigh-high boot as well as thigh. Then I rang the bell . . . only to be embarrassed. Instead of Chauncey answering the door, his friend Geester did.

Geester looked at me and smiled. "Yo, Chaunce, you have company, man."

"Hey." I covered myself as best I could as I entered the house.

Geester went into the media room with his guest, I assumed. Chauncey walked up to me, looking stunned by my attire.

"You didn't tell me you were going to have company."

"I didn't think it would be a problem. I knew you missed me, but not *this* much," he said giving me a kiss.

"You're always telling me to unwind, have fun. I thought it was just you and me tonight."

"It is all about you and me. You know I love to love ya love ya. I want to see your entire outfit."

"That can be arranged *after* your guests leave."

"Nah, I can't wait that long. I want you now."

"How many people are here anyway?"

"Don't worry about them. It's about you and me."

I am one for spontaneity so I tongue him down.

"*That's* what I'm talking about." Chauncey led me to the game room.

Once the door was closed I dropped my coat and did my signature runway strut over to him. I didn't want to waste any more time talking so I grabbed him by the collar and kissed him hard. I tugged at his belt until it was off.

As usual, Chauncey took over. He picked me up and tried to enter me. I slipped my way out of his grasp.

"What's wrong?"

I reached in my boot to retrieve a condom.

He hesitated a minute but then put it on. He got right back to where I stopped him at. This time when he picked me up, he pinned me to the wall. He moved my thong to the side, and then entered me with force. I was a little caught off guard. He was fucking me rough, knocking shit down. It took some getting used to, but I matched his groove. Chauncey started biting on my nipples and slapping my ass. I didn't think he had it in him. I knew he was trying to put on a show for his friends. I was ready to put an end to his fiasco so I wrapped my legs around his waist and started to give it back to him. With all the bouncing, my clit constantly rubbed against his dick. Needless to say, I was stimulated.

Definitely enjoying this, I should have done this sooner. "Fuck me, Chaunce." I boosted his ego.

Chauncey went into a groove, goddamn. I continued to stroke that ego, moaning and groaning.

"Damn, baby, you feel so good," he groaned.

Chauncey went in. I wanted to scream, "About Damn Time," but I moaned and enjoyed this much-needed pleasure. If he keeps fucking me like this I may fall in love. As I was coming, I felt Chauncey's body begin to shake. His legs were weak so he leaned on one of the game tables. That was a mistake. The table collapsed, I fell back hitting my back on the wall. If that wasn't bad enough, Chauncey's weight came crashing down on my ankle and me.

"Awwwww, shit," I yelled.

"Damn, Yas, I'm sorry. Are you OK?"

"No, my ankle is fucked up." It was throbbing.

Geester and his female companion heard the commotion and rushed in. I thought I was embarrassed before, but this took it. Luckily, Chauncey was quick and was able to cover me up.

"Man, you all right?" Geester asked, trying to get a glimpse.

"Yeah, man, I got this."

Once Geester was out of the room, Chauncey attempted to help me up. I couldn't stand on my ankle so he picked me up and carried me to a chair. He managed to pull off my boots. My left ankle began to swell immediately.

"I think you need to go to the hospital."

"I think you're right. And you're bleeding on your arm."

Chauncey looked at his arm. "I must have scratched it when we fell."

"You mean when I fell and you fell on top of me."

He laughed. "I'm glad you still have your sense of humor. Are you ready to go to the hospital?"

"No, look at me. I don't have any clothes on. How am I supposed to explain this?"

"That's true. But it was good, wasn't it? You handled it."

What I wanted to say was I've had better. And when I did, it did not require an ER visit, but I gave him a phony smile with a little laugh. "I figured I was staying the night. I have some jeans, but I don't want to irritate my ankle. Get me one of your T-shirts and a pair of socks."

"What are you going to do for pants?"

"In addition to panties, add jeans. Give me the scissors. I'm going to have to cut them." I noticed Chauncey still had the condom dangling from his dick. Good, the last thing I needed is to pop up pregnant. "Chauncey, you may want to dispose of *that*," I said, pointing to the condom.

"Good idea."

By the time he made it back I was crying. I put my newly cut shorts on, but my ankle and back were killing me. Chauncey scooped me up and carried me to his truck. He sat in the back with me. Geester and his female companion took the front. I saw a smirk on Geester's face. Years from now I may be able to look back on this and find it amusing, but right now, at this moment, it wasn't.

"Are you comfortable, Yas?" Chauncey asked.

"What do you think?" I said, irritated.

Geester couldn't hold it in and bust out laughing. I tried to hold it in, but this was crazy. Being freaky landed my ass in the hospital. Chauncey and Geester's companion were laughing now too.

"Seriously, Yasmin, are you OK?" Geester asked, trying to be serious.

"OK, joke on me tonight. Go ahead, get your laughs out now, because when we get to the hospital, the story is I tripped over Chauncey's big-ass feet. Chauncey, you tried to grab me but scratched your arm on some glass."

"That's what I like. You think quickly on your feet," Chauncey teased.

"Yo, that shit was funny. You should have seen how y'all looked on the floor," Geester added.

We all laughed at that. Although it was embarrassing, I knew it was a sight.

"Chaunce, reach in my bag and get my cell. Call Landon for me, please."

Chauncey called Landon and gave her the fabricated story. She was going to meet us at the hospital.

I was in pain but tried to minimize it. Chauncey kept trying to make me more comfortable, but it wasn't helping. When the tears fell, I knew he felt bad for what happened. Geester stopped with the jokes too.

Once we arrived at the hospital Chauncey insisted on carrying me in. Of course, the female staff recognized Chauncey and Geester. Chauncey wasn't trying to do the celeb thing and demanded I get attention now. I was in the back within five minutes. I had x-rays done of my back as well as left ankle, while Chauncey got his arm checked out.

I was waiting for the doctor when Landon came in the room frantic. "Yas?"

"Landon."

"Yas, are you OK? Why weren't you paying attention to what you were doing? I can't believe you were so clumsy. Were you drinking?"

"Calm down, Momma Diva."

"Well, answer me."

I told Landon the true story. She thought it was the funniest thing she'd ever heard.

One of the doctors had to come in to ask if she was OK.

"Yas, I'm sorry. I just have this mental picture of what it looked like. Answer this, was it that good? Did Chauncey really break your back? Really, was it good?"

I leaned into Landon. "Hell, no."

"Damn."

She laughed some more. "Is he that bad, Yas?"

"Chauncey thinks he's a lover. He has to control everything. Don't get me wrong, he's not the worst, but I've had someone better, so he's good for the moment."

Landon shook her head. "Please don't start with the Braxton song. Braxton has a tacky girlfriend. Move the hell on. Look at Chauncey. You need to stop playing and get serious with Chauncey. Braxton is over; he's history. He's not moping over you. Wake up."

"Yes, Mama."

The doctor came in and told me that I only had some sprains and prescribed some pain medicine. He wanted me to stay off my feet and, of course, rest my back. I was set to stay at Landon's for the next week and make her wait on me. I was looking forward to paying her back from when she was pregnant with Eric. Chauncey wasn't going for that, though, and I ended up at his place.

Staying at Chauncey's was a mistake. It was the end to what I was trying to make in a relationship. Just when I started to fall I got a reality check.

The first couple of days were relaxing. Chauncey kept me laughing and occupied. I did give him some pussy. Truthfully, however, there were no love sparks. He was like a cool friend. He had a nurse for me, and I lay around like I was a queen. My back was feeling much better. I was able to move around, however, my ankle was still a little swollen. Since Chauncey had a few games left, I was left alone. Now I was bored.

I was missing Chauncey's company. I went into his drawers looking for a T-shirt and found a picture of his baby mother. The one he loved along with a letter. The letter said she missed him and couldn't wait until they could be together. She made mention he'd better not be messing with those stank-ass-ho bitch groupies or she would kick their ass, then his. I flipped over the back of the picture.

> *Chauncey*
> *You will always have my heart.*
> *Love always,*
> *Toya*

Chauncey still had feelings for her if he held on to the letter. I wanted to say something to him, but who am I? I can't because I feel the same way about Braxton. Maybe I should see what's going on. Chauncey wasn't scheduled to come back until next week, therefore, I still had time to decide. His phone rang so I answered.

"Hello."

"Who's this?" the female caller asked with attitude.

I was not going to entertain whoever the caller was so I hung up.

It rang again, but I ignored it. An hour later it rang again.

"Hello."

"Well, I just wanted to let you know, don't get too comfortable. Chauncey will get tired of you soon, and when he does, I'll be there."

This bitch does not realize how stupid she sounded. I knew I should have hung up, but I was bored. "OK."

"You think you the shit because you're answering the phone, but he was with me last week."

"OK, I heard you the first time. You made your point. He's not here, and obviously, he's not there with you, now, so what do you want?"

"Oh, you just some dumb bitch."

I started to cuss the bitch out, but I figured, what for? I just hoped Chauncey wasn't so sloppy and trashy with his choice of females. "Whatever. Good-bye."

Of course, the chick kept calling so I turned off the ringer. I was tired anyway.

After my nap I woke up hungry. I sent the nurse home early so I was on my own. I was heading downstairs, but then I saw my cell phone lighting up. I checked and saw I had twenty-one missed calls. Some were from Landon, the other ones were out of area, so it had to be Chauncey. I even had a call from my mother. I'd call her later when I was really bored. Just as I was about to call Landon, Chauncey called.

"Hey, Chaunce."

"Girl, where are you at?"

"At your house."

"You need to answer the phone then."

"I forgot to turn the ringer back on."

"Why are you turning ringers off?" He sounded annoyed.

"Because some dumb-ass bitch keeps calling."

His tone changed to a calmer one. "Oh yeah? Who was it?"

"I don't know nor do I care. I didn't ask."

"OK, well, what did she say?"

"Chauncey, you know me well enough to know that I don't entertain the young shit." I knew from the way he was asking questions something was up, but we'd discuss that when I saw him.

"Cool, so how you feeling?"

"Better. How's it going with you? I see you're working hard."

"Yeah, we just have these two games left, then I'll be back."

"Good, because I'm bored."

"Well, I'll make sure you're entertained when I get back."

"I'm sure you will."

"I have to get back. I'm going to call you later."

"All right, I'll make sure the ringer's on."

I didn't hear from Chauncey that night or the next morning. Now that I have nothing but time, I realized I rarely talked to Chauncey. I was usually busy with work or hanging with Landon and Kevin. This time was really making me think. Chauncey and I weren't going to work. He had females waiting for him every night, in every city. The phone call was just a preview. I had neither the time nor desire to chase chickenheads away each day. Like the article stated, I was just a main chick, but Yasmin was an only-chick type of girl. I dealt with being second all of my life. I didn't like it then, and I damn sure wasn't going to settle for it now. While I have love for Chauncey, I never could marry him. Chauncey was my rebound guy.

As if I needed confirmation that this relationship was doomed, the Internet sealed it. I was surfing the net and came across an entertainment blog Web site. I was just about to click off when I saw a picture of Chauncey carrying me into the hospital with Geester behind. The caption read: HERE YOU SEE MS. SINCLAIR CRYING, BEGGING FOR SOMEONE TO SAVE HER UNBORN CHILD. I just stared for a moment in disbelief.

> **Miami Heat's Chauncey Smith rushes pregnant fiancée to Emergency Room to avoid miscarriage.** *Unfortunately, he was unsuccessful.*

>> *Miami Heat's player* **Chauncey Smith,** *28, fiancée 26-year-old* **Yasmin Sinclair,** *rushed to the hospital on May 28, 2005. According to the private nurse who has asked to keep her name "unknown" to the public, "The basketball star rushed his fiancée into the emergency room after she fell." It is also reported Mr. Smith tried to avoid falling and suffered injuries as well. As you can see from the photo, there is blood on his shirt. The nurse said that she "felt very bad for his fiancée as she cried, 'Please save my baby.'" . . . Ms. Sinclair's ultrasound revealed that she was expecting a baby boy!*

>> *I'm sure the news is more devastating considering Mr. Smith was served with a paternity suit days prior from 22-year-old Monica Scott. Ms. Scott claims Mr. Smith fathered her 2-week-old infant.*

There were even medical records attached to this article. Upon further review, I realized it was doctored from my actual miscarriage. I couldn't believe this. This was it. I was not dealing with this. I couldn't have my personal life on display. That was private. I was still dealing with that. This relationship was going to end today. I called Landon for support. As soon as she picked up I lost it.

"Hello."

I tried to talk, but I couldn't. All I could do was cry.

"Yas?"

"Land, I nee—" I sniffed and cried some more.

"Yas, take a deep breath. Breathe, talk to me."

"I need you to come get me."

"OK, but tell me what's wrong."

Somehow I managed to tell Landon what was going on.

She rushed over and was there within twenty minutes. Landon grabbed me and cried with me and even stayed over with me that night.

"Yas, how are you feeling?"

"Better."

"Good. Unfortunately, it isn't easy being with an athlete, but you'll be OK. You're strong. Don't let the media upset you."

"Land, they brought up my son."

"I know. It can be cruel. Does Chauncey know?"

"I never told him about my son. As far as the article, I don't know. I doubt it. I haven't heard from him."

"Well, talk to him. You're in a relationship."

"Yes, we are, but Land, I can't do this."

"Yas, don't let the media get to you."

"Land, it's more than that. Chauncey and I are more like friends with benefits. He's fun to hang out with, but honestly, I can't commit to him. All this drama with other females, you have no privacy. I'm not feeling this. How do you deal with it?"

"I don't restrict myself."

"Diva, later on you with that, but your ass needs to slow down before Eric zaps out on you."

"You're right, later on that about Eric. So you're just going to break up with Chauncey?"

"Yes."

"How are you going to do that?"

"How am I going to do it? Good question."

"Yas, seriously, Chauncey is a good guy. I know you're hurt, but it's not his fault your business was put out there. You know he's into you. He left you alone in his house while he was gone. You've met his mother, kids. Next is the wedding. You deserve to be happy after dumb-ass Braxton. Chauncey is always attentive and treats you well."

"You're right, Land, but this is too much."

"Yas, don't punish him because of the media. You know the media. Next week it will be a different story. He's just making a living. It's not his fault. Think about it. Don't ruin a good thing."

"All right, Landon."

Landon caused me to have second thoughts. She was right. It wasn't his fault but seeing that brought back undesired memories of Braxton.

Being bored, I went roaming through the house. I came across a lot of VHS movies. I knew they were sex tapes. I was surprised he wasn't more discreet; they were only semihidden. He had them in a file cabinet that wasn't locked. The tapes had dates and states. He was smart about that. I guess he figured if any the girls came back crying rape, he would have proof. Curiosity got the best of me. I popped one in.

The first tape was interesting. He was in what I assume was a hotel room having sex with some girl. The girl looked like the average groupie: the weave, silicon breasts, big ass, fake nails, and hooker outfit. She started stripping for him. I gave in to the chick. She had skills. She was doing splits and cartwheels. The girl took the bottle of champagne they were sipping on and placed it the floor. She stood over the bottle and swirled her body down on top of it. She took in more than half. I know her pussy had to be worn out, hanging to accomplish that. Why would anyone want to fuck her? What could they feel? But she stood up, holding it in place. Chauncey was clearly amused. This chick wasn't loose at all.

Next she took a blunt, stuffed it in her pussy, and proceeded to puff. In fact, she held that shit in. Even though the shit was nasty, I had to give it to her. She must be the Donna Richardson of the Kegel exercise. That's what I call getting high off some pussy. What happened next was obvious. Chauncey was fucking the shit out of her. The chick was oohing and ahhing, but I knew the deal. Their fucking didn't even get me wet.

The second tape was just straight-up nasty. The girl fit the part too. She reminded me of the girl in the hotel room. I guess I was wrong. Chauncey fucked anything. Well, he treated her like shit too. This tape involved Geester as well. They took turns fucking her. Chauncey would be getting a professional while Geester fucked her doggy-style.

Geester was good size from what I can see. I was impressed with the way he was banging her. When they alternated, I lost any interest for Geester. His dumb ass took off the condom and let her give him a professional raw. Dumb ass, your ass can catch something. Chauncey, I see, works better in competition with the way he was handling the girl. Afterward, they had her sit Indian position. My mouth dropped when I saw them both give her a golden shower. The bitch actually sat there welcoming it. She looked like she was in heaven, moving her face from side to side accepting their urine. They were urinating all over her, in her hair, mouth, wherever. When I thought it couldn't get worse, I saw Geester bring in his pit bull and had her suck its dick. These fools were calling her a nasty ho while she was doing it. Didn't they just fuck her? Y'all dumb asses for fucking the chick. I had seen enough.

Chauncey was on another level. Yeah, he was right for doing that nasty shit with groupies. I was not down for any of that. I really had no desire to be with him now. I didn't want him kissing or fucking me. He fucks anything. I saw he had protection, but what if the condom broke or fell off? He's HIV or a STD waiting to happen. Hell no. I'm glad the NBA tests for HIV regularly, and we always used protection. I wasn't too nervous, but I wasn't taken any more chances. Now I just have to figure out how to break things off.

Chauncey came in two days later. I didn't want him trying to sex me, so after he ate I was going to have the talk.

He gave me a kiss on the cheek. I could handle that. I decided to put the blame on me.

"Chauncey, we need to talk."

"Yeah, what's up?"

"Do you still have feelings for your ex?"

"What? Where did that come from?"

"Just thinking. We've been in this relationship for a while."

"Yeah?"

"I'm going to be honest. I know you have groupies. You have pussy thrown at you every day."

"I do, but I'm not messing with those girls. That shit gets real old quick."

"Chaunce, I'm not one of those naïve females who think my sex will keep you faithful."

"Yas, where is all this coming from?"

"It's not important. I just brought it up because I can't deal with it."

"Yas, we straight. I thought we had an understanding. Yeah, you know how it is, but you know you're my wifey."

I rolled my eyes. I did not tell this fool I was OK with him sleeping with whomever, but I'd get to that in a few. "It was cool until I saw the latest entertainment column with you carrying me into the hospital."

"What is you talking about?"

"The miscarriage."

"Oh, that. Look, I was going to tell you about that. That bitch seduced me that night. She slipped something in my drink. I don't even think the kid is mine. I'm getting the paternity thing checked now."

"What?" I said it but didn't mean to say it aloud. I read that part in the article but only focused on me. I *know* I'm definitely not staying in this relationship.

"That happened when we first got together. You and me weren't even like that then. Like I said, that bitch got me drunk and is trying to trap me."

I just looked at him like, yeah . . . right. "I was referring to the miscarriage but thanks for the additional info."

"You were pregnant?"

"Yes, I was, but that was prior to our relationship. I was pissed because my business was tampered with, then put out there."

"I'm sorry it went down like that, but I can't control the media."

"Let's just call this a loss. I can't deal with my life being open to the public."

"Yas, don't get upset. There'll be another story tomorrow. That didn't even cause much of a buzz."

"Yeah, I know, but I'm still hurt over that. That's private."

Chauncey came over and gave me a hug. "You want to talk about it?"

He was so sweet. I hate to end it, but the tapes . . . I gave him the story. "I was five months pregnant when I was rear-ended by a drunk driver. The impact caused me to hit another car. I lost my baby."

"Damn, I'm sorry." He gave me another kiss on the cheek. "What happened to the dude you were pregnant by?"

He just had to go there, but I was honest. In fact, I was going to use it to my advantage. "It was too much for him. He couldn't deal with a serious relationship. He wanted freedom and to be with other people. I thanked him for his honesty, and we went separate ways."

"That's why you've been holding out on me. It's that the dude Javon hangs with."

"Yes. I didn't want to get hurt again."

"I feel you, Yasmin. I'm not trying to hurt you. You think I would have left you in my house if I wasn't serious about you?"

"I know that. It's just with the groupies, and now this new baby."

"Yas, I told you. I'm taking care of that."

"What if the kid is yours?"

He took a deep breath. "I'll pay the support, but that bitch is definitely not a threat."

Time for the kill. I gave him my sincerest look. "Chaunce, you know I always have been up front with you. I believe you. I have a confession. While you were away I missed you. One day I was missing you so much that I wanted to smell you, so I went and grabbed one of your T-shirts." I paused.

He was smiling. Good, I had him.

"Well, I saw a picture and a letter from your ex."

The smile disappeared.

"I asked about your ex earlier because I know you still have feelings. I expect that. You have history, and if it weren't for choices you made, you would still be together. You still love her, don't you?"

"Of course, she has my kid."

"So does the other girl, but you don't love her like Toya. Chaunce, I'm sure she still has feelings for you too. I've seen how she looks at you, and the way she looks at me."

He laughed. "What are you trying to say, Yasmin?"

"I think you should get back with Toya. I told you I'm not trying to get hurt again. I know you still love her. I respect that. I know I can't compete with that. Honestly, I'm not trying. So go be with her. I want you too."

Chauncey just stared at me.

"Why are you looking at me like that?"

"Yassy, damn, I really like you. You're always real up front, honest. You could have, but never tried to, take advantage of me. I have a lot of respect for you. Your ex was dumb as shit to let you go."

"Thank you, Chauncey. You're a sweetheart too. So are you going to stop bullshitting and go get your girl back?"

"You're too much."

"No, I'm just keeping it real."

"So we're still cool?"

"Why wouldn't we be?"

"Good, than can I get some of that, as you say, sweet stuff, one more time."

I was screaming in my head *Hell fucking NO,* but I replied calmly, "Nope."

"You're all right with me."

I stayed at Chauncey's that night. There was no sex at all. We hung out watching *Fridays* and *Rush Hour.* We had a good time. Like I said before, Chauncey was a cool friend. I even gave him ideas on how to get Toya back.

The next day, when I returned to my condo, I saw my mother had left me another message to call her. I called and my father answered.

"Hey, Daddy, how are you?"

"Fine, despite the fact that you're in magazines looking like a whore."

"What?"

"You heard me."

Here we go. I could clearly hear my mother in the background rambling. Apparently, she's disgusted with me as well. She took the phone and wasted no time lecturing me.

"Yasmin Elaine Sinclair, how dare you embarrass us like that. You have your father all upset and disgusted. You went from bad to worse. First, you sleep with someone you work with. Then you get pregnant by him, giving it all up without a commitment. You had nothing left to offer so he left. You can't be mad at that. Now, you're on the cover of magazines looking like a slut, a low-down common whore with a NBA player. I taught you morals, yet you act as if you have none. I don't know what your problem is. What kind of example can you set for your sister? I thank God Ashley is respectable. God knows it's been hard with the example you've set. Now the latest news is you were pregnant by Chauncey. Are you retarded? When are going to learn to stop having kids or sex without being married? You see, you had another miscarriage. Don't you get it God doesn't approve of your lifestyle? I swear I don't believe you. I've taught you morals. You make me so ashamed."

Tears were falling from my eyes. I was numb. Sad thing is, I'm not shocked by anything she's saying. She's just saying what she wanted to say for years. I hate the fact that she feels that way, but at the same time, I'm not pleading for her approval anymore.

"Well, I'm sorry you feel that way. I have nothing to be sorry for. As you stated earlier, dating an athlete comes with a lot of attention. The media showed us holding hands, kissing. That's what couples do. Was I on a pole? On a strip? Was I even naked? Not that it matters, you've already formed your opinion, but I never was pregnant by Chauncey. The media, unfortunately, has a tendency to fabricate stories. Its opinions, like yours, keep them circulating." I hung up went to the mirror and looked at myself.

"Yasmin, I love you. Yasmin, you are beautiful, smart, and worth holding on to. Yasmin, you are special and here for a reason. No matter what anyone says, you are beautiful inside and out; a gift. I love you, Yasmin."

24
Lost Without U

It's been some weeks since I'd broken up with Chauncey. Ironically, I'm not sad. After evaluating everything, I'm satisfied with my decision. Overall, Chauncey was a good guy. Granted, he needed to get a lot of things in perspective but could be future husband material, just not for me. What we had was plenty of physical attraction, but that's it. Yes, I had feelings for him, but as a friend. I didn't care if I was with him or not. Honestly, I didn't want to wake up next to him, nor have kids with him. My heart was never in it. It didn't skip beats or anticipate his arrival. I didn't get that feeling in my gut or chest known as love. He was my something to do. Someone who came along to help me deal with self, teach me how to have fun. Chauncey served his purpose. He opened my eyes to new things and reinforced what I now know and what Braxton always told me: I am beautiful. For that, I appreciate Chauncey, especially his generous gifts. Especially his last. Chauncey recently sent me a nice package that included jeans, jewelry, fragrances, candles, and of course, bras and panties. Attached was a note.

Hey, Miss Lady,
I got nothing but love for you, baby.
Ha-ha, you miss my songs, don't you?
I hope all is well.
Just wanted to let you know you're definitely a lady.
But you knew that.
Thanks for keeping it real with me.
I hope you find that person who will be real with you.
But I know he won't be as sexy as me.
I'm going to keep it real now.
This is your last gift package.

I do thank God for the memories.
That black and red set, damn, girl, only you can rock it.

I got a hard-on just remembering that feeling, DAMN!
You a BADD . . . *******
Anyway, my underwear debt is now paid in full.
I repeat, no more underwear.
Especially since I won't get to see. (Whoa, black and red)

Besides, I can't have Toya kicking my ass.
Smile,
Chaunce

P.S. If you ever need anything, holla.

Such a sweetheart. I'm happy for him. He got his girl back, and I wish them the best of luck. She's going to need it with those whores. I told Landon she could have the life. She was more upset over the breakup than I was. No more celebrities for me.

I miss Chauncey only for conversation. Who I really miss and want is Braxton. How pathetic. I haven't seen Braxton since the last time I was at BET. I don't know how many times I've picked up the phone to call him, but I've remained strong and haven't. It's over I keep reminding myself. Despite me missing him, I'm coming to terms with our breakup, realizing it was for the best.

There have been other changes in my life. I bought a two-bedroom condo. I now can look in the mirror without hating my eyes. I can say, "I love Yasmin." It was a long, difficult process, but I finally love me. It was time and long overdue. I see my eyes as special, like me. I don't allow my parents to make me feel ashamed anymore.

Little Eric, who recently turned one, and I were hanging out today, and although he is new to walking, he thinks he can run. I decided to let him run in the mall. Unfortunately, while chasing him, I ran into Derek.

"Hey, Yassy, You look good, real good. Can I get a hug?"

"Hello, Derek."

"You know I miss you, girl. When we going to hook up? Let me take you out."

"You can do that? Don't you have child support to pay? Funny, how you told me you didn't have any kids."

He laughed. "I had to get a paternity test done first. But you have a kid now. We can be one big family your kid and mines. Stop acting funny, you know you want me."

"Good-bye, Derek."

"Well, you think you can get Chauncey to hook me up with some tickets?"

I walked away from the fool. Why I talk to him is beyond me. What was I thinking? I plead temporary insanity. After the cookout he's really showed his true colors.

Eric still wanted to run at the mall. That boy had way too much energy for me. I was so tired. I tried to carry him, but he wanted to run. I gave up and let him do his thing.

"Iccce . . ."

Eric couldn't say ice cream, but I knew what my baby wanted. "Say ice cream."

"Iccce."

All I could do was laugh. He tried. I went into Baskin Robbins to order him a cone. As I reached in my purse to get my wallet he ran off.

I ran after him. "Eric!" I yelled. He stopped, laughed at me, and kept going. I ran after him and bumped someone accidentally. I would have stopped to make sure they were OK, but I had to get Eric. Instead, I apologized and kept going.

Eric was at the door laughing.

"Eric, why did you do that to Auntie?" I picked him up and kissed him.

"Iccce."

"You're not getting down this time." I went back to get his ice cream. Rushing after him caused me to leave my wallet. I looked on the counter but didn't see it.

"Looking for something?"

I looked up and saw Braxton standing there with my wallet. "Yeah, thanks." I tried to grab my wallet, but he held it up. "So are you going to talk to me now?"

"I didn't know I wasn't talking to you."

He chuckled. "You know I wanted to talk to you that other day."

"My numbers are still the same."

"I didn't want to call you and cause problems with your *friend*."

He was playing a game. I was not in the mood for more games after Derek. I rolled my eyes. "Well, I'm not in the mood for games. You can keep the wallet. That too can be replaced."

"Ooh, you're so mean and such a smart-ass."

I hit him. "Watch your mouth."

"I'm sorry," he said looking at the baby. He just stared at him. "Hey, buddy."

"Say hello, Eric."

"Heddo," Eric replied.

We both smiled.

"Can we talk for a minute?"

I decide to be nice. "OK, but let me get him an ice cream first. Can I have my wallet back?"

He gave me the wallet. "I'll get the ice cream. Do you want anything?"

I shook my head no.

Eric and I took a seat in the corner of the store. Dating Chauncey has caused me to avoid people when possible.

Braxton found us. "You don't want to be seen with me now?" he joked.

"You said it."

He looked at me like, *are you serious?*

"Hurry up, have a seat, I need you to be inconspicuous. I can't have you ruin my image or have any photos with you and me together. Oh no, that wouldn't look good at all." I tried to keep a straight face but bust out with laughter.

He sat down and handed me the ice cream. He didn't look amused.

"I see you're still uptight."

"I'm not uptight."

"OK, whatever. Not my problem.

"So you're hiding out?"

"Basically, I've had enough pictures taken of me the last few months. You know I like my privacy. I'm just used to avoiding attention now."

"Yeah, you were popular."

"Too popular. Some things should be left private."

"Yeah, they should." He paused. "I'm sorry to hear about the miscarriage," he said, sincerely.

I looked at him feeling the tears swell up. One escaped, but I quickly wiped it away. "Braxton, you work in the entertainment industry. You should know you can't believe everything. Someone at the hospital released my old records. That file was from my miscarriage with *our* son."

He was quiet for about a minute, "Damn, I'm sorry. I didn't know."

I ignored him. "Is the ice cream good?" I asked Eric. Eric smiled.

"Landon named him Eric Bryan Ayers to honor our son."

Braxton looked at Eric. "That was nice."

"What did you want to talk to me about, Braxton?"

"I just wanted to see how you were. What you've been up to."

"I told you everything was lovely when I saw you a couple of months ago."

"Your ring finger is empty. So, that means you're not engaged."

"Nosy. Yes, I never was engaged."

"So what's the status on you and Chauncey?"

"Why you all in my business?"

"I can't ask questions?"

"No, you can't."

"You're still beautiful."

"I know."

He laughed. "Conceited now."

"No, that title belongs to you."

"Does Chauncey make you happy?"

"Really, it isn't any of your business, but Chauncey and I are no longer together."

"Sorry to hear that."

"No, you're not."

I saw him smirk. He tried to hide it, but it was too late, I saw it. I wanted to mess with him. "I just got tired of seeing me on a magazine hugging and kissing him. There were so many pictures of us at the beach cuddling, kissing, being intimate. I guess I should be glad none of the sex tapes got out," I said, making sure I was a little dramatic, dragging out some of the words.

"I get the point."

He was mad. I could see the vein in his neck throb. I laughed to myself.

"What's going on with you? How's *your* girlfriend?"

"What girlfriend?"

"That's right. You like being free."

He laughed but got serious. "I was going through a lot of things back then. I didn't know how to talk to you. It was easier to push you away. I'm sorry. I paid for it, though."

I was getting weak. "Is that so?"

He looked at me with sincerity. "Yes, I did. I lost you, my best friend."

"Well, it's time for me and Eric to go. I'll see you around."

"Yasmin, stay. I miss you."

"Braxton, please, this is not the time or place."

"You're right. Can we go out later?"

"I'm babysitting."

"I can come past your place later on."

"I don't think that'll be a good idea."

"Yasmin, just to talk."

"Why don't you just call?"

"Are you going to answer?"

"Maybe. Depends on my mood." I gathered Eric. He, of course, was a mess but happy.

"Why are you being difficult?"

"I'm being honest." I laughed. I wrote down my number and handed it to him. "Here's my new number."

"You know you were wrong."

"The other number is still good, I just rarely check it. Besides, you have my work number. That hasn't changed."

"So you're leaving me."

"You left me."

Braxton stood up to escort me out, ignoring my comment.

"I'm a big girl. I don't need an escort."

"I'm just being a gentleman."

We were on our way out when an older woman stopped us to admire Eric. "Aww, he's so cute. Look at him. He's so handsome. How old is he?"

"One," I smiled.

"He's so adorable. He looks just like you," she said looking at Braxton.

I didn't feel like correcting her. "Thank you."

"Well, let me let you go. I just had to see this handsome little fella. You're such a beautiful family." She walked off.

Good. That was an awkward moment. I looked at Braxton. "That's why I like the corners. People always assume."

He shrugged.

He walked me out to my truck. After I loaded Eric in, I faced him. "Well, I have to go. Nice seeing you again."

He walked up close to me, too close. I could feel my nipples tingling. "You say that like you don't expect to hear from me."

"No, now you're assuming."

He pulled out his cell, retrieved the number I gave him, and dialed.

"What was the purpose of that?"

"I know you. You can be a smart-ass. I had to make sure it was the right number."

"I told you watch your mouth. I don't have to lie. If I didn't want you to have my number, I wouldn't have given it to you."

He didn't say anything at first. "Are you going to answer when I call?"

"Maybe," I said getting into my truck.

He closed my door and stared at me. "I know where you live. If you don't answer, then I'll have to stalk you," he joked.

I laughed. "You can try, but I've since moved."

He smiled. I pulled off.

I took the baby home to his mama and relaxed with her.

"Hey, Mommy, baby," Landon said grabbing him. Eric's face immediately lit up. Motherhood has changed Landon for the better. She hasn't completely calmed down, but it's a start.

"Land, I ran into Braxton when I was at the mall."

Landon looked at me strangely. "What did he want?"

"To talk."

"About?"

"Us. He started talking about how he misses me."

Landon cut in. "Yas, it took you a long time to get over him. Shoot, you're still not over him. I don't want you to get hurt. He probably still has his games."

"I was thinking the same thing. But, he seemed more mature."

"Don't start getting weak on me. You remember how you were when you broke up."

"True, but he was honest. He didn't cheat on me. I know it was for the best. I've grown. We both needed this space."

"You don't know that. I can't tell you not to talk to him. Please don't have sex with him because you'll get hooked again. I still can't believe Miss Conservative had sex on the first date. You have a weakness for the Joker."

"I know. I'm glad he doesn't know where I live. I'll just talk to him on the phone."

Landon looked at me like, *yeah, right.* "If he hurts you this time, I'm putting a hit out."

"Landon, I'm going to take it slow. Just talk on the phone. No dates."

"Yeah, whatever. Don't depress me anymore. You know you still have Kevin."

"Land, Kevin is with Nicole. I've told you a thousand times I don't like Kevin like that."

"You never know until you try. Kevin still wants you. I see how he looks at you."

"Now *you* sound like Braxton."

"Damn, does every conversation have to include him? It's pathetic how you're still naïve when it comes to him. Wake up. I didn't want to tell you before because you were hurt enough. He cheated. That's why he broke up with you."

I just looked at her. I was hurt. "What? Why are you telling me this now? What do you know?"

Her voice softened. "I'm sorry. Yas, I just didn't want to hurt you. I never saw Braxton cheat, but you said it yourself, we have a lot of similarities. The way he was acting and the reason he gave you when he broke up, that's one of my lines. I've used it quite often, actually. Then Javon made mention that he and Braxton are notorious for female company. I've heard stories from other sources. But that's not important. Yas, please don't fall for him again. Leave him in the past. Braxton is nothing but games."

25
Ain't Nothing but Love

"Hey, Miss Y.E.S.," Kevin said somberly.

"Kev, what's wrong?"

"Can we go out tonight? I don't feel like talking about it over the phone."

I was scared now. "Kevin, is everything all right? It's not anything life threatening?"

He chuckled. "No, it's not that serious. Nicole and I broke up."

"I'm sorry, Kev."

"Thanks, but I'll talk to you about it later."

"OK, I'll see you later. I'll pick you up at five."

"All right, Yas, I appreciate this."

"Kev, you know I love you. Anytime."

It was only twelve so I had time to lounge around and think. I was still sorting out my feelings for Braxton. I've been true to my word since I've seen him at the mall. I've only talked to him. I try to keep the conversations short. The conversations were good. Like always, he made me laugh. We talked about everything, but I purposely avoided the conversation of us. He's tried to get me to go out with him, but I keep declining. Landon's words keep replaying in my mind. I knew he was getting frustrated, but, oh well, I had to do what was best for me.

I didn't realize I'd dozed off until my phone rang.

"Hello," I answered groggily.

"Hey, Beautiful."

Here we go with the beautiful. I'm not going to get weak. "Hey."

"I didn't mean to wake you."

I looked at the clock and saw it was three. "That's OK. I need to get up anyway."

"What's on your agenda today?"

"Nothing much. I'm hanging out with Kevin later."

"OK, where are you going? Landon isn't going with you?"

He said that calmly. I'm impressed.

"Nope, it's just me and Kevin."

"Well, don't let me hold you. But before you go, I really called to see what you were doing tomorrow."

"I don't have any plans."

"I want you to come to a cookout with me tomorrow."

"Whose?"

"My parents. I know my mother would love to see you."

"Oh, thanks for the invitation, but I'm going to decline."

"May I ask why?" I could hear his frustration.

"I don't want to give your mother the wrong idea. I definitely want to see her, but she'll assume we're back together."

"Yasmin, what are we doing?" he asked.

"We're talking."

"You know what I mean," he said annoyed.

"Don't get upset with me. This is how you wanted it. We're talking as friends. Nothing more, nothing less."

"How long are we supposed to talk as friends?" he asked very irritated.

"I don't know. Right now, I'm just living my life like it's golden."

"So you're playing games?"

"Games? What are you talking about? I just said I'm not ready. I just got out of a long public relationship with Chauncey. I'm still sorting out some things."

"Bye." He hung up.

I know his ass did not hang up on me. "If you would like to make a call . . ." I heard the operator announce.

This is the stuff that irritates me. His damn temper. He has no patience. He expects me to just fall back in bed with him and we just pick up where we left off. No. If he couldn't wait, then I'll have to get the strength to say good-bye. I looked at the clock. It was 3:30.

I rushed and showered. Since it's only Kevin I didn't make a fuss. I was presentable though, wearing a jean sundress.

It's been awhile since I hung out with Kevin, and I was looking forward to hanging with my friend. I just wished it was on better circumstances. We've all been busy with relationships, unfortunately neglecting each other.

Kevin answered looking sad. "I don't feel like going out now. Don't feel like being around a lot of people."

"Yeah, neither do I." Braxton had plucked my nerves.

"Blockbuster night?"

"OK, but I'm not trying to watch some crazy *Matrix* movie with you."

"Ha-ha. I have a decent collection. Go check it out. Nicole added some things."

I looked through his movie collection. It was decent. I pulled out *Bad Boys* and *The Best Man*. "Do you have anything to drink?"

"Depends on what you want."

"I'll just take some juice."

Kevin made me a piña colada. He popped in the movie and took a seat beside me.

"You know what I like." I hungrily accepted the drink. "So, why did you break up?"

"She wanted marriage. I wasn't ready."

I was with Nicole on this subject. "You've been together three years. Why did it take you so long to realize you weren't ready? You should have called it quits instead of leading her on. Why is it always what *you* want? What about *our* feelings?"

"Hold up. Don't take your frustrations with Braxton out on me."

"I apologize. You're right, but really, did you think she wasn't going to want more?"

"Don't get me wrong. I love Nicole. I just want everything in order before I get married."

"Kevin, you're a twenty-nine-year-old successful attorney that owns his own house and is very financially secure, thanks to me. How much more order do you need?"

"True, but if I get married, then she'll want kids, and I don't think I'm ready."

"You're good with Eric, and I know you want kids, so don't BS me."

He laughed. "OK, I don't know if she's the one. I'm a lawyer. I don't want to end up in divorce court a couple of years from now."

I looked at him. "Why isn't she the one?"

"She may be. I just don't want to wake up years from now wondering if there was someone else."

"Is there someone at work or someone you met that you want to be with?"

"No. I don't know. I'm just not sure."

"Whatever, Kevin."

We watched *Bad Boys* and laughed at Will Smith and Martin Lawrence the entire movie. *The Best Man* was good, but I dozed off. I looked at Kevin, and he had dozed off with his head in my chest.

I nudged him. "Kev, get up."

Kevin moved slightly but didn't get up, so I nudged him again.

"Huh?" he said, half out of it.

"Get your big head off of my chest."

That's when he sat up and kissed me. He kissed me with his tongue and all.

I should have rejected him, pushed him away, but I didn't. We kissed for what had to be five minutes, maybe longer. He was caressing me in the right spots. He moved his tongue to my neck, and we knew that's my weakness. Then I let him lead me to his bedroom. I should have stopped right then, but I wanted him, and I was curious.

He laid me on the bed and started to kiss me again. "Yasmin, I've wanted to do this for a long time," he said tenderly.

He focused back on my neck and started placing light kisses down my neck to my chest. "Do you like that?"

I moaned.

He pulled my spaghetti straps down, exposing my breasts. My nipples were ready. He took one into his mouth and licked nice and slow.

He was turning me the hell on. All this time, I didn't know Kevin had skills. Who'd have thought?

"You like that, Miss Y.E.S.? Talk to me."

"Umm-hmm."

He moved onto the other breast and gave it the same amount of attention. He smashed my breasts together and put both nipples in his mouth and started sucking.

"*Ummmmmmmm*," I moaned.

"You like that? You're so sexy."

Kevin stood up and went in his drawer to get a condom. He removed his shirt, and I was definitely impressed. Kevin's body looked way better than Braxton's.

Did I want to go here with Kevin? I should have objected when I felt his hands pull my panties down, stopped him when he lowered me to his bed. Instead, I let him have his way with me, spread my legs, allowed him to insert his two fingers into me. I moaned, "Fuck me."

"Nice and wet, just the way I like it," he grinned as he placed his two fingers in his mouth. "You taste even better than I thought," he whispered.

He dove in me with his tongue.

"Ohhh, um." I had to look down. Kevin has a long, thick tongue. It felt like a minidick. He was licking my insides, while I was pulling my hair. Damn. He pulled his tongue out, and then vigorously he began licking and sucking my clit, like he was trying to get to the center of the tootsie roll pop. I can truthfully say, never has anyone licked me this good. I couldn't take it anymore. I needed the dick. "Fuck me, Kevin, give me some dick," I begged.

He stopped. He positioned himself between my legs. He put on the condom and plunged in hard. "*Aarghhh,*" I moaned.

"Damn, I've wanted to do this too long. You feel so good, baby. You like how that feels, Yassy?"

He held his dick there for a long minute, then he started taking long, deep, forceful strokes. His dick felt so good inside me. We continued at this pace for a while. Soon, Kevin stopped, leaving his dick inside me. He bent down, kissing me passionately. "You feel so good."

I wrapped my legs around his waist.

He grabbed my butt and started pumping fast. "Tell me how you like it. Give it to me, Ms. Y.E.S. You like this, don't you? Damn, right there. Talk to me."

He was killing my vibe with the talking. Some is cool during certain times, but not a lot. I liked to just go off of the vibe. My actions will tell you if you're pleasing me or not. Besides, right now, I wanted to fuck, not talk. Nonetheless, I should have expected it. He does talk for a living. Anyway, I blocked him out and went into a zone.

I squeezed my vaginal walls and started pumping Kevin just as hard. We wrestled back and forth, trying to reach that ultimate haven. Just when I thought I couldn't take any more, Kevin had new tricks. His dick seemed to be getting longer and stronger, satisfying me more. He was handling it. I remembered moaning and saying what, I don't know. Kevin definitely gets props.

Kevin pinned one of my legs behind my head and pounded me so purposely. Oh, how I was loving that. The icing was him putting my nipple in his mouth and nibbling. Next thing you know I was shaking. Kevin let go seconds later, collapsing on top of me.

He rolled off of me, smirking. "I see why your milkshake brings all the boys to the yard. You got some stripper techniques."

I look at him shocked, although offended depicted my feeling. "You wrong for saying that. Actually, what's that supposed to mean? Why did you say that?"

"Nothing," he chuckled.

"You wouldn't have made the comment if it was nothing."

"Calm down, Ms. Y.E.S. You just have that aura about you that attracts people."

"And?"

"I see the fascination."

This must be a new asshole Kevin, the lawyer. The Kevin I usually know doesn't make insensitive comments. Matter of fact, where was all this coming from? "What are you talking about? That comment makes it seem like I sleep with a lot of men."

"I didn't say that."

"You implied it."

He sighed. "I know you don't sleep around; you just tease."

I got up and started dressing.

"Why are you getting dressed?"

"To go home."

"Yas, I didn't mean to offend you. Truthfully, I'm shocked we took it this far. I've been trying to get with you for a long time. Why did you let me get close to you tonight?"

How could I answer this question? I couldn't tell him the truth. I was pissed at Braxton but was horny and curious. "I don't know. It felt right."

"That's bullshit, and you know it."

"What? Why are you flipping on me? What's with the attitude?"

"I apologize if I came off harsh. But the truth, is we both just used each other. You probably had an argument with Braxton, and I'm upset with the breakup with Nicole. Don't get me wrong. It was good, real, real good, but we shouldn't have gone there."

What the fuck was going on? I was hurt, Kevin talking shit to me, and I don't like it. "You're right, Kevin, this should not have happened. You could have stopped it, but you didn't. I will tell you one thing. You're not going to continue to talk to me like I'm some trick you met on the street, all right? You're the one who always wanted me like you said. The feeling was not mutual. Tonight happened. We were two consensual adults, so this entire jib jab is unnecessary."

He just looked at me. "You're right. We're still cool."

I don't know where this Kevin came from. He definitely isn't as sweet as I thought he was. I knew he had a reputation for being a shark in the courtroom, but damn. I guess it's like they say, you never know a person until you sleep with them. "We're cool, Kevin," I lied.

"Yasmin, seriously, I really apologize if I offended you. You said it. I have wanted you for a long time, but you chose Braxton. I just had to be direct with you. I told myself I wasn't going to get caught up with your drama. I know you still love Braxton, and I realize that I love Nicole. Tonight was special, something we both needed; closure. Go ahead and do what you want to do. Go be with Braxton."

"Kevin, for the record, I never led you on. You were just too stubborn to see that. As far as Braxton, that's my business about what I choose to do. Regarding the closure, there was nothing to close."

"Yasmin, you know you flirted with me too. But I'll let you have the last word." He kissed me on the cheek and proceeded to put his clothes on.

I was standing in shock. This motherfucker than got too damn cocky. I was mad at myself for sleeping with his ass. "Kevin, I don't know what the hell is wrong with you but don't call me anymore."

"All that isn't necessary, Yasmin. Answer this. Prior to tonight, did you have any intention of pursuing a relationship with me?"

I didn't say anything. I just looked at him like the crazy ass he was.

"Fine, don't answer. I will for you. No, you did not. After we had sex, were you interested in pursuing a relationship? No, you weren't. You know how I know? I could see it in your eyes. Feel it in your body language. There is no reason for you to catch an attitude with me. We can still be friends. This should not complicate things. You're right. We are two consensual adults. With that said, I rest my case."

"You are not in a courtroom." I grabbed my stuff and left. As soon as I got home I called Landon.

"Hello," Landon answered.

"Laand," I said in an angry tone.

"Yasmin, what's wrong? Do you need me to come over?"

"No, I'm mad at myself. I shouldn't have slept with him. He treated me like a trick. Then he said we can still be friends. Tonight we used each other for pleasure."

"What the fuck! I knew you shouldn't have messed with that motherfucker. He's nothing but a user. That's his problem. He thinks he's a pimp. I told you I would put my foot up Braxton's ass if he messed with you."

"Landon, it wasn't Braxton," I mumbled.

"What? Who? Chauncey?"

"No."

Who?"

"Kevin."

"Who?"

"You heard me," I growled.

"Kevin—*our* Kevin? Kevin Anderson? The one we call our brother Kevin?"

"Yes." I spilled the story.

"I can't believe that. I'm through with him. Yas, one question."

"Yeah?"

"How was he?"

"Leave me alone."

"No, you can't keep this inquiring mind wondering, now, how was it?"

I had to laugh at her. "No one has ever licked my pussy so good. He tongue is long and thick. It reached far in there, woo. Felt just like a dick. I give him his props. He has skills in the fucking department as well." I admit I felt better after venting, but I still wasn't talking to his ass.

"Damn, Yas."

"He definitely has skills."

"I don't like the way he said it. However, he's a lawyer, and growing up with Daddy and Mommy I know lawyers can be harsh. I'm not taking sides, but he told you the truth."

"I thought you were on my side," I whined.

"Yassy, he was a little too blunt; however, you know he was only telling the truth."

"You're right. Now that I've vented, I admit it, he was right."

"Good."

"Landon, I feel guilty for sleeping with Kevin. Braxton and I aren't together, but we're slowing working toward it."

"Yassy, this does not mean go be with Braxton again."

"I know you don't want to hear this, but I still love Braxton."

"I swear he has you under some spell."

"Should I tell him? Hell no. He can't deal with it. He can't stand Kevin now."

"I agree, some things are just better left in the dark."

"I don't know what to do. I want Braxton, but at the same time, I'm not ready to see or be with him."

Landon laughed. "Good. I still can't believe you slept with Kevin."

"Why not? You been throwing slurs about me being with Kevin forever."

"I know, but after a while, I knew it wouldn't work. I just said it to piss you off when you were with Braxton. Notice I stopped when you broke up."

"I'm going to sleep. I need to clear my head."

Before going to sleep, I checked my messages. Braxton had left me a message apologizing for earlier and asked me to reconsider his invitation. I still wasn't feeling that, especially after my night with Kevin. I decided I would not be talking to him for a while. I knew me. I get weak. I always do with Braxton, and sleeping with Kevin and then him—hell no, not an option or possibility.

*

It's been three weeks since my episode with Kevin. I've been avoiding him, along with Braxton. Both of them are too much right now. Kevin has left several messages, but as soon as I hear his voice I delete. Landon told me to be nice. Doesn't she have nerve? She says since I admitted Kevin was right I should talk to him. He was, but I didn't like his tone, so later for him.

As far as Braxton, he's been just as persistent. Luckily, he doesn't know where I live so I can't get any pop-ups. Unfortunately, he knows where I work. He's been sending me flowers, candy, fruit baskets, notes saying he's sorry. One gift I did love was a heart for my charm bracelet. Too bad I threw the bracelet away when we broke up. I'm tired of them both, truthfully, but you know I have this weakness for Mr. Simms.

Yesterday, when I was leaving work, this guy approached me. He was cute, 5 foot 9, brown skin, low haircut, medium build. Later, I would realize it was Donell Jones. At first, I thought he was trying to ask me out, so I ignored him. Anyway, he handed me a note from Braxton, but advised me I'm not allowed to read it until after he finished. Before I could object or ask what he was planning to do, he began to sing. Most people would have cried, smiled, or showed emotion. I silently cursed Braxton with a look of disbelief on my face. He knows I hate crowds, and I had one praising him with *ohhs* and *ahhs*. The guy could definitely sing, and I'd be lying if I'd say his voice, along with the words, didn't affect me. A tear or two fell by the second bar. He serenaded me with "Where You Are (Is Where I Wanna Be)":

I'm saying I'm sorry for leaving you
But I wanted to start my life brand new
I was going through changes and could not see
That with you is where I wanna be
Nothing compares to you
And I hurt from the pain that I put you through
Baby, I need you desperately
Cuz I gotta be
Where you are
Now to the note, it read:

Hey, Beautiful,
Don't be too mad
I know you HATE attention
But you left me no choice
You won't talk to me
I chose this song to convey some of my feelings
I miss you
All I want are a few moments of your time; talk to
me
If you don't, I'll do it all over again tomorrow
You know I will, but this time I'll do the singing

I love you, Beautiful
—Braxton

I was stubborn so I still didn't call Braxton after the performance. I'd call him next week.

Today I'm irritable and in the *leave-me-alone* mood. I couldn't wait to go home, pull out my Carol's Daughter, and soak in my bathtub.

When I reached my car, I noticed another car blocking me in. I was so not in the mood. The windows were tinted, but I could tell the driver was in the car, so I tapped on the window. "Excuse me. Could you please move your vehicle?" I asked, annoyed.

The window rolled down. "Depends if you stop being difficult."

"What do you want?" I sighed.

"You know what I want. Go out with me."

"No, now go home."

"You put a man to work. Come on, Beautiful."

"No."

"I'm not leaving. I'm about to sing."

Seeing that he wasn't going to move and was serious I quickly agreed. "OK, when?"

"Now. Get in."

"You're getting on my nerves now."

"Well, get in. I'll take care of you."

"I bet you will," I said sarcastically.

"Seriously, Yasmin, get in."

I got in. "New car?"

"Company car."

"Where are we going?"

"To talk."

We drove to Columbia Lake in silence. We sat there for a while, taking in the scenery, before Braxton finally turned to me.

"Yasmin, I apologize for the way things ended. I should have handled things differently. I know I should have talked to you, but I couldn't."

"What was going on with you?"

"I was adjusting to things at work, the baby. Things were crazy. I couldn't comfort you. I was scared. I told you, I'd never been with anyone as long as you. I didn't know what to do, how to handle it."

I remembered what Landon said. "You cheated, didn't you?"

He gave me a surprised look that I couldn't read. "No."

"Braxton, don't lie to me. We're not together. If you did, now is the time to tell me."

He took my hand.

"Don't lie. Are you telling me the truth?"

"I'm telling the truth."

"I got the apology, now, what do you want from me?"

"I don't want anything from you. I just want you."

"No."

"Yasmin, I want you back."

"How do you know you can handle a relationship?"

"I know I can because I know how it feels not having you in my life."

"I'm not trying to get hurt again."

"I'm not trying to hurt you."

"You already did that."

"And I'm so sorry for doing that. I regret it every day."

"Whatever."

"Honestly, I am so miserable without you. I need you. No one can love me like you."

"Oh, it's a sex thing."

He chuckled. "You know the sex was, um, good, but it's more than that. I love you. I'm not going to push you away. I'm in it for the long haul. For better or worse, I miss you, Beautiful."

"I can't tell. It's been a long time. I wasn't missed that much."

He shook his head. "You just don't know how much I missed you."

I rolled my eyes and shook my head.

"You can be so mean. Those green eyes are evil, but so sexy."

"Aarghhhh."

He looked at me like I was crazy. "What was that for?"

"You just don't know what to say out of your mouth."

"I'm sorry, you're right."

"No, I apologize. It's me. I'll let you in on a little secret. You hurt me badly, I admit it, especially when you commented about my eyes. As you know, I'm not close to my parents. But you don't know why. I never felt wanted or accepted. My paternal grandmother is who really hurt me the most. She would always say, 'Those green, evil, monstrous eyes, you think they'll get you anything you want. Well, they won't. All they will ever cause you is trouble. Men will tell you how pretty they are because they're fascinated, but that'll wear off. They don't want you. They never will want you for nothing more than a fling. You're good for nothing, just a waste of time. Nobody wants you now or ever will. I'll give you some advice: Don't fall in love because all you will ever have is heartache.'

"Those words always stuck to me. Every time a guy would comment on my eyes those words replayed. And when we broke up, you made a comment about my eyes. Your excuse validated her claim, and it pissed me the hell off," I said, crying.

"Yasmin, I'm so sorry. Damn! I didn't mean to hurt you at all. I never felt that way. I loved you then, and I love you now. I don't want you as a fling. I want you permanently. I did then, but I was stupid. I couldn't admit it to myself. I wish I handled things a lot differently. This year and a half has been a waste. I promise not to hurt you. Let me in. I want to show you how much I love you, make up for the pain I caused you. Yasmin, you are beautiful, all of you."

"I know that now. The breakup was for the best. I know the space did us some good. We both needed to mature on some things. You shouldn't have had to tell me I was beautiful. I should have known. It didn't hurt that the media agreed," I joked.

He didn't find that amusing. "You know damn well I don't want to acknowledge your relationship with Chauncey."

"Still jealous?"

"I don't care about Chauncey, I care about us. Yasmin, I want you. Let's stop wasting more time. We need to get back together."

"We need to take it slow."

"We've been taking it slow. Now it's time we commit."

"Braxton, no."

"Yasmin, yes."

"Let's just take it slow."

"We have. I know what I want and need."

"Braxton, I don't think you're ready."

"I am," he said grabbing my hands.

"I'm not ready."

"Yes, you are. You want to be with me like I want to be with you."

"Braxton, don't fuck with me. Are you in this for the long haul? You're not going to push me away when you get stressed?"

"I'm with you through it all. No matter what. Besides, my mother will kill me if I do."

Chuckling, I asked. "Your mother gave you a hard time?"

"Did she. She told me I am not allowed to bring any females to her residence unless it is you. Practically every time I go over there she's had choice words. She called me today and asked if I had begged for your forgiveness."

"Your mother is my girl. I called her a couple of times, but she would start about you and me. When are we getting back together. She told me that Chauncey guy wasn't right for me."

"I agree with her on that. I hated seeing you with him. I'm not going to lie. I was jealous, but you know all of this."

"So it's you and me now?"

He kissed me.

I quivered from the touch of his lips. It felt so right. I missed my baby.

"It's been too long," he smiled.

"Now can you take me to my truck?"

"Nope, I'm not letting you go that easily. Where do you live?"

I laughed, "What?"

"You heard me."

"I don't know if I want to divulge that information yet. I can't have you just popping up at my place."

"Stop playing."

"Who said I was playing?"

"OK, well, we've been apart too long. Let's go back to my place."

"We've been back together one minute and you trying to fuck me? So you missed fucking me."

"Stop twisting my words. I've missed your smart mouth, holding you, kissing you, and, yes, hearing you scream out my name."

"So cocky."

"No, I just know I love you, and I've been without you too long. I don't want anyone but you, Beautiful. It's all about you."

"Take me to my truck. You can follow me home." I wasn't even going to play the *let's wait* game. "Before we go back to my place, we need to get some condoms."

He smiled. "No need." He reached in the back and pulled out a box of Magnums.

"That sure of yourself? You're so arrogant. And if I wouldn't have taken you back?"

"Well, you did, but if you didn't, we would have been sitting here until you said yes. You're stuck with me for life."

He followed me to my place. When we made it inside my condo it was on. He stripped me and I he. He kissed me like I was his breath of air. He took his time reintroducing himself to my body. Braxton still remembered my spots. He sucked on my neck, my nipples, me. He lowered me to the bed and began to love me like he never has before. When he did penetrate me I wanted to scream. He filled me, and I felt so complete. I missed my Sugar Daddy, so nice, long, and sweet. Sex with Kevin and Chauncey was good, Kevin ten times better, but it wasn't anything like being with the man you love. It wasn't just sex; it was deeper; it was a mental, emotional, spiritual connection. He always made love to my mind, body, and soul. I missed everything. But what I really missed was how he held me afterward, telling me he loved me without uttering a word.

After our lovemaking session, Braxton lay in bed facing me. He stroked my face, then kissed my lips.

I looked deeply in his eyes. "Braxton, I love you too. I never stopped."

"I know, Beautiful. I was stupid to let you go, but I'm not making that mistake again. I told you, you're the only one for me. You're where I want to be." He pulled me on top of him. I lay my head on his chest and listened to the sound of his heartbeat before drifting off to sleep.

26
Brother to the Night

It was the morning after our reunion, and I was still tired from last night. We made up for lost time, making love throughout the night. Braxton was surprisingly still energized, looking like he was ready for another round. I needed a minute. I swear he had to have a Red Bull and a five-hour energy drink stashed somewhere.

"Good morning, Beautiful."

"Hey, you."

"You always leave underwear out for display?"

I looked over to see my underwear drawer open with underwear falling out.

Braxton went to my dresser and took a peek at my underwear. "Nice underwear. Are you going to model these for me later?"

"Maybe. Depends on what I get out of it." I rolled on my stomach attempting to get some sleep.

He laughed and continued to pull out stuff from my drawer. "Damn, you have a lot of underwear. Is this your new fetish?"

I laughed. "You never can have too many. You know you like them."

Suddenly, Braxton was silent. I turned around to see he was looking at something. "Reading anything interesting?" I joked.

"Yeah, I am," he said seriously.

"Really? Well, enjoy."

"Yasmin, what happened between you and Chauncey?"

I rolled over on my back. Why was he asking about Chauncey? "Nothing. We broke up."

"Why?" he asked.

"He wasn't for me."

He just looked at me. I could tell he was trying to control his temper. But why? I looked at his hand to see he was holding a note. *Damn.* In my underwear drawer was the last note Chauncey sent. The note he sent with my last underwear package. Something told me to throw it away, but it was cute and special. It's not like I was expecting Braxton to be back in my life yesterday. I sat up to get ready for the drill and attitude.

"When was the last time you talked to him?"

"Months ago."

"Any unresolved feelings?"

"No, Chauncey is more like a brother."

"Another brother?"

"What I mean . . . well . . . We both had unresolved feelings for people in our past."

"Why didn't you just say that from the beginning?"

"You caught me off guard. I didn't know how you would deal with it."

"Who else did you hook up with?"

"No one," I lied. I knew he would flip if he ever found out about Kevin. "Are you mad?"

"I'm not mad. I don't like it, but I'll deal with it. Yasmin . . ." he said calmly.

"Yes?"

"I know it was my fault you hooked up, but I don't want to hear about him. I'm also going to need you to get rid of this stuff."

I smiled. Braxton had lost his mind. I was not getting rid of anything. He said it. It's his fault I hooked up with Chauncey. He's just going to have to deal. My pretty panties are staying. Now it was my turn for the interrogations. "How many people did you sleep with?"

"Enough."

"Enough is not a number. I know you wrapped it up, but were there any accidents with the condoms?"

"No accidents."

"You still haven't answered my first question."

"You don't want details about my past sex life, and I definitely don't want any details 0of yours."

"Braxton, I asked you how many women, not details. Obviously, it was a lot. When were you last tested?" I hated going to get tested every six months. It is so much easier when you're in a committed monogamous relationship. You can go with the flow without having to worry about the condom breaking, or if you're putting yourself at risk for a moment of pleasure. But this is the world we live in, and you had to do what you had to do. Testing was a must. It is what it is.

"I knew you were going to ask that. So I was tested last week. Yes, it was negative."

"How long has it been since you were with someone?"

"Almost three months."

I just shook my head. "How many?"

"That's not important. I wrapped it up each time; no accidents."

"Well, when it's been six months and your test is negative and you're ready to be honest, you can call me."

"Yasmin, it's not that serious. I told you, I used protection always. I'll get tested again tomorrow if that makes you happy."

"You need to. But no one told you to go out and fuck every chick that had her legs open."

"Now you're exaggerating."

"I'm going off of your actions. I have no problem being honest with you. We just had this conversation last night. You promised me you would be honest. If you can't be honest, then we need to end this now."

Braxton took a seat next to me. "I don't want to argue with you. I was a little out there. Truthfully, I was with about 35–45 females."

My mouth dropped open. "Damn, in one year? Braxton, you've just killed the moment. I hope you weren't performing oral sex too." I was mad as shit. I went off.

"Don't be like that, and hell, no. No oral sex!" he shouted.

"Don't be like *what*? *Honest*? We've already had sex. I can't change that, but I'm not having sex with you again until you're tested."

"Are you serious?"

"Yes. Do you have a problem? Another reason I ended it with Chauncey was because of the groupies. Not condoning it, but he had females waiting in the room. You went out and got it. I'm not going to sit here and say Chauncey never slept around when we were together, but I know it wasn't that many females. And with his career, he gets tested on a regular, so there was minimal risk."

"Don't compare me to Chauncey. You don't know what he did when you weren't around. I know you're not that naïve."

"I'm not naïve. I was just stating the facts. Here's another. When I'm with someone sexually I don't want to be scared that if the condom pops or slip off I could get something. You know I can be buck-wild when it comes to sex, and it's likely to happen. So if your results come back positive, you're on your own."

He looked at me like I was being irrational.

"Don't look at me like that. I'm being honest, like you were with me. I'm not going to limit myself and take precautions because you couldn't keep your dick in your pants. I know some women can do it, but not me. Damn, this is what happens when you have sex first and ask questions last."

"That's how you feel?"

"Yes."

"So where does that leave us?"

"You know, this is all your fault. Why couldn't you settle with 2–3? You said 45."

"Can you calm down? What, did you want me to lie?" he said with his voice elevating.

"No, but I wasn't expecting you to be so damn promiscuous. How? Why did you have sex with so many females?"

He didn't say anything, but had a dumb expression on his face.

"*Hello*? I asked you a question."

"Oh, you know the answer to that. I went to a lot of parties with Javon. Woman were always there."

"I should have known you were with his ass Javon. Ugh."

"What's that supposed to mean?" He sounded offended.

"Nothing." Bottom line, Javon was Braxton's friend. Although he was wrong for approaching me the way he did, he never really physically crossed the line. If he did, then Braxton would have been told. Besides, I didn't want to start any problems between them. Even though I couldn't stand him, he was supposedly one of Braxton's best friends. He's an ass but definitely not worth my breath. His devious ways would come to surface.

"This is why I didn't want you know where I live. I didn't want to go here again, but you wouldn't leave me alone."

"Are you done?"

I knew he was annoyed, but I wasn't done venting. "No. Well, I hope all the women you fucked weren't tacky like the date you took to the awards ceremony."

He shook his head.

I laughed. "She was tacky. I wasn't even close to her and could tell she was wearing a track. Then she had the nerve to be staring at me."

"Any more jokes?"

"You have to admit she was tacky. I was expecting better from you."

"Yasmin, you are better. No one is better for me but you. That wasn't her purpose. I knew no one could compare to you, so I wasn't with her or any of them for that. When I saw you that night it made me get my shit in order."

The break was good, I know that, but why did he have to sex everything he met? I had calmed down. "Braxton, I apologize for going off on you. I wasn't expecting you to say you were so out there. I'm not going to lie and say I'm cool with this info, but I won't dismiss you. Let's just take it slow. Definitely no sex. Regarding your promiscuity, let's see what the test says and take it from there. It's more of a relationship than sex. We shouldn't just be with each other because of sex. We need to work on communication anyway. Sex is not always the answer."

He gave me a kiss on the cheek. "You're going to make me suffer."

"Yes. One more thing. You will only be seeing me once a week. You can talk to me as much as you like, but we need distance."

"Yasmin, seriously, you're pushing it. I told you I used protection each time. Now I can't see you? Whatever."

"I'm not playing. Once a week."

27
Kiss of Life

This has been a long, long, did I say *long,* four months. The first month was the worst. Braxton was at my house every day. He got me on that one. I know I was really wrong considering I had sex with Kevin three weeks prior to us getting back together. I'd be lying if I said I was completely celibate.

Braxton and I fell asleep one night on the couch. I was awakened by his tongue between my thighs. Of course, I didn't stop him then, but when he tried to penetrate me, I put a halt to it. He was mad and tried to get me to give him some, telling me he had condoms, but I ever so kindly went into the bathroom and returned with some Vaseline telling him to work it out. Of course, he didn't like that; instead, he made a valid point. When we first met I did fuck him on the first date and never pressed the issue about the number of people he was with. He was absolutely right. However, this was now, and *45* females? Come on. After that incident, he pretty much left me alone. To be on the safe side, I wore pants when he was around. Typically, we would just cuddle, talk, or listen to each other. We just enjoyed each other. As a result, our commitment and bond was stronger.

We also agreed not to tell his mother we were back together until we got it together. She would have us married the next day. That element of our relationship has been fun and crazy. I've talked to Mrs. Simms quite a few times. She still had no clue we were together and was still hinting that she wanted me back with her son. Braxton, on the other hand, was grilled. It was funny. I heard a few conversations where she told him she knows he's seeing someone, but he better remember what she said: no other females.

When the time did come for us to get tested I was a little nervous. This would be my third since I broke up with

Chauncey. Fortunately, both of our results were negative. Thank GOD.

"Why are you so restless?" I asked Braxton. I was thinking it was due to the lack of sex. We were on the plane taking a trip to the islands. Braxton surprised me after our negative HIV results with tickets. Our results came back three weeks ago, and we've still managed to sustain from having sex. In fact, Braxton turned the tables. I propositioned him twice but was turned down. He's been avoiding me too. Not coming over, limiting the number of calls, as well as length. If I didn't see the results myself, I would think something was up. I was shocked when he asked me to take a trip.

"I'm fine, just a little tired."

"Well, take a nap."

"I'll wait until I get to my room."

"*MY* room? Do we have separate rooms now?"

"Yes." He started laughing. "I'll wait until we get to OUR room."

"I didn't come to the Cayman Islands to watch you sleep."

"Well, go sightseeing, shopping, to the spa or something. I'm taking a nap."

"I don't want to go by myself. You know I have no sense of direction."

"I don't know what to tell you then. I'm sleeping today. Later, we can go somewhere to eat."

I just looked at him. Fine. I'll just have to have fun all by myself.

Grand Cayman Island is mesmerizing. Immediately, I was hypnotized by the alluring turquoise water with white sand. The shining sun, the bright, beautiful, colored birds flying, and warm, welcoming breeze enhanced the scene. The air as well as the aroma was clear, fresh, and clean. This is paradise. I just wanted to check out the scenery, enjoy the ambiance.

Braxton, however, was on a schedule. Even though I hated to check into our resort, I followed him to the Aqua Bay Club. Once we were in our room, I was disappointed. The condo had an oceanfront view of the sea accompanied with a private, screened balcony. The facility included a freshwater pool, tennis court, and Jacuzzi.

"It is so beautiful."

"Just like you."

I walked over to Braxton giving him a passionate kiss. "Let's go out. I know you don't want to sleep now."

To my dismay he did.

"Nah, Beautiful. Go enjoy the island. We'll do something later."

"Braxton, come on, I don't want to go alone," I said, pouting.

Braxton yawned, and then lay on the bed. "Meet me back here at six."

I was not going to stay cooped up in a room. I stormed off, and I could have sworn I heard him chuckle. First, I showered and slipped on my one-piece blue bathing suit that dipped low in the front and had long slits on the side. I knew Braxton would have a fit with me in this. I thought about wrapping a sarong around myself but changed my mind. I walked out to see Braxton lying on the bed. "Enjoy your nap."

He rolled over. "You don't leave much for the imagination, do you?"

"This is an island. I'm not the supposed to be covered."

"I didn't say that. All I was pointing out was that you'll be all alone. I know you don't like attention."

I grabbed my purse, sarong, and left.

Once on the island I did a little sightseeing, but I ended up in the stores. I was nice buying Braxton a watch. He always needs help with telling time. For myself, I bought a black coral necklace and a Caymanite amber stone ring. Even though we still had issues, for Kevin, I decided to get some rum and island sauces since he liked to cook. For

Landon, I picked her up jewelry and swimwear from La Perla. The store even had lingerie. You know I had to add to my collection. Of course, I picked up things for my baby, Eric. I missed my little cutie.

By the time six came, I was ready to experience Cayman nightlife. I went back to the room. Braxton wasn't there. I changed into a floral print sundress and pulled my hair up. By the time 6:45 rolled around, I was pissed, wondering where the hell he was. Just when I was about to give up on him, he walked in like nothing was wrong. "You forget about me?"

"No. I decided to take a walk."

"I thought the reason for the trip was to spend quality time together," I said irritated.

"It is. I wasn't as tired as I thought. Are you ready?"

Even though I was still upset I went to the door.

Nightlife is just as beautiful as the day. The way the moon reflected off the water was soothing. The ambiance of the island at night was one of tranquility and serenity; pure ecstasy.

We ate dinner at a nice restaurant called The Wharf. The Wharf was located right on the water's edge, complete with huge tarpons under the deck and live music. While I wanted to partake in the activities, Braxton was real antsy and didn't have much to say. If I wasn't so into the atmosphere, I would have been bored because Braxton was ignoring me. He definitely was preoccupied with what, I don't know. After dinner, we went to The Planet Niteclub. The island liquor was a lot more potent then in the States, so it didn't take much to give me a buzz. Along with the alcohol and the beating of the drums, I wanted some love. When I danced with Braxton I could tell he was getting aroused, but he backed off. He really was taking this to another level. He took a seat, leaving me all alone on the dance floor. He was acting too weird for me. I even danced with some Islander men, yet Braxton remained still. Something was up. No temper tantrum. Where is my bipolar lover? After a few dances with strangers I was done. I went to be with my baby.

"Why are you so anti?"

"Yasmin, what are you talking about?"

"You're boring. You're acting like an old man. Usually, I'm the one who stays in the back. You're sitting calm. Not even overeating."

He laughed "I'm just enjoying the music and atmosphere."

"Well, enjoy it with me. Dance with me," I whined.

"I'm fine right here. Go ahead, dance. Enjoy yourself. Someone out there will dance with you."

"I don't want to dance with anybody. I want to dance with you." I kissed him on the cheek.

"I'm tired. I don't feel like it." He yawned.

"Braxton, you want someone else to dance with this body?" I stood up to show him my assets. "You want their hands all over me? Touching me, breathing on my neck, telling me how good I smell and feel?"

"I trust you."

Oh hell, no. What is up with him? His jealous ass gets upset if someone just looks at me. All right, let's see how he handles this. I spotted a tall, dark chocolate Adonis with a pretty smile. He was sexy, but my baby was sexier, but he would do. I went on the dance floor, found the sexy little local, and danced. He matched my dance moves, and I matched his. I looked over to see Braxton was dancing with some female. What happened to just enjoying the atmosphere? I was too tired. He can't dance with me but with her. I'll give it to her, she was cute, but not beautiful like me. She's a petite size four, 5 foot 7, light skin, curly wild hair. We made eye contact, and I rolled my eyes. I no longer felt like dancing anymore so I went to the bar. My dancing partner thought he could follow. He tried to slip me his number, but I politely turned him down.

"Your man don't appreciate you. If he did, you wouldn't be alone."

"Don't worry about my man or me. All that matters is I'm content."

"No, you're not, Pretty Lady."

"I'm not going to sit here and debate you. Thanks for the dances. Good night." I turned around hoping he got the hint, but he didn't. I looked to see Braxton was still dancing, oblivious to my dilemma.

"Pretty Lady, let me take you for a walk. We can talk. Tell me about yourself. I want to get to know you."

"Let's be honest, you want to fuck me, don't you?"

He smiled. "Yes, I do. I'll take good care of you."

"I appreciate your honesty, now listen to mine. It ain't going to happen." I got up leaving him with a stupid look on his face. I saw Braxton was still dancing so I interrupted. His dance partner didn't look too happy, but I didn't care. I cut right in, wrapped my arms around his waist, and lay my head on his chest. "Let's go to our room. I'm tired."

"Relax. I'm not ready yet. Wait around for a while."

"I'm just letting you know you are being an ass. Come on."

"No, I'm not ready."

I pushed him and left.

"All right, come on, crybaby," he said as he followed behind me.

We took a walk along the beach. Braxton tried to initiate a conversation, but I chose to ignore him. When we made it back to the condo, I took a long hot bath. I came out wearing a long spaghetti strap red silk nightgown with a split that reached my upper thigh—to find Braxton fast asleep. He was really ruining my vacation.

The second day Braxton woke me up with a kiss and a flower. I was still pissed, but I welcomed some affection. As he kissed me, I pulled him on top of me and wrapped my legs around his waist, putting him in a headlock with my thighs. I could tell Braxton was aroused because Sugar Daddy was standing up, ready to be stroked.

Braxton then took my arms and pinned them to the bed. I thought it was an indication he was going to fuck me nice and hard. *Good, it's been awhile. I don't mind being ruffed up a little.* I could feel my other lips watering and getting prepared for its treat. Instead, Braxton gave me a peck and freed himself from my headlock.

"What's up with you?" I asked, annoyed.

"What you talking about?"

"You know what I'm talking about. Why aren't you giving me love?"

"I'm giving you love. I surprised you with this vacation."

"Blah, blah. I want you to enjoy the island with me. Maybe even feel you inside me."

"I am enjoying the island."

"What about me?"

"Damn, girl, you'll be all right. You need to seek counseling. I think you're a nymphomaniac. I may need to take a break from you." He chuckled, but I didn't find it amusing.

"You didn't have a problem before."

"This is now. Change is good sometimes. Are you open to change?"

"It depends on the change. But anyway, are we hanging out today together?" I asked, annoyed.

"Well, this morning, I'm getting a massage. I made you an appointment also. Later on, we'll see."

"How you know I want a damn massage?"

"You look tired. You need to relax. You're too uptight."

"Well, I know what I'm *not* tired from."

"Yeah, yeah. Are you going to keep yapping or get the massage?"

"Both. You're ruining my vacation. Next time I come, it won't be with you."

"I'm not ruining anything. That's your attitude."

I ignored his comment and got dressed. Today, I wore a white smocked dress, my hair was down, and no makeup except for gloss. When I came out of the bathroom, Braxton was on the phone. In what seemed to be the norm lately, he ignored my presence. I slipped on my shades and waited by the window taking in the view. Braxton took me to breakfast, and then we took a tour of the island. Throughout the day, we had minimal conversation. Braxton was nervous about something; he was only half paying attention. I made up my mind after the spa I was enjoying this trip by myself. Once I receive my aromatherapy facial with massage and the pedicure I forgot I was mad.

Afterward, I looked for Braxton, only to discover he's disappeared on me. Just when I was about to leave, the masseuse hands me a note along with a flower from Braxton saying he would see me later. The note also instructed me to go to Duty Free Mall to some store to pick out a dress for a blissful evening. Braxton even arranged for me to have a chauffeur/assistant to carry my bags.

Although annoyed because I wanted to spend this time with him, I decided to go. As soon as I walked in the store someone approached me ready to assist. She had me try on several gowns, but we reduced the number to three. The first dress was a pink satin strapless with a sweetheart neckline, plain and simple. The second was a white satin and chiffon V-neck with a crystal-beaded bodice A-line that layered at the bottom. Finally, the third was a white satin and chiffon gown with crystal beading. The dress was A-line with an empire waist, and the bottom had a variation of hem lengths in the layers of chiffon. I tried on all three but fell in love with the second. It was formal yet free. The saleswoman then handed me a flower attached with another note instructing me to go the jewelry store to pick out accessories.

I followed this trail practically the entire afternoon, accumulating shoes, perfumes, accessories, jewelry, lingerie, and a bouquet of flowers. After my spree, my chaperone led me to a villa. The villa was lit with candles and had rose petals scattered throughout that read, "Beautiful, you are my life." Immediately, I began to cry. He loves me. Another flower along with another note instructed me to meet him on the beach for a blissful evening.

Anxiously, I prepared for the evening. My hair was in loose spiral curls, the back hung loosely, the front was pulled back with a crystal clip. Once ready, my chaperone led me to a secluded area on Seven Mile Beach. I stood watching as the sun danced along the water anticipating Braxton.

"Yasmin Sinclair?"

I spun around to see Braxton wearing all-white. He was so handsome. He was wearing shades, but I could still sense his nervousness. "Are we formal now, Braxton Joseph Simms?"

He laughed. "Yasmin Sinclair, do you love me?"

"Yes, I love you. You know that."

He walked over and kissed me passionately. "I made a lot of mistakes before. Now, I can say, no matter what obstacles we may face, I won't leave you or push you away again. Will you do the same for me?"

"Where is all this coming from?"

He grabbed my hands. "Yasmin, I just want you to know how I feel. Do you feel the same way?"

"Yes."

"Tell me."

"Braxton, I love you. I've always loved you. I never stopped. You're my other half. You complete me. I will love you through the good times as well as the bad. I'll never desert you. I love only you."

"Do you promise?"

"Yes." I smiled. Then I asked, "Do you love me?"

"Do I love you? The last four months you put me through so much grief, and I've had to use a lot of restraint. No kissing or sex. I'm still here. That's love," he laughed.

"I kissed you."

"Seriously, yes, I love you. I'm a better person when I'm with you, and I'm miserable without you. I'm not taking any chances on losing you again. I can't take it. I'm lost without you. Let's make it official."

"OK, we are."

"Yasmin Elaine Sinclair."

"OK, is this a new thing? You're calling me by my whole name."

"No, I just wanted to say it one more time."

"What do you mean one more time?" I asked, confused.

"On more time before it becomes Yasmin Elaine Simms. Let's get married."

"What? We just got back together."

"So? I know you're the one, the only one for me. The only one I want."

My mouth opened from shock.

"Now."

"Now?"

"Yes. Here. Today. Right now."

"We don't have the paperwork. No one is here."

Braxton kneeled down on one knee and pulled out the most beautiful ring. "All that matters is you and me. Marry me now."

"Braxton . . ."

"Beautiful, I love you. Marry me."

"Yes."

Braxton then guided me to a pier of alluring crystal clear water, Rums Point. The flowers I collected throughout the day served as my bouquet. Braxton had arranged everything from the decorations to officiate, to the rings, to the ceremony. Even a photographer and videographer were present to capture the moment. They'd captured all of the events leading up to this moment. I was speechless. His love . . . wow, no word or words can describe the magnitude. Everything was so charismatic, so romantic. When the sun kissed the azure water the ceremony began. It was intimate and sweet. I cried, of course. I had no idea who the witnesses were nor did I care. Like he said, all that mattered was he and I.

When it was time to recite our vows, Braxton went first. I saw tears in his eyes before he spoke.

"Yasmin, my beautiful, beautiful, Yasmin, where do I begin? You've changed me. I never wanted or thought I'd end up here. But you came into my life, changing everything, and I'm so fortunate you did. You gave me what I didn't know I needed, love. Now I know how to love, and I've been lucky to have you love me. I make you this promise to always be there and to make you happy. You are my life. I loved you then. I love you today. I'll love you through eternity."

Through tears I managed to get my vows out. "Braxton, I remember the first time I saw you. My heart skipped a beat, I knew then you had my heart. Like a warm, embracing breeze, you came into my life. I had so much pain, but with you, I felt love. You inspired me, helped me to love me. With you, I have no fear or insecurities. I have trust and my missing beat. I am complete. I am happy. You are my blessing from God, the love of my life, my light in the darkness. And just like our first encounter, my heart still skips, because my heart you will always have."

Following our vows, we were announced man and wife. Gazing into the heavens, I saw the moon and stars beaming, creating a mesmerizing radiance. To me, it symbolized this was our destiny.

We elected to go back to our room after the ceremony. It was just the two of us. Braxton, however, was not done. He had even more surprises for me. The room was lit with candles, chilled champagne, fresh fruit, chocolates, and even more rose petals. Now I understood why he was "tired" and antsy so much of the time.

"When did you plan this?"

"Last month. I didn't want to waste any time."

I cried even more. "I love you, Braxton. I can't believe you planned all of this."

"I love you too. Now can you stop talking so I can make love to my wife?"

"I finally get some love. You've been so mea—"

Braxton tackled me on the bed, kissing me deeply. Somehow or other while kissing me, he managed to undress himself and me.

Once we were undressed, he escorted me to our private balcony, whispering to me all the while how he loves the way my body glows under the moonlight. I took the clip out of my hair, letting it fall all around my face. Braxton motioned for me to come over. I complied. Once I was close, he picked me up, flipped me over, and started to give me the best oral I'd ever received.

Stimulating my clit with his tongue, then wrapping his mouth around my swollen clit, I could feel his tongue in me drinking like a bee drowning in sweet nectar. This made me dizzy, or maybe it was the fact that he had me completely upside down, and blood was rushing to my head. Either way, the feeling was fabulous. This new trick, stripper move, I am *ohh* loving this. He flipped me back, and my legs were like jelly. He then swept me in his arms, laying me on a lounge chair. Braxton spread my legs apart and glided in. We both let out loud moans. He stayed still while my kitty automatically began to pulsate. I could feel him exploding inside me. "My wife, my wife, my wife," he whispered.

Grabbing me while he's still hard inside me, he rolled on his back. He wanted me to ride. I love to ride. I took my time satisfying my husband. I bent down and kissed him intensely while my kitty kat sucked in all of Sugar Daddy. Sugar Daddy was growing, and kitty continued to stroke. Kitty kat was so wet from all that licking that Sugar Daddy just slipped out. I could feel kitty kat's juices flowing. They were flowing down my inner thighs, on his lap, all that sweetness making our bodies sticky and hot. Sugar Daddy was jumping, pleading to be stroked. I obliged. Braxton grabbed my ass, held on tight, and let Sugar Daddy give her a workout. Kitty was purring, and I was screaming, going thrust for thrust. Braxton tried to muffle my screams with his mouth, but he wasn't successful.

Apparently my screams were so loud that I created an appreciative audience. Normally, I would have been embarrassed, but not this time. This was long overdue; besides, Sugar Daddy was feeling too good. All I could do was moan, words no longer an option.

Braxton must have been oblivious to the audience and into kitty because his next move surprised me. He lifted me up, exposing my body. I wrapped my legs around his waist. While still inside of me, he walked me over to the balcony, pinning me, bending me over, and fucking me hard. His body was driving in me with so much force that his balls were smacking my ass, causing it to jiggle. At this point I was panting, in a zone. Braxton was both biting my nipples and massaging my ass. He was definitely taking me to another level. I was damn near out of breath.

Braxton got a burst of energy from somewhere and dug deep, deeper. He couldn't get enough, going deeper and harder and longer. I don't know how he could continue at this pace, but I couldn't take any more. I felt my body tremble as my limbs went numb. I was dizzy, disoriented, seeing stars, rainbows, and doubles. I literally was fucked unconscious because the next thing I remember was Braxton kissing me on the neck and being in a bed.

For the remainder of the night, Braxton had me twisted in too many positions, positions I didn't know I was capable of doing, from the full spits to him entering me upside down. It was some deep Kumar Sutra. I even let him enter me in the back door. Well, he tried anyway. Shit, Sugar Daddy was way too much for me to handle. Overall, our lovemaking was a love experience, a marathon that resulted in countless orgasms.

The next morning, however, I was walking around like I was in need of a hip replacement and a walker. Braxton's cocky self really thought he was the king. Yeah, he worked me good, real good.

We stayed in for the next three days, making more love. Braxton showed me some mercy, doing it nice and slow, allowing me to get my back together.

We enjoyed the remainder of our Cayman Island honeymoon. Braxton was brave and did some scuba diving. I cheered from the sidelines. He captured some nice underwater shots. We made more use of the island the following week. It was incredible. We went swimming, did some more clubbing, cruised to Pirate Island, and saw some shows. I hated to leave, but I was eager to tell my girl my news and show her my ring.

My ring was breathtaking, just like this vacation. Braxton outdid himself. A five carat emerald cut center that was raised, with countless diamonds surrounding it. From across the room it sparkled. In a dimly lit room, it gave off a magnificent glow, simply beautiful.

28
Giving You the Best That I Got

"Where are we going?"

Our flight had just come in two hours ago from Cayman Island. I was tired, wanting just to wrap up in my blankets with my husband.

"To an anniversary party."

"We just got married," I teased.

"I know, but we have to tell everybody."

"Braxton, are you serious?"

"Sort of. It's not ours, but my parents'."

"Your mother is going to kill you for making her miss the wedding. First, for not knowing we were back together, then for finding out we're married."

"No, she's going to kill both of us," he joked.

"You're right. But you could have given me more notice. Look at what I have on." I was wearing a cream mid-length skirt and gold silk blouse.

"You know you look beautiful, Beautiful."

I smiled and gave him a kiss on the cheek. "So, what are you going to do? Just walk in there and say, 'Guess what? I'm married.' Um, I don't think that's a good idea."

"Yeah, well, that's what I'm going to do."

I gave him a look like *are you serious?* He shot me back one letting me know *he is.*

The party was being held at Newton White Mansion in Mitchellville. When we got there I was so tense. To calm my nerves, I tried to take in the mansion's lavish décor. Despite the mansion being over ten thousand square feet, I could hear everyone enjoying the festivities, which only amplified my anxiety.

"Stay right here, Beautiful. I'll be right back." He kissed me before rushing off to the back.

I watched as Braxton entered the room.

"Hello, everyone."

"Hey, Braxton, hey, baby," I heard him get greeted.

"Where have you been? I was worried. I didn't think you were going to make it," Mrs. Simms grilled.

"I went away."

"Braxton, don't play with me. I know that much. You could have called. Well, at least you made it to my party. If you didn't, you *really* would have had it," Mrs. Simms lectured.

"Sorry, Ma."

"Boy, I swear, out of all my kids you—"

"Calm down, Bev," Mr. Simms coaxed.

I couldn't help but laugh at my husband getting grilled.

"I have announcement I need to make."

"Braxton, what is it? You just got here. Already you've come in, stirring up trouble," Mrs. Simms commented.

"I just want both you and Daddy to know how much I appreciated you when I was growing up. You've always been there, even though I was one that stayed in trouble."

"You sure did. I was worried about you for a minute. I still worry," I heard Uncle Charles say.

Everyone laughed.

"Well, I've been fortunate to experience your love and see the love you have for each other."

"Aww, thank you, baby, give me a hug," his mama said.

"Ma, Daddy, I say this because I've found a love of my own."

"Here we go," Uncle Charles commented.

"Son, that's good, but don't rush anything," his father advised.

"It's too late. I married her. My vacation was really a honeymoon."

"Braxton Joseph Simms, you *better* be lying to me," Mrs. Simms dared.

"Calm down, Bev," Mr. Simms coaxed.

"I hope this is a joke. I don't believe you. You really want me to kill you today? I *know* you did not come here to ruin my party. Why are you telling me this now? How are you going to marry someone, how can you love someone? Married? What do you know about love or commitment? The last person you loved you ran off because you were scared of commitment. Please, tell me you're lying," she said angrily.

"Ahh, shucks, she brought up Sweet Thing," Uncle Charles instigated.

"Speaking of Yasmin, you're not even over her. I told you she's the only one you can marry or should marry, but that's beside the point. What were you thinking? You really disappointed me."

"Ma, please. Calm down, my wife is out there."

"Braxton, what is *wrong* with you? You can't just tell us all this and expect for us to be OK with it," Mr. Simms stated.

"You brought her here? First, you tell me you're married, now you're telling me you brought her here. What am I supposed to do? Accept her with open arms?"

I couldn't take it anymore so I walked in. "I hope so."

"*Ahhhhhhhhh*, Yasmin!" Mrs. Simms hugged me and started crying. "You were very close to becoming a widow. You two got me good. I'm so shocked. I don't believe you two."

"I'm sorry, but this was your son's idea," I said, hugging her back.

Braxton shot me a look. I laughed.

"You know, I had that wedding planned, but it's about time. Right now, I'm happy both of you came to your senses."

We received congratulations from the family.

"Thank you, everyone, now can I please dance with my wife?" Braxton asked.

"That boy has always been so impatient," Braxton's father chuckled.

Braxton directed me to the dance floor. "My mother was ready to kill me and disown me over you. See what you do? Yeah, and I like how you shifted the blame on me."

"That's right," I teased.

The DJ was playing old school. The first song was followed by Marvin Gaye's "Let's Get It On." Uncle Charles came over when the DJ played "Sweet Thing."

"Excuse me, this is *our* song. You're going to have to take a seat. Let Uncle Charles show you how it's done."

Braxton was nice and let him take over. "One dance."

"You put that whip appeal on that boy, didn't you?"

"I don't know what you're talking about. Whip appeal? What's that?" I asked innocently.

He pretended to be crying. "Well, Sweet Thing, I guess it's really over. You have left me for that fool."

"I'm sorry, Uncle Charles, but I love him," I joked back.

"I know you do. Congratulations. You keep that boy in check. I like that. You're good for him. Uncle Charles now is about to lay some wisdom on you. Remember, in marriage you face problems. I want you to always remember to communicate and love each other, through the good times and bad. Be there for each other. Be willing to work it out; fight for your marriage, compromise. Like I said before, you two are good for each other. You have something special and rare. So continue to make each other happy. Put each other first."

"Yes sir."

"You know you remind me a lot of my first wife, Gladys. She was pretty just like you. Like you do with Braxton, she kept me in check, but I didn't appreciate her until it was too late. She died fifteen years ago. She was in a fatal car accident. Not a day goes by that I don't wish I had more time with her."

"I'm so sorry, Uncle Charles," I said, giving him a hug.

"So am I. I want you to be good to each other. Remember the love you have for each other and why. Promise me, please, no more breakups. That boy was the most pathetic, sorriest thing I ever seen. Then he had the nerve to be mean."

"I promise," I said, laughing.

As if on cue, the song ended and Braxton was standing there. "Your song is over." "Boy, I was trying to teach you something."

"You missed me, big baby?"

"You got jokes. What's wrong with wanting to dance with my wife?"

"I didn't say anything was wrong with that. I was just dancing with my buddy."

"What did Uncle Charles have to say?"

"You know Uncles Charles, but he gave me some old wisdom."

"I hear that."

"Well, hubby, I'm yours for the rest of my life."

We danced for a couple more songs. Oblivious to the guests, I swayed back and forth with Braxton communicating through dance the depth of my love. When the DJ played Anita Baker's "Giving You the Best that I've Got," I looked him in the eyes while I sang to him. I was gone, not realizing what I had just done until I heard the applause. I buried my head in Braxton's chest.

"I love you too, Beautiful."

"I got caught up in the moment."

"Don't be embarrassed. You know you can sing. Not as good as me, but you're all right."

"No, baby, you have other talents," I said, laughing.

"Well, how about I take you home?" He kissed me on the neck. "Show you some of my talents."

I laughed.

"What's so funny?"

"Where is home?"

"I don't know. Wherever you want it to be. My focus was to get you to say yes. I didn't think about where we were going to live."

"Since my place is closer tonight, that'll be home. We'll figure out the rest tomorrow. Mr. Simms, are you ready?"

"Yes, Mrs. Simms."

We were on the way out the door when we were stopped by his mother.

"Hold it, you two. I know you're not leaving. You deprived me of the wedding. Y'all know how I was planning for that day. The least you can do is stay for my party. We're not even going to talk about how you came in here earlier."

"Ma, we're newlyweds."

"My baby boy, the one who gave me the most trouble growing up, the one who had me in labor the longest. You know I was going to try to have another baby. I wanted a girl, but you put a hurting on me. You were so stubborn. Then—"

"All right, Ma."

"That's what I thought." She pointed to where we were supposed to sit.

We went back into the hall, but Braxton wasn't happy at all. He really is a big baby. An hour later his parents made a little speech.

"We would like to thank everyone for coming to celebrate our joyous event. We've had thirty-five good years and look to the next thirty-five years. We've been blessed with four sons and wonderful family and friends. We are extremely happy to welcome our new daughter-in-law, Yasmin. I wish you and Braxton nothing but the best. I'm sure you two will be here thirty-five years from now. Please, everyone, join me in congratulating them."

His mother walked over to give us each a hug and kiss. "You can leave now, Braxton."

"Thank you. We love you." Before I could respond Braxton grabbed me and had us out the door.

What usually is a twenty-minute drive took Braxton ten. As soon as I opened the door, he swept me in his arms and carried me over the threshold. Taking me straight into the bedroom, my husband made it clear he wanted my love. And my love is what he got.

In the privacy of our room, I jumped on Sugar Daddy and rode him backward, frontward, sideways. I made sure I was thorough, gyrating, clapping my ass. It was rather intense as I slithered up and down his pole. From the sound of his moans to the thick milky cum, I knew he was loving every bit of me.

The sun woke us up the next morning.

"Good morning, Mrs. Simms," Braxton said with his arms still wrapped around me.

"Hey, you."

"What are we going to do today?"

"Decide where to live."

"So where do you want to live, Beautiful?"

"I want something new. We need a single-family home."

"I like the idea of having a single-family home. This way, you won't disturb the neighbors with all that screaming, 'Ooh, Braxton!'"

I hit him with my pillow.

"You know you like that."

"I never said I didn't."

"Anyway, your house is too small, and this place is definitely too small. I figure we should sell your place. Take the profit, invest half into a new home. I taught you some of my tricks, so I know your place is paid for. We'll see a larger profit. My condo is too new so I won't get that big of a profit. I figure we could rent it out."

"Damn, you taking my house and money already. You think you know me that well? You all in my finances, then you get to keep your stuff," he joked.

"You know finance is my specialty, but anyway, it's *our* stuff."

"I know, that'll work. I was just playing."

"I'll call Landon."

"Landon? For what?"

"She's a realtor."

"I forgot. She actually sells houses? Are you sure?"

"You just have a lot of jokes, don't you?"

"I'll show you what I got."

Braxton stood up. "Turn around."

I complied. Next thing I feel is him entering me from the back. It was feeling *ooh* too good. He took his fingers and started playing with my clit. He knew just how to please me.

*

"Landon Taylor."

"Hey, Diva, what's going on?"

"Not a thing. How was your trip?"

"That's what I called you about. Are you sitting?"

"Uh-oh, what's wrong?"

"Everything is good. Braxton and I went to Cayman Island. We got married. He set up the whole thing. It was a surprise."

"You did *what*? Ugh, Yasssy, umm um um unh unh."

"Land?"

"What were you thinking? You just got back together. You have the Diva speechless. Why? Are you sure? You did—"

"Yes I'm sure I love him. He makes me happy."

"I'm sorry, Yasmin. Congratulations," she said nonchalantly.

"Landon, what's the problem? I know you not a huge fan of Braxton's, but I was hoping for a genuine congratulations. Maybe even an, 'I'm happy for you.'"

"You right. I'm just surprised. I thought I would be at your wedding. But I have to go."

"Sorry you weren't there, Landon. It was spur of the moment. I need your help."

"Yeah? What's up?"

"I need you to help us find a house."

"You have two. What do you need a third for?"

"Land, we need something bigger."

"Well, I'll refer you to someone."

"What? Are you that fucking upset you missed the wedding? You're supposed to be my girl. I called you, not another realtor. You can be really selfish at times."

She took a deep breath. "All right, all right, all right. I apologize. You're right. I'm so happy for you, Yasmin. Congratulations," she said in an obnoxious voice.

"I didn't say be phony. If it's too much for you to sell me a house, I'll get a new realtor. Give me a reference. Another thing, don't give me a realtor that'll show me anything for a profit."

"Yassy, you're my girl. I'm sorry. Tell me what you want. I'll get some properties to show you. When are you trying to see some properties?"

"Saturday." I gave Landon our wish list and hung up. That definitely was not the reaction I was hoping for.

29
Family Reunion

It took a couple of weeks, but Braxton and I eventually found a house. I didn't plan to spend a lot on the house, but I wanted it. The listing price was $985,000, but with a lot of negotiations, we settled on $870,000. We used the check from selling Braxton's townhouse as a down payment. With that, it left a balance of $350,000. To say the least, I was happy. It was a five-bedroom stone colonial with seven bathrooms, five fireplaces, nine-inch ceilings, a pool, sunroom, a sunken living room, complete with a three-car garage. It was set on three acres, and as Braxton said, gave me a lot of freedom to scream.

Married life has been marvelous. I didn't think it possible, but I love Braxton more each day. Landon eventually got over the shock and genuinely seemed happy for me.

I was in the midst of our housewarming/post wedding party doing the hostess thing, making sure everyone was having a good time. We had a good crowd, about sixty people, consisting mostly of Braxton's friends, family, and coworkers. Among his guests were Mike and his now wife Tiffany, Kim and her husband Paul, along with his coworker Sean. Landon and Eric were also here. Landon was busy doing her, as she says, "networking," while poor Eric was looking like a lost dog. Kevin along with his new girlfriend Cara were here. Our relationship was still awkward, but I was being cordial. Braxton even was very sociable with Kevin. If I didn't know any better I would have thought they were best friends.

There were a couple of people present that could have stayed home, such as Ms. Stevens. Right now, she was being phony. Her husband was with her. He reminded me of

Steve Urkel, and come to find out, is a CEO of a local insurance company. It figures. Even still, despite her being married, I know she still has eyes for my husband. Therefore, I made sure she used her eyes for what they were for—to see my five carat emerald cut treasure.

Javon was also here, but he hasn't bothered me. Other guests that could have stayed faraway were my parents. What was the purpose of their visit? Braxton had to have invited them. I was staying positive, so I never mentioned to him our last conversation. You know, the conversation where my mother told me she was ashamed of me, and it's my fault my son died. The more I tried to ignore their presence, the more it irked me.

Ashley and her boyfriend were here as well. She was welcomed. I do feel bad for not working harder to build a sisterly bond. I've spoken to her only once since our last encounter.

"Hey, Beautiful." Braxton came behind me and wrapped his arms around me.

"Hey, you," I said, tilting my neck so he could kiss my cheek.

"Why are you over here looking so serious?"

"No reason. Thinking why my parents are here."

"Because they're your parents."

I led Braxton to our bedroom and closed the door. As soon as the door was closed, he hugged me and kissed me on the forehead.

"What's going on?"

"I neglected to tell you, I'm not dealing with my parents. I mentioned when we first got together how my parents were when I was growing up. Well, my mother and I had this big argument."

"OK."

I recapped the argument, and Braxton was irate. Before he could walk out the door I grabbed him.

"She said that? Oh, their asses are getting out of here now. They're not welcome anymore," he barked. He then grabbed me. "I'm sorry, I didn't know."

"That's all right. I'm going to stay positive. I've spent too much time trying to get them to accept me. I love me, and that's all that matters. Yasmin is happy."

He pulled me in his lap. "Well, you know I got you. I love you, and I'll be there for you. I still can make them leave."

"Thank you, baby. I love you. Leave them. They can't hurt me anymore. Besides, being here will prove how wrong they were."

He kissed me. "I love you. I told you I never want to see you hurt again. I just want to love you and make you happy. That's my job."

"Aww, you're so sweet, and you're doing such a wonderful job."

"Yes, I am. So can I get a quickie?"

I smiled.

Twenty minutes later, Braxton and I returned looking guilty. We got a couple of stares, then smiles, but I didn't care. Shoot, this is my house. Braxton was still holding on to me when my parents approached. I pinched Braxton and gave him a look indicating I didn't want a scene.

"Yasmin and Braxton, we haven't had the chance to congratulate you. Yasmin, I apologize for the things I said to you during our last conversation, but you could have called. I don't want to argue. I was wrong to say those things," my mother confessed.

I was speechless.

Before I could think of a reply, my favorite aunt Patti appeared. "Hey, sweetie, you're looking good, and I see why. I finally get to met Braxton," she said looking at him.

I hadn't seen my aunt in years. Since her move to North Carolina, I'd only seen her twice. I'd talked to her on holidays, birthdays, the usual, but felt bad for not calling or visiting more often.

"Aunt Patti, I've missed you. Yes, this is Braxton."

Braxton and I both gave her a hug.

"I'm so happy for you, baby. You two look good together."

By now my parents had walked away. I was happy, and I was ready to enjoy my party. Braxton and I continued to entertain our guests, and everything was going well. Uncle Charles, in true character, kept everyone laughing. My lovely in-laws were dancing, showing us how it was done back in the day. There was never a dull moment, so my job was done.

The party finally started winding down around eight. Practically everyone had left with the exception of the immediate family, which basically included Landon, Eric, Kevin, Cara, Ashley, Daniel, Aunt Patti, Braxton's parents, and mine. I was in the kitchen when Landon came grabbing my arm.

"Yassy, your baby is looking for you. He's asking for you."

"Which baby?" I teased.

"Ha-ha. From what I saw earlier, you took care of Braxton already. Yes, I saw you two freaks sneak off. Came back looking crazy. I don't know what was worse, Braxton's smile or your hair."

"Land, I *know* you did not have me walking around looking crazy."

She laughed.

"Diva, you're just jealous because you couldn't get a quickie."

She gave me her famous smile. "Remember, I sold you this house. I know all the hidden getaways. Anyway, are you coming to see my baby or not?"

I laughed. "You know I am. Where's my cutie?"

"In the living room with my parents. They're dropping him off."

I walked in, and little Eric literally jumped out of Mr. Taylor's arms into mine.

"Hey, Auntie's baby, can I get a kiss?"

"Mimi." This was Eric's nickname for me. He grabbed my face and gave me this sloppy kiss.

"I see he loves you," Mr. Taylor commented.

"That's because Yassy spoils him, Daddy," Landon commented.

"Like you can talk," I commented back.

We all laughed.

"Yasmin, this is a nice place," Mrs. Taylor said.

"Thank you. You know Diva. She wouldn't have sold it to me if it didn't meet her standards. Let me give you a tour."

We took a tour of my house and ended in the media room with the remaining guests. Immediately I was overwhelmed with this weird vibe.

"Hey, everyone, this is Mr. and Mrs. Taylor, Landon's parents."

"I didn't notice how much the two of you look alike earlier. All three of you look alike truthfully," Daniel said, pointing to Landon and me, along with Mr. Taylor.

"I used to say the same thing," Eric added.

"But you *are* related, right? You all are cousins," Daniel said.

"No, just friends. People say that all the time because of the eyes. We're best friends, although she's more like my sister. The older sister I don't listen to but irritate," Landon giggled.

We both laughed.

My mother dropped the cup she was holding. "I don't believe. Oh no. No. Not now. Why is this happening?"

Everyone stared at my mother like, *what is wrong with you?* I looked at the Taylors, and they looked like they'd seen a ghost. My father was looking angry. I was lost.

I handed little Eric to his daddy and finally asked, "What's going on?"

"I need to get out of here. Michele, come on."

Earlier, I would have been rejoicing at their departure, but something was up. "Daddy, why are you so upset? What's the problem?"

"Michele, it's time you tell her the truth," Aunt Patti advised.

"Patti, you stay out of this. Shut your mouth," my mother yelled.

"No, somebody better say something. If neither one of you will . . ." Aunt Patti paused and pointed to Mr. Taylor, then my mother, "I will."

"Patti, don't you dare."

"Michelle, she's right." Mr. Taylor agreed.

"Lawrence, you promised. Just keep your mouth shut." My mother was now hysterical.

By now, Braxton was standing behind me with hands on my shoulders.

"Yasmin, Landon, I—" Mr. Taylor paused. I looked at Mrs. Taylor to see her crying.

"Daddy, why is Mommy crying? How do you know Yasmin's mother?" Landon asked.

"I'll tell you how. He took advantage of my wife and made her have sex with him," my father yelled.

"Hold it! No one took advantage of anybody," Mr. Taylor yelled back.

My head was spinning trying to decipher this newfound information. Automatically, I assumed the worst and took a step away from Mr. Taylor with Braxton right behind me. "What are you saying? Were you raped?"

"In so many words. Your mother didn't want to have sex with him, but he got her drunk. Took advantage of her and he threatened her job if she said anything. He knew we were having problems and used it to his advantage," my father said matter-of-factly.

"That's a damn lie. What we did was consensual. She was never forced to do anything. She's the one who initiated the affair. Michele, you've always been manipulative. I should have known you would have concocted a lie such as that one. You need to tell the truth for once."

"Don't try to blame this all on me. You weren't complaining before," my mother yelled back.

My mother and Mr. Taylor—oh my God, I can't believe this. They had an affair? When?

"Michele, what is he saying? You told me you were drunk. It was a mistake. Told me he tricked you and if you said anything you would lose your job and be blackballed. When I threatened to have him disbarred, you begged me not to. I begged you to file rape charges, but you said you couldn't deal with the humiliation. Is what he's saying true?"

By now, my mother was crying hysterically.

"I don't believe this. You lied to me all this time. I got over the affair. I accepted Yasmin like she was mine. I even signed the birth certificate, accepted his child. Do you know how hard that was for me? Every time I looked at her, I saw *him*."

I fell back in Braxton's arms. What? This has got to be some joke; a nightmare or something. No way possible this is true. I was numb, mute.

"Daddy, is he telling the truth?" Landon asked with tears running down her face.

Landon's father came over. "Landon, sweetheart, listen to me. I love you."

"Is it *true?*" Landon demanded.

"Yes, it is."

"All this time you lied to me. Why, Daddy? What happened? Why didn't you tell me the truth, especially when Yasmin and I became close? I used to beg for a sister, and I referred to Yasmin as the sister I never had. Why didn't you tell me?"

"We thought it was best that you didn't know," Landon's mother spoke up.

"How did this happen?"

He hesitated.

"Tell me," Landon demanded.

"I met Michelle at the law firm I was working at. We were never serious."

"You led me on. You made me believe that we were going to be together," my mother yelled.

"That's a lie. I never promised you anything," he yelled back at her. He then focused on Landon. "I didn't even know she was pregnant until after your mother and I were married. After I found out about Yasmin, I was prepared to take responsibility, but Michele insisted that John was your father." He looked at me. "After you were born, I had the paternity test done. Michele wanted John to raise you. She said I was married and she wasn't doing the joint custody thing." He focused his attention back to Landon. "At that time, I found out your mother was pregnant with you. We thought it was the best decision to go separate ways. I allowed John to adopt Yasmin, and I provided a trust for school and other financial assistance."

"Well, guess what? While you lived happily ever after, my life was miserable. John never accepted me. In fact, he made me hate the fact I was born. He wouldn't even hug me or talk to me. Neither he nor Michele never even told me 'I love you.' There was no love because I looked so much like you. These eyes, your eyes, I was told were evil and basically would never be good for anything. And that trust fund you set up, guess what? I never got it, not one cent. I worked through school," I spewed out angrily.

Braxton wrapped his arms around my shoulders and pulled me close.

"Yasmin, I'm sorry. I never knew," Mr. Taylor apologized.

"I don't want your apologies. You're just as bad as they were. You easily gave me up without a second thought."

"You're right. I want to be a part of your life now."

"Now I'm good enough?"

"Yasmin, I just was respecting your mother's wishes. I thought it was for the best. I didn't want to complicate things."

"No, you were just doing what was convenient for you. You had a reputation to uphold. Out of sight out of mind."

"I'm so sorry. You're right, I have no excuse. I failed you. You are my daughter, and although it's hard to believe, I love you too. Honestly, I never wanted to hurt you or see you hurt. Please allow me the opportunity to be in your life. I know I haven't been, but I want to be your father," Mr. Taylor said.

"Yasmin, I'm sorry as well, sweetie. We never wanted you to feel that way. You and Landon are sisters. We know now we should have handled this differently. We need—want—to build a relationship," Mrs. Taylor spoke.

I looked both of them in the eye and wiped my tears. "I am not one of your clients or some court case where you can tell me a few words and think it will be OK. You've had years, and more than one opportunity, to reach out to me, but you didn't. Your actions prove to me you don't want to be bothered. I managed this long without you and will continue to without you."

Braxton hugged me tighter.

My mother was crying. "I thought Lawrence loved me. I thought he would leave his girlfriend Jackie for me, but I was just a fling. When I found out I was pregnant, I didn't know who your father was. Your father found out about the affair, but he forgave me. I didn't want anything to do with Lawrence, so I told him to let John adopt you. I resigned and was humiliated. All through my pregnancy I prayed that you were John's. But when you were born, I knew. You had his eyes. You looked just like him. Your father, John, raised you like his own. You were fortunate that he did."

"Stop calling him my father!" I yelled.

"You're an ungrateful child. You need to stay in your place. I accepted you. I raised you like my own. Don't you ever talk to me that way, after all I've done for you."

"Ungrateful? *I'm* ungrateful? My childhood was a fucking joke."

"You had a roof over your head, clothes on your back, food, a stable home. You weren't beaten or abused. You act like you were in foster care," my mother lashed out.

"That's what you wanted all along. I never was wanted. Neither of you should be bragging about how well you raised me. My entire life all I wanted was to be accepted by you. I got good grades, it was like, 'Oh, that's good.' In middle school, high school, you never showed any interest in me or came out for support. I bet you can't tell me what activities I participated in. He just said a trust was provided. So why did I have to work to pay for college? What happened to that money? *I'm* ungrateful? You accepted me? You think so. The truth is, neither one of you were there for me. Do you know what it's like to not have your mother or father tell you 'I love you, I'm proud of you' or even hug you? Do you know how it feels when your parents forget your birthday? Tell me this, if I was so much of a burden, then why did you have me?"

They both were silent.

"So why am I here?"

"I did raise you like my own. I just couldn't get that close to you. When you were born you looked just like him. Every time I look at you I see Lawrence. I still can't accept that."

"Honey, I'm sorry you felt that way," my mother said to me.

"Don't call me honey now. You can keep your apologies. You know what really hurt me the most? When I lost my son, I wanted my mother to hold me. Tell me it's going to be OK. Instead, you told me 'sometimes things happen for the best. Next time, don't give the cow away for free.' That I got what I deserved. You were nothing but a fucking hypocrite."

"You said *what?*" Aunt Patti jumped in. "You are a sorry excuse for a mother."

"One more thing. You got your wish. I'm dead to you. You can forget I ever existed." The tears were running down my face, but I didn't care.

It seemed after that, everything went into complete chaos. It was like a riot. The scene played like a movie with no sound. Landon was crying and screaming at her parents. Ashley was screaming at Mrs. Taylor for what I don't know. My aunt Patti and mother were going at it and had to be restrained. My two fathers were fighting. Poor little Eric, he was scared, screaming at the top of his little lungs from witnessing this craziness.

I felt my head exploding, my legs collapse, and my body being lifted into Braxton's arms. I don't remember much after that. Everything was a blur. So much pain, hurt. It was too much. I don't remember everyone leaving. I don't remember getting in my bed.

What I do remember is Braxton holding me. He kept telling me he loved me. He promised he would always be there and telling me I was beautiful inside and out. He held me tight the whole night, telling me how he thanked God every day for me. I thanked God for him. He being there meant more to me than anything. I knew he was with me for better or worse. One day hopefully I can show him how much I love him and appreciate him for this.

Funny how when I thought I finally had my shit together, this drama unfolds. It took me twenty-six years, but finally, I loved me. I was happy, in love, doing me, and then this. It hurt like hell, but it made sense. When I think about how I was treated, it all made sense. All the time, the truth was right there. Now it had come to light, and I refused to feel sorry for myself. Refused to feel sorry anymore for being born, because I am here for a purpose.

A long time ago, I heard your family isn't always your relatives. I never understood that until now. My biology does not define who I am. I do. My life has come with so many obstacles and challenges. I've struggled, but I never gave up. I survived. I've learned a lot of lessons along the way, the most important—to love me.

If only I knew, this was just the beginning of a series of life lessons.

Stay tuned . . .